"How does Annette Smith [...] the voice, heart, and all-to[...] dad Joel. Now in *A Crooked Path* she beautifully brings to life the honest, faithful, hardworking Manny, who with his quiet integrity and servant's heart shatters stereotypes and prejudices we may not even realize we had. Bravo! An honest, real story that will speak to your soul."

—LAURA JENSEN WALKER, author of *Miss Invisible* and *Reconstructing Natalie*

"*A Crooked Path* once again demonstrates Annette Smith's talent for creating unique characters who capture our hearts from the opening paragraphs. She tackles potentially divisive issues with grace and empathy, helping her readers experience points of view they might not have previously considered. *A Crooked Path* kept me turning the pages until I reluctantly reached its deeply satisfying conclusion."

—JANELLE CLARE SCHNEIDER, author

"Rarely do I cry when I read a novel, but Annette Smith's *A Crooked Path* left me no choice: spare, beautiful prose, a captivating story, and a main character you can't help but fall in love with. *A Crooked Path* is everything I enjoy about fiction."

—MARY E. DEMUTH, author of *Watching the Tree Limbs* and *Wishing on Dandelions*

"Annette Smith is a master of rhythmic fiction. Her characters develop in their own time. Smith's subtle, gently nuanced prose provides a welcome respite from the world of mass-produced, pulp fiction. Sit down, slow down, and savor the story of how three lost souls find their place in this world."

—TERRY MATHEWS, arts editor, *The Sulphur Springs News-Telegram*

An eden plain novel

A CROOKED PATH

ANNETTE SMITH

OUR GUARANTEE TO YOU

We believe so strongly in the message of our books that we are making this quality guarantee to you. If for any reason you are disappointed with the content of this book, return the title page to us with your name and address and we will refund to you the list price of the book. To help us serve you better, please briefly describe why you were disappointed. Mail your refund request to: NavPress, P.O. Box 35002, Colorado Springs, CO 80935.

NavPress
P.O. Box 35001
Colorado Springs, Colorado 80935

ISBN-10: 1-57683-996-6
ISBN-13: 978-1-57683-996-6

Cover design by Kirk DouPonce, DogEared Design
Cover image by Getty, SuperStock
Author photo by Jenny Leigh
Creative Team: Rod Morris, Darla Hightower, Arvid Wallen, Kathy Guist

This novel is a work of fiction. Names, characters, places, and incidents are either the product of the author's imagination or are used fictitiously. Any resemblance to actual events, locales, organizations, or persons, living or dead, is entirely coincidental and beyond the intent of either the author or publisher.

Published in association with the literary agency of Alive Communications, Inc., 7680 Goddard Street, Suite 200, Colorado Springs, CO 80920 (www.alivecommunications.com).

Smith, Annette Gail, 1959-
  A crooked path : an Eden Plain novel / Annette Smith.
    p. cm.
  ISBN 978-1-57683-996-6
  1. Ranch life--Texas--Fiction. I. Title.
PS3619.M55C76 2007
813'.6--dc22
                          2007015651

Printed in the United States of America

1 2 3 4 5 6 7 8 9 10 / 10 09 08 07

FOR A FREE CATALOG OF NAVPRESS BOOKS & BIBLE STUDIES, CALL
1-800-366-7788 (USA) OR 1-800-839-4769 (CANADA).

To the memory of Arnulfo Santillán

acknowledgments

I OFFER APPLAUSE TO MY agent, Beth Jusino, for her behind-the-scenes work on my behalf. Thanks are also due the gracious, energetic, and creative folks at NavPress, especially editor, Rod Morris, and Kris Wallen.

I so value the support of friends who encourage me on my writing journey. This time around, special thanks go to Sheila Cook, Susan Duke, Kelli Standish, Laura Walker, and Mindy Ward. These dear ones provided encouraging words when I needed them most.

I am blessed by my extended family. I so appreciate the enthusiastic support of my parents, Louie and Marolyn Woodall, and my children, Russell and Sarah Smith, and Rachel and James Silvester.

My husband, Randy, is simply the best. There are no words adequate to express the love and gratitude I feel for him. He is my heart's home, my safe place, the beginning and ending of my days.

To God be the glory.

chapter one

FOUR DAYS AFTER MY TWELFTH birthday, my mother came to the bed I was sharing with my younger brother, Thomas, and my two little sisters, Maria and Sophia. She put her warm hand on my shoulder and gave me a little shake. "Manuel," she whispered, her lips close to my ear, "get up. Don't wake the others. Come to the kitchen."

I sat up and rubbed my eyes, not really awake, a little bit confused.

I was accustomed to being awakened at daylight by crowing roosters and braying donkeys, not by my mother while it was still night. I slid out from the covers and put on my sandals. Since I slept in my clothes, I was already dressed. It was dark in our room, but I could see from the oil lamp in my mother's hand that the curtain separating my parents' bed from ours was pulled back and my father was not there. This was in August, a month when the sun rises before seven. Yet it was still so dark outside, my path to the outhouse was lit by the moon, as was the short trail to the kitchen. It was built of adobe, the same as the structure where we slept.

When I stepped inside the kitchen, my mother was heating tortillas and cooking eggs and potatoes over the fire. My father was sitting at the table, drinking coffee. I was surprised when he told my mother to pour a cup for me, too, since the only coffee I'd tasted before was the rare, sticky, cold drops my brother and sisters and I gleaned from the bottoms of our parents' cups.

"Sit down, Manuel," my father said.

I looked first at him, then at my mother. My father's eyes met mine, but when my gaze fell upon my mother, she turned away to make my coffee, dark brown, rich-smelling Nescafé powder, stirred into boiling water. I sat down opposite my father and wondered why, if something was happening early today, my brother and sisters were still sleeping. Rarely was one of us singled out from the other three. So why was I sitting here at the table, while they slept?

I wondered, but I did not ask.

My mother set the cup on the table in front of me. My father pushed the bowl of sugar and the can of milk toward me. My mother set plates of food and a cloth-wrapped stack of corn tortillas on the table between where my father and I sat, but she didn't join us. She wiped her hands on her apron, made the sign of the cross, then turned away from us again.

My father reached for a tortilla, tore it in two, then began to scoop his breakfast into his mouth.

I did the same. Not talking, it did not take us long to finish the meal.

"You're twelve years old now," my father said after he pushed back his plate.

My mother stood beside where he sat. She smiled at me, then wiped at her eyes.

"No longer a boy. A man."

I sat up taller. Took a sip of my coffee. Even though it was still so hot it burned my tongue, I didn't flinch. There were no words in the world I wanted to hear more than these.

"Today, I go to the city," he said.

I tried to make my face stay the same. For as long as I could remember, every year near this time my father left to go work in Mexico City. He would be gone for three months. We would see him when he came home for the month of December. But soon after Christmas, he would leave again, not to return until spring. No matter how many times it happened, I was always surprised when he left. As the end of summer came near, filled with dread at the thought of his absence, I would tell myself lies. *Maybe this time he won't go.*

But there was no work for my father in our village. No jobs like in the city, where he worked building fancy hotels and restaurants to make the money we needed. For food. Taxes on our land. School uniforms and fees. When he came home, my father always brought presents. New shoes. New clothes. Dolls for my sisters. Balls or toy guns for my brother. Paper and colored pencils or paints for me, because I loved to make pictures. He always brought a new dress for my mother and yarn for her crochet. Once my father brought us a weed eater. You put petrol in it to make it run. The machine made lots of noise, but it didn't work nearly as good as our goat.

You would think knowing there would be presents when he came back would make telling my father good-bye easier, but it did not. I cannot express how we all hated it when he was gone. For days my mother and my sisters would cry. My brother and I would pick fights with each other and then with our friends.

My mother was a nervous woman and we were nervous children. Terribly afraid. All four of us. We worried every day that our father was gone. While picking up apples, or bringing up water from the well, or in the evening when our mother was asleep in her bed and we were supposed to be asleep in ours, we would talk, always in whispers or very low, about all the terrible things that could happen.

"Who will protect us if a bad man comes to our house?"

"What will we do if Mommy gets sick? What if she dies? Who will take care of us?"

"What if someone from the government comes and tells us we have to move from our land?" That happened once to my friend Pedro. His mother came and got him out of school. I never saw him again. If something like that could happen to another family, that meant it could happen to us, and if it did, and we had to move far away, how would our father ever find us?

Always after my father had been gone for about three or four days, my mother would stop crying and begin to crochet. She never did handwork when he was at home, but when my father was gone, every time she sat down to take a rest from her work, she would pull out her thread and her hook, and her fingers would fly. She made doilies. Dozens of them in every color and pattern you can imagine. Ones with flowers, horses, chickens even. Our house had doilies everywhere you looked. So many there was no place to put anything without moving a doily first. She made aprons and dresses for my sisters' dolls. Pillow covers. Tablecloths. Even the salt shaker and the bowl where we kept the sugar wore little dresses my mother crocheted for them.

After he had been gone a few weeks, my brother and sisters and I would begin asking our mother, "When will Papa be home? Tomorrow? The next day? Please. He'll be home soon. Right?" After telling us over and over that he had only just left and that it would be many days before we would see him again, our mother would finally tell us we could not say his name again where she could hear.

And so on that morning, I sat there in the kitchen, across from my father, who was leaving, but who had just told me that I was now a man. I willed myself not to be a baby. Not to cry. My feet did not touch the hard-packed dirt that was our floor, but I sat up tall, though I kept my eyes on my plate.

"You are going with me."

My head popped up. I heard my mother let out a little sob, but I didn't look at her. I had eyes only for my father.

"Really? To the city? To work?" I could not believe my good fortune. To go with my dad, to be deemed old enough to go where a man goes, to see what a man sees, to do a man's work—well such a day as this is the dream of every boy!

In my twelve years, I had never traveled more than a couple hours from the central Mexican village where I was born. Nor had any of my friends. But we had heard stories and seen pictures in books at school. We knew there were wonderful things in the city. Big shiny cars. Tall buildings. Lots of other things, too. When the father of one of my friends came home with a TV and hooked it up to their generator, we sat in front of it for hours. We saw huge stadiums full of people watching soccer. Beautiful women who wore fancy dresses and sang songs about love. McDonald's hamburgers. Cheer detergent. *The Price Is Right* and *The Dukes of Hazzard*.

"Pack your satchel. Your clothes, nothing else. Remember your coat. It will be cold before we return," my father said. "When the sun is up, we must leave. It is a two-day walk to get to where the bus comes that will take us to the city."

My brother and my sisters woke up when I went in to gather my things. They sat up in bed.

"What are you doing?" Maria rubbed at her eyes. It was just starting to get light outside.

I knelt on the floor, pulling clothing from the box I kept under the bed. I wished to take my art supplies, but my father had said I should take only my clothes. "I'm packing."

"Why?" Thomas slid from the bed.

"I'm going with Papa."

"Where you going?" Sophia was the baby. Only five.

"To the city. To work."

"You can't go with Papa," Thomas said.

"Yes, I can. I'm twelve now. He says I get to go with him."

Sophia and Maria started crying. They grabbed at my arms. Sophia got out of bed and began taking things out of my satchel while I put them in. "No! No! You can't leave us! You have to stay."

I pulled away from her and grabbed my clothes and my satchel and took them outside, where I set them on a bench so I could stuff my clothes back inside.

Thomas followed me outside. He stood beside me and watched everything I did. Even though he didn't make a sound, I knew he was crying because I could see him wiping his eyes and his nose with his arm.

"Here," I said. I didn't look up, but I handed him my red T-shirt, one I knew he liked. "You can have it. It's too small for me."

There are some moments in a man's life that are forever imprinted on his heart. They divide his life into before and after. Into what was and what came to be. That morning, the one when I told my mother and my brother and my sisters good-bye, is one I will never forget. They were all crying. But I was not even a small bit sad. I was happy. Excited. Only a little scared. My sisters hung on to me. They begged me not to go, but I did not look at them. I pried their hands from my arms. I pushed my brother away when, at the last minute, he, too, tried to make me stay.

My mother did not hug me, for a mother does not cling to her grown-up son.

I was a man now.

A man who had someplace to go.

My father and I walked for what felt like many hours. At first along the side of the dirt road that went from our mountain village downhill to the next small village, then on farther to the next one after that. Along the way we met only a few people, most walking like us, a few on donkeys, and one man in a truck, but no one my father knew. Every person we met kept their head down. Not one of them spoke to us. Finally, when we stopped going downhill, we took off on a trail with few trees and only a little grass, a path that was sometimes so faint and so crooked I did not know how my father knew which way to go.

"See the sun?" he said. "The shadows? We are traveling west. As long as we go west, we will get to the highway. There is no way not to cross it as long as we walk west. You say you cannot see the trail. Here it is." He pointed to the ground. "See? The way the rocks lie? The way the grass grows here, but not here? You must look to see the signs of where other men have walked. You think we are alone. And today, we are. But many others travel this way."

So I looked. And I could now see what my father saw. I, too, could make out the trail.

When we first started walking, I turned and looked back every few minutes. For a long time I was able to locate our house. It got smaller and smaller, but I could still see our village. Now, when I turned around, I could not locate anything that looked familiar to me, only the mountain, green and brown, with blue sky above it. No clouds. When I could no longer see anything I knew, I felt strange for a few minutes. Never before in my life had I spent a night away from my mother's house. But being with my father, walking beside him, sometimes behind him, I was not afraid.

Only tired.

"How long will it take us to get to where the bus picks us up?" I asked my father.

"We will walk all of today. Part of tomorrow."

"And how long will we ride the bus?"

"Two more days."

"We'll go to sleep on the bus?"

"Yes."

"They will let us eat on the bus?"

"Yes."

"Where will we sleep tonight?" I asked, a bit worried.

"On the ground. Under the stars," he said.

"What about the snakes?" We had already seen two. Small ones. But they were rattlesnakes. Mean and sneaky. The color of the sand. After seeing them I had become careful to watch every step I took. I thought maybe we should take turns sleeping so we could watch for them.

"Don't worry," my father said. "I have some special powder we'll sprinkle on the ground around us before we lie down. It will keep the snakes away."

My mother had packed us food, which I was carrying. Tortillas, beans, eggs, and apples from our trees. Because he was stronger than I, my father carried the heavy water jugs. Four of them. Tied together with rope, looped around his neck, hanging from his back.

"May I have some water?" I asked. The sun was already hot on my back. I was sweating. My mouth was dry.

"Only a little. We must make it last."

We stopped so I could drink. After I took three careful sips, I held the jug out for him, but he shook his head and put the lid back on. Even though it felt good to quench my thirst, when my father showed me his choice was to wait longer to drink, I wished I hadn't asked for any for myself.

After the sun had passed overhead and started its way toward the west, my father and I found a place to rest under the shade of a small tree. It felt good to sit down. My legs were strong, and I was young and lean, but we had been walking for what felt like ten hours. I was tired. And by then so hungry my stomach was talking to me. I suppose my father was feeling the same way because we ate, then stretched out our legs, put our hats over our faces, and slept for a little while. Only once, before I slept, did I sit up because I thought I'd heard a snake.

When we woke up, we drank more water, then started out again.

My father had never been a man of many words, so I did not think it odd when he did not speak to me much as we walked. I only wished he would tell me about what it would be like when we got to the city.

Where would we stay? What would we eat? What kind of work would there be for me to do? Would there be other boys, men, like me, or would they all be older, bigger, stronger like my dad? There were so many questions I wanted to ask, but the more I asked, the more quiet he became, so I tried to keep my thoughts inside.

When it got to be nearly night, my father and I stopped to sleep. There were no trees. Only cactus and a few scrubby bushes. Mostly sand and rocks. We had blankets, which we spread out on the ground. My father lay down on his side with his arm curled to give him a place to rest his head. I lay beside him, my back to his back. Soon he began to snore, but I could not sleep. Because of clouds, the night was dark as though we had heavy, wet blankets over our heads. I looked around but I could see nothing. No moon. No stars. But I could hear. Coyotes in the distance. Rustling grass nearby from rabbits, I hoped; maybe mice or rats looking for their dinner. Didn't they know one should sleep when it is night? Then began the sound of birds that sing to the dark, calling to each other in a contest to see who could sing the loudest.

My bed of earth was hard and uneven. Before we'd put our blankets down, my father and I had moved all the rocks we could see, but some of them were still there. I could feel a sharp one under my hip. Another one at my shoulder. I tried to wriggle myself around so they didn't poke me, but I didn't want to wake my father. Because the night air was cool and his back was warm, I moved myself closer to him and did my best to lie still.

Finally, after what felt like hours lying awake, I fell asleep.

The next morning when I woke up, I saw the beginning of the sun, rising in a pink and blue sky. At first I couldn't remember where I was. My mouth was so dry my tongue had no moisture for my lips, and my body was sore from sleeping on rocks. Then I saw my father. He was standing a little ways off, his back to me, a puddle forming near his feet.

Seeing him, I suddenly had to go too. I threw back the blanket and stood up.

While I was a ways off, with my back turned like his, my father returned to our campsite and put out some food for us to eat. Tortillas, a few beans, apples — two for him, one for me.

"Good morning," I said. "Today we get on the bus?" I already knew the answer to my question, but I was so anxious I could not keep myself from asking.

"Yes. Today," he said.

I sat down on the ground and ate my breakfast quickly. While my father finished his, I rolled up our blankets and tied them with rope. The land was flat except for the mountains behind us, which were now a day's journey away. In the daylight, off a very far way, I could see a distant road, with tiny cars and trucks on it. I could hardly keep myself calm. Would the bus be crowded? What if there weren't enough seats? And what if I had to go to the bathroom? My friend Thomas once rode a bus. He said the bus driver had a radio. He played it loud enough that everyone could hear. I hoped the man who drove for us would have one too.

"Are we going to that road?" I asked. I shielded my eyes with my hand so I could see a little better. Every time a car or truck passed by, a cloud of dust followed behind. "Is that where the bus will be?"

"Yes. We will go to that road, and the bus will pick us up," he said.

My satchel was packed and already slung over my shoulder, but my father was taking his time packing his. I wanted to tell him to hurry, but I didn't. Instead I picked up rocks and started throwing them toward the road. Twice my rocks caused a rabbit to jump up and run.

My father stood up. "Manuel. Your shoes."

My sandals were not buckled.

"And your pants."

I was not zipped.

"Now," he said, after I'd fixed myself. "We go."

When we started out, I thought we would walk for only a little while before we got to the road. But even though I thought it looked like it was a small distance away, it seemed that we walked and walked but did not get any closer at all. It was as if the road was moving away from us as we tried to get closer to it.

"Slow down, Manuel," my father said to me more than once, when I got too far ahead of him. "The sun is hot. You will get too tired. Stop and drink."

I could not take my eyes off the stream of cars and trucks that moved so quickly from left to right in front of my eyes. I wanted to see everything. We were close enough now that I could make out the colors of the vehicles. I could tell that many of them were large trucks, the kind used to haul heavy loads from one part of Mexico to the other. Even back and forth from the United States, my father said.

It was some time after noon when we got close enough to the highway that I could hear the sounds of the trucks. We stopped for a short rest and to drink. By now three of our water jugs were empty. We had nothing more to eat, but my father said not to worry. We could buy food when we got to the road. There would be many people traveling like us. On foot to catch the bus. In their own cars and trucks. There would be merchants selling things. While we were stopped, my father took a short nap, but I could not make my eyes stay closed. They kept popping back open to see the road.

As we got closer, the sounds got louder. Finally, our trail led us to the edge of the highway. We turned and began walking north along the side. Trucks zoomed past us. About a quarter kilometer ahead of us was a place where the edge of the highway was wide and where trucks and cars and people on motorbikes and bicycles pulled off and stopped. It was like a little village. My father said it was a place where trucks and cars stopped for fuel and where people got on the bus.

We met men alone and men with their wives and children. People were talking, walking, sitting down in the shade, eating, and drinking. I heard the sounds of radios playing music and of people calling out what it was they had to sell. There was the smell of sweat, garbage, diesel, and of food cooking. Lots of dust. After nothing but dirt and grass and sky, here on the highway there were so many things to see, my eyes jumped around.

But not my feet. For while I had been so eager the past hour, walking, sometimes running, far ahead of my father, now I hung back and walked close to his side, matching my steps to his. The dirt at our feet was soft and red. In my sandals, it felt greasy between my toes. My father said that was because so many cars and trucks leaked oil into the earth.

We walked past a big petrol station where trucks and cars were lined up to buy fuel. We passed places to get tires fixed and rows of booths where people were selling food, soft drinks, and beer. One place sold medicine and herbs. At another the dried skins of snakes hung on wires in the sun like when my mother washed our clothes. Most of the booths were shacks of sticks stuck into the ground with blankets over them to make shade from the sun. A few of them were made of adobe. My father said those were not just booths, but the houses where some people lived. There was one building, a restaurant, made of concrete blocks like my school.

A few booths had roofs of tin. My father and I stopped at one of these. He bought tacos for us. Beefsteak, with onions and garlic. A man cooked the meat while his wife warmed the tortillas. We sat in plastic chairs under a tin shade and ate our food, which was good. My father bought us cold Cokes to drink. Before we were finished a group of children ran up to us. They tried to sell my father sweets and gum, but he told them no.

After we had eaten, my father asked the man cooking to make four more tacos and to wrap them up in foil. When they were ready, he gave them to me to put in my satchel. There was a place to get water there too, so my father stopped and filled three of our jugs. The fourth one he left there. When I asked him why, he said we wouldn't be needing it, but someone else might.

"When does the bus come?" I asked. I was getting a little bit nervous. We had taken a lot of time getting food. After filling our water jugs, my father had come and sat back down in the shade a little ways back from the road. What if the bus pulled up and we were too far away to get there before it left again? In my mind I could see the two of us chasing the bus in a cloud of red dust, yelling as loud as we could for it to wait.

"Soon," he said, but nothing more.

"Where?" I asked.

"There." He pointed to the petrol station, which was close to where we sat.

I stood up and looked down the highway.

"It will come from the south." My father pointed the other way. "You remember. We came from the east."

"Yes."

"On the trail, which is that way." He pointed to the place where we had first come to the highway. "You see where that is? Near where the road curves. Beside that big rock."

"Yes, I see."

But I did not care about the trail. All I wanted to see was our bus. The one that would take us to Mexico City. So I watched and watched until finally off in the distance I saw something I thought might be it. I kept my eyes on the highway. Yes. It was a bus!

"It's coming!" I said. "Look, Papa, it's here." I slung my satchel over my shoulder and picked up one of the water jugs. "Should we hurry? It will be here soon." What if the driver didn't stop? What if we had to run to get on? It would be better to be close to the highway rather than far off like we were now.

"Not yet." My father was not concerned. "The bus will stop. People will get off to buy food and to walk around. The bus will stay here almost an hour before it leaves again. We'll wait here in the shade until time to get on."

I didn't believe I could bear more waiting.

Finally, the bus pulled in. Like my father had told me, people got off. Some of them went into the restaurant made of blocks. Some people went to the booths to buy food. Some only walked around for a few minutes, then got back on.

All of this I saw from our spot in the shade. I could not sit still. I put my satchel over my shoulder, then took it off. I got a drink from our jug. I went behind the booth to relieve myself, but quickly, in case the bus got ready to leave.

Finally, the people who had gotten off began to head back to the bus. Some, who like us were only now getting on, made a line. They were waiting for the bus driver to take their money so they, too, could get on the bus.

When I saw all this happening, I looked at my father. He saw what I saw, but he did not move. "Papa? Isn't it time? What if there aren't enough seats? Shouldn't we go stand in the line?"

"Not yet. The best seats are always the last ones sold."

I looked at the people at the front of the line. Too bad they didn't have my father's knowledge about how to get the best seats.

Not until there were only two people left waiting to get on did my father stand up, pick up his bag and the water jugs, and start out to the bus. I walked beside him, so eager to see what the bus was like inside, so glad it was finally time for us to get on. My hands were sweaty. My heart was beating nearly out of my chest. I couldn't wait to sit up so high and to see what it would be like to watch the land rush by. Were the best seats the ones in the front or the ones near the back? Would my father let me sit by the window, or was that where he would sit?

The driver was standing near the bottom step of the bus. It was just him, my father, and me. Everyone else had already gotten on. My father set the water jugs in the dirt beside where I stood. From the ground, I could see inside the bus. Four steps up was the driver's seat and the steering wheel. The bus had air-conditioning, something I'd heard about but never experienced. I could feel the cool air coming out into the heat where we stood.

Soon I would climb those steps.

I would board this bus. And it would take me someplace I'd never been before. I would see sights I'd never seen. I'd work hard. Make money. Help my family. Getting on the bus would mark the beginning of my life as a man.

"One. To Mexico City," my father said. He handed the man some money.

I stood, waiting. Holding tightly to my satchel. Looking up at my father. He knew what to do.

"Is the boy going?" the bus driver asked.

My father shook his head and climbed the first step onto the bus.

I put my hand on the frame of the door to follow my father up the steps.

"You can't get on without a ticket," the man said.

"Papa?" Again, I tried to climb the first step. Again, the man blocked my way.

"Papa, what should I do?"

My father turned around, and he was no longer my papa. His face was hard and mean like a sharp stone. He was someone I did not know. He put his hand on my chest to keep me from following him up the steps. I struggled, but he pushed harder to keep me from getting on the bus.

"You are not going," he said.

"But Papa!" My heart could not hear the words in my ears. "What do you mean? I'm coming with you. I'm going to work with you."

"No. Listen to my voice. Go home to your mother. Tell her you saw me get on the bus. Tell her I am gone forever. Tell her I said I'm not coming back."

"No! Papa!" I was not a man, for my eyes filled with tears. "Don't leave me!" I grabbed hold of his arm. "No!" I screamed. "I'm going with you. I have to. Don't leave me!"

My father twisted my wrist to make me let go of his arm.

"Let go of me. Stop crying like a baby. Let go of me now!"

I grabbed him with my other hand, but he twisted it, too.

"No! I am supposed to go with you. Papa, I do not under-stand. Please."

I reached for him but he had stepped up onto the third step. I caught hold of his leg and tried to hold on, but he bent down and put his hand on my chest. He shoved me so hard I fell backward into the dirt beside the bus.

"Wait! Don't leave me!"

I scrambled to get up. I kept saying the same words over and over again. But it was as if I was whispering for as much as I was heard. The bus driver jumped on the bus behind my father. He took his seat and slammed the opening of the bus shut. I pounded and kicked the doors and begged the man to let me in. When I heard him put the bus in gear, when I felt it lurch forward, I tried to pry the two doors apart with my hands, but I could not.

I ran and ran after the bus until I could not run anymore. Then I stood watching until I could see only a trail of red dust where it had been. My tears fell like a stream. My heart swelled until it was so heavy I believed it would break out of my chest. My belly cried too, and I vomited, over and over again, onto the oily, red dirt.

chapter two

HOW LONG I STOOD AT the edge of the highway, my eyes on the road where the bus had been, I do not know. What I remember is that suddenly my thirst became so great I could think of nothing but quenching it. My legs trembled so that I was not sure they would carry me, but my throat was so dry I was almost crazy with thirst. I think I had cried so many tears, there was no water left in me. My father had taken one of our water jugs with him. The other two were where he had left them, tied together with the rope, sitting in the dirt next to where the bus had been. When I reached them, I squatted down and drank and drank.

Finally, I wiped my mouth, stood up, and looked around. Not one person met my eyes. There had been people standing nearby when my father pushed me away from the bus. Mothers and fathers, shopkeepers, and children selling sweets had seen what had happened. But not one person spoke a word to me. No one asked me if I was all right, if I was lost, or if I needed help.

Standing there, wondering what to do, the words of my father repeated themselves over and over in my mind. *Go home to your mother. Tell her I'm gone forever. I'm not coming back.* My heart was flooded with shame. I did not know what my terrible deed had been, but I knew I had done something wrong, something so unforgivable it had turned my father against all of us. He had treated me as a man, but I had acted like a child. I had failed him. I had failed my mother. My brother. My little sisters.

The sun was a good ways past the middle of the sky. My shirt was wet from my sweat. My arms felt heavy and weak, but I swung the jugs over my shoulders and set my way toward the path to my home. What else could I do? I had no money, no friends, no family in this place.

The jugs were so heavy, I staggered when I walked. Every step I took, they swung outward, then came back to knock against my thighs. The rope rubbed and cut into my neck, causing pain like a burn from my mother's cooking fire. I tried to walk with my hands under the rope, holding it away from my neck, but I couldn't for very long. When I spotted an empty cardboard box on the side of the highway, I tore a piece off the end of it and put it between the rope and my neck.

I followed the highway to the big rock where the path to my home began. Now I knew why my father had pointed it out to me. When had he decided I would be traveling back to our village without him? Why had he done this? What had I done wrong? Over and over, fresh tears filled my eyes and spilled down my dusty cheeks. I kept wiping and wiping at my face with the sleeve of my shirt.

I started off down the path. Two days of fear lay before me. Never before had I walked alone. What if I came to a fork? Which way would I go? What if I got lost? I had not paid attention to the path, to the way we had come. I had been a child, walking where my father told me to walk. Sleeping when he told me to sleep. Eating what he told me to eat.

My stomach called, but I did not answer. The tacos in my satchel were all the food I had for my two-day journey. I would wait until the sun was gone to eat my first meal.

I had been nervous traveling with my father. But that nervousness had been mixed with excitement and anticipation of the great adventures that waited for me. Walking alone, I was terrified, and my terror was mixed with confusion, grief, and dread. My mother. How could I face her? How was I going to tell her my terrible news? And what would we do without my father?

These thoughts did not leave me as I walked. While the sun was up, I stopped only to drink. The sun kept its march across the sky, and I watched as my shadow became longer and longer, as the sky turned from blue to pink to orange. Finally, when it became too dim for me to see my path, I stopped, ate a taco, spread my blanket, and tried to sleep.

But sleep would not come. I didn't have special powder to keep snakes away, and I was afraid. The ground was hard and the night air was cold. I did not feel like a man. I shivered and I wished for the warmth and protection of my father. I thought of my home. I longed for the comforting noise of my brother's snore as he slept next to me in the bed, for the sounds of my sisters, whispering to each other before they dreamed, and for the muffled voices of my parents behind the curtain that separated their bed from ours.

In my whole life, I had not slept one night by myself.

I lay on my back and looked at the stars and the half moon above me. Never had I felt so alone. Never had I seen myself so small and so very weak. My heart raced in my chest. My stomach hurt. My legs would not be still. I heard noises all around me and I was so afraid, I wondered if I might die. I had heard stories of people who died because of great fright.

I did not want to die.

So I prayed. To God. To the saints. To the virgin Mary. I asked for protection.

And it was given to me.

For the next morning, when I woke with the first light of dawn, I saw I had not died in my sleep. I looked all around. Flat, dry ground to the west, from where I'd come. No sign of the highway. No sounds of trucks or cars, for I had already come too far. But to the east I could see the blue gray mountain of my village. I would walk all day, and by nightfall, unless I lost my way, I would be home. So I ate two tacos and rolled up my blanket. One of my water jugs was full, the other one about one-third. To make my load more balanced, I poured water from the full jug into the other one so that they were even. I tried to be careful, but my arms quivered, and I spilled some on the ground. Today, I decided, instead of drinking from one jug, I would drink some from both.

It was when I set out toward the mountain, with my satchel over my shoulder and the jugs around my neck, that I first saw him—a small dog with shaggy tan hair and pointed, standing-up ears. He was on the path ahead, sitting with his back to me, but he was looking over his shoulder my way, as if he was waiting for me to catch up. I stopped. The dog looked friendly, but one can never tell about animals. Many of them are mean or sick. Sometimes they bite.

Still the dog waited.

So slowly, I walked toward him. But I didn't get any closer, for as soon as I walked, he did too. He stayed ahead of me, picking his way around rocks and bushes, staying on the path. Ever so often, he would look back to see if I was still behind him. When I stepped off the trail to relieve myself, he waited for me. When I stopped to drink, he stopped too. Though he was only a dog, the sight of him gave me comfort, and I did not feel so alone or quite so afraid.

Together we walked and walked, until the sun was past the middle of the sky. I was hungry and tired. I thought perhaps the dog was too. So I stopped to rest and to eat. I had one taco left, but still water in both of my jugs. I broke off part of my taco and called to the dog. But he didn't come. He was lying down at the edge of the path, panting in the heat. I eased toward him, slowly, in case he decided to bite. But when I did, he got up and moved farther down the trail, keeping a space between the two of us. So I set the food down for him. I shaped the foil the taco had been wrapped in into a bowl for him. I poured him some water from my jug, then moved back to where I'd left my satchel and the other water jug.

The dog watched all of this. He waited until I moved away, then he came back, sniffed the taco, and gulped it down in one bite. He lapped up the water in the little foil bowl. I knew he needed more water than what I'd given him, so I took my knife and cut the top off one of my jugs so he could drink from it. When I took it to him, he moved away again, but when I stepped back, he returned to drink and drink.

Afterward, I stretched out to rest before beginning the last part of my journey. Before I closed my eyes I saw that the dog, too, had laid himself down.

The first portion of my walk back toward my home, I had hurried, walking as fast as I could and sometimes running under the blazing sun. That morning, too, I had walked quickly, my eyes never leaving the mountain before me.

But after my meal and my nap, my pace slowed. I was no longer afraid of not finding my way because even though I recognized no landmarks on my path, I could see, far ahead, the rooftops of my village. Soon, I would come to the dirt road that would take me there. I could see smoke from cooking fires. By night, I would be home. Home. Where my mother and my sisters and my brother were passing this day unaware of the terrible news I was bringing.

My mother spent much of her time preparing our meals. She

made tortillas and cooked beans and rice every day. She washed our clothes and hung them on the fence to dry. We children had tasks to do too. My brother's job was to milk the goat and to pull weeds from the garden. My little sisters helped my mother sweep the hard ground around our compound. They brought up water from the well every evening.

I felt no joy as my feet took me closer and closer to my home. It had been three days since I'd seen my family, but it felt like three years. My mind could not tell my tongue what words to say to them. And so the closer I got to my home, the slower my steps became.

My family's compound—two adobe buildings, an outhouse, a garden, and a fenced place for the goat—stood at the edge of our tiny village. It was surrounded by apple trees. I came close, just as the sun was beginning to set, but I stood a ways off, where I was not seen but where I could see them.

The day was nearly done, and the four of them were sitting outside, in the cool of the evening, the best time of the day. My mother sat in a chair near the door of our sleeping house, her hands working green yarn. At her feet, red geraniums spilled over the sides of the tin cans they were planted in. My brother was throwing rocks, trying to hit a jar stuck on top of one of the posts of the fence. Two times he missed. The third time he knocked the jar off the fence. My sisters squatted in the dirt playing one of their clapping hand games. I heard them laugh, saw the littlest one fall over into the dirt. In the low branches of the trees above them, our little flock of chickens had already settled in for the night.

Watching my family, seeing my home, a part of me wanted to run toward them as fast as I could. After two days of fear and loneliness, I longed to feel safe, to fill my empty stomach with food from my mother's kitchen. I wanted to feel Sophia's arms around my knees. I wanted to wash my feet and my hands, then lay my body down in the bed I shared with my brother and my sisters. I wanted to see their smiles and hear their laughter.

But another part of me did not want to enter our compound. In my shame and grief, I wanted to turn away, to leave forever, to go somewhere, anywhere. I wished to leave them behind as my father had done, for I did not know how I would bear their disappointment, their fear, their disbelief.

So I stood on the outside looking in like a stranger, an unseen observer of my own family. My feet felt stuck to the ground. I knew I should go to my mother, that I should deliver my news to her now, that I should not wait any longer. But I dreaded this thing more than anything I'd ever dreaded in my life.

With my father gone, I was now the man of my mother's house. This thought had come to me while I was on the path. I was not ready. I was weak. I was not wise. I did not know how to do so many things.

My mother's tears would be ones I could not dry.

It was only seeing her motion to my brother and my sisters that it was time for them all to go inside that made me move ahead. To come to them when they were already in bed would be worse. It would frighten them.

The dog had been sitting, waiting, still a distance from me. But when I made my move to go forward, he came close to me, not near enough for me to touch him, but closer to my side than he'd been all day.

It was he my family saw first. "Look," my brother said to my sisters, "a dog."

"Stay away from him," my mother said. "Shoo!" She clapped her hands and tried to chase the dog away. He moved back up the trail, which led my mother's eyes to me.

"Manuel."

Her face was like that of a woman who has seen a ghost. Her eyes did not want to believe, and her feet did not move from her place in front of our house. Her hands made the sign of the cross.

But my brother and sisters ran to me. Grabbed me. My sisters hugged me and kissed me. They took my hands and pulled me toward my mother.

"Manuel, you're back! You're home! Mama, look! Manuel is home. But where is Papa? Is he coming home too?"

I did not answer them. My arms stayed at my sides. I did not return their hugs. I was too afraid. My sorrow was too great. I went to my mother. I stood before her, but I could not find my voice.

My mother spoke. "Your father. Something has happened to him. He is sick?"

"No, Mama," I said.

"He is hurt?"

"No." I shook my head.

My mother began to weep. She fell into my arms. "He is dead." Her tears wet my shirt. "My son, my son, I knew. I saw it in a dream. Tell me. How did it happen?"

I held my mother. "Papa is not dead. He is gone. Forever. He is not coming back."

"No."

Even though my mother made me tell her over and over again during the next several days exactly what had happened, she was sure I had misunderstood my father's words. So she watched for him. Day and night, whenever she paused from her work, I would see her fix her eyes on the path that led away from our home. Her hope was so great, even I wondered if perhaps I had been wrong. Could it have been a dream? A vision that was not true? Perhaps my ears had not heard what they heard. Perhaps my eyes had not seen what they saw.

My sisters insisted their papa was coming back. It was as if nothing I'd told them was real. They talked every day about when he would be back and about the presents he would bring them. Pretty new dolls. New dresses and new shoes.

But my father did not come back. Not after a week. Not after a month. Not after two months. Still my mother watched. But when December—the month my father would normally return with money and gifts—passed, I saw hope leave her eyes.

A boy grows up believing nothing but good of his father. His papa is everything to him. A boy wants to walk like his father and talk like his father. He hopes, one day, to look like his father. In some ways a boy's father is like a god to him.

Until the day my father left us, I believed him to be a perfect man.

In the years since my father disappeared from my sight, I have spent many hours thinking about why he left us. Did his love for our family die? He had a wife and four children. Were our needs too great for him? Did he break under our weight? It has crossed my mind that my father may have had another family. There were no signs that I can recall, but I have heard of men who live double lives.

I will always love my father, and as years have passed, I believe I have come to forgive him. But here is one truth that will never change: My father's greatest sin was that he was a coward. What kind of man would trick his son as he tricked me? What kind of husband would ask a son to deliver such news to his wife?

A man with courage would not have left his family with no explanation, without any good-byes. Forgive me for saying these words, but a man of good character would not have left at all.

I suppose there is one thing you can say about my father.

He kept his word.

None of us has seen him since the day he left on the bus.

Thankfully, our trees had borne more fruit that fall than ever before. Not a woman who wasted anything, my mother had stored lots of apples. There had been so many she had run out of room in the kitchen and so put boxes and crates of them in our bedroom. There were apples everywhere. On the shelves. In the corners. Even under our beds.

That first year, our family survived eating those apples, eggs from our chickens, and little else. There was no money for coffee, for milk, for sugar, for meat. My brother and my sisters stopped going to school because my mother could not pay the fees.

There was great sadness in our house. No laughter. Only hunger and fear. My sisters did not play. My brother and I did not make up games. Our shame was great. We kept to ourselves, for the bad luck that had fallen on our family was known throughout our village. Neighbors stayed away, though occasionally we would wake up to find a little sack of beans or some corn left on top of the fence.

During the day, my mother kept a strong face. She went about her work. But at night, I often heard her crying after she thought we were asleep.

The dog I had met on the trail stayed near us for several months. He never came close enough for any of us to touch him, but every morning, when we woke up, he would be asleep just inside our gate. We grew accustomed to his presence. Then one day he was not there anymore.

My sister heard from someone that thirteen dogs, nearly every one in our village, had disappeared on the same night, a night when there was no moon. No one knew for sure what happened, but people claimed an old woman had passed through on a white horse. Everyone had thought she was a good woman, but it turned out she was a witch who put a hex on all the dogs. The hex made them go crazy. They ran around in circles three times, then fell over dead.

When my mother overheard us talking about the old woman and the hex, she told us to hush. Our village was still full of dogs. If we stopped for a moment we could hear them barking. She said the story about the thirteen dogs was a lie and that the dog at our house had simply moved on to someplace where he could find food.

That first winter was the hardest. The hungriest. The next year was bad too, but at least we knew what to expect. We planted a bigger garden. We killed our goat and sold the meat.

When I was fourteen, life for my family became a little easier. I got a job at the petrol station on the highway, where I could work five and a half days a week. I cannot tell you how much the life of my family improved because of the money I made. No longer did my mother go without food so that my brother and sisters could eat. She was able to cook enough beans and rice for them all to have enough every day, as well as a small piece of pork or a chicken at least once a week. I can still remember the change I saw in my mother's face when she no longer had to worry about food.

The man who owned the station let me sleep in a little room at the back. His wife sold me food. I was lonely but not afraid, because the man locked me inside when he went home every night. Today, the thought of this frightens me. What if there had been a fire? I would have been trapped. But at the time, that thought never came to me.

I was so tired at the end of every day, sleep came quickly. On Friday, the man would give me my wages, and on Saturday, when the station closed at noon, I went home. I had a bicycle I could use most of the way. By riding as fast as I could, getting off and pushing when I couldn't pedal because of deep sand or big rocks, I nearly always made it home before dark.

As soon as I arrived, my mother would give me some hot food. Then, even though it was night, she would get out the rubboard and the tub. She would wash my clothes and hang them on the fence to dry so they would be ready for me to wear at my job the next week.

I looked forward all week to my night at home. I was happy I had a job, and it gave me great pleasure to give my mother money, but I missed my family. I loved seeing my brother, listening to my sisters talk, and sitting at my mother's table. I loved sleeping in the bed next to my brother, with my sisters and my mother close by.

Sunday noon, the time I had to leave to go back, always came too soon. One night with my family was not long enough. But I would pack my clothes and get on my bicycle. My sisters would hug me. My mother would make the sign of the cross. Leaving my family caused my heart to ache, and as I pedaled away, I was careful not to look back.

I had been working for almost a year when my brother, Thomas, began working at the petrol station alongside me. In some ways, this made things better for all of us—I had a companion during the week, and my mother and sisters had extra money. With the two of us working, my mother was able to buy coffee, milk, and sometimes sweet bread or cookies for a treat. There was even enough money for our sisters to go back to school, but by then, Maria was twelve and had missed so much she didn't want to go back. Sophia was eight. She did return to school. It was difficult for her at first, but she was smart. Maria helped her, and soon she caught up with the other children her age. Sophia loved to read stories about fairies and princesses and beautiful things. She brought books home from school. She would read a story to me every time I came home. Hearing her voice moving over the words brought great joy to me.

When I was fifteen years old, I paid a man two hundred dollars to help me come to the United States. For while there was still work for me at the petrol station, I knew I could make much higher wages if I went north. I would be able to provide a better life for my mother. I could help my sisters. They were getting older and more beautiful every day. It was not good for them to be without a man to look after them six days out of the week. If I made more money, my brother could leave the petrol station. He could return home to be the man of the house. His presence would provide protection for them. He could help my mother with the garden, tend to some goats, and rebuild the fence around our compound, which was in very bad repair.

My mother cried when I told her my plan. She tried to talk

me out of leaving. She told me everything was all right the way it was. But I was already a man. It was my job to provide. Going to the U.S. was the best thing I could do. On the day that I left, I promised her that she could count on me to come back.

It is difficult and dangerous to cross into the U.S. today. There are many dishonest coyotes, men who will take a person's money, demand more, then not do what they have been paid to do. Many desperate Mexicans lose their lives in the desert trying to get across. Some die in the backs of trucks that have no air-conditioning, no circulation, no water, and no food. Whenever I hear of such stories, I feel a great sorrow for these people. For their families. I understand the desperation that makes it worth it to them to take such risks.

It was difficult and dangerous when I made my trip as well. The first leg of my journey, I walked with five other men for one and one-half days across the desert to get to where we had been told to meet the man who would smuggle us across. The other men were much older than I, but they were no more determined. I kept up with them. I did not complain. We saw scorpions and rattlesnakes along the way, which made me remember my father's magic powder and wish I had some of my own. The other men did not appear so afraid, but I have always been terribly fearful of snakes. Each time I saw one, my heart would pound for what felt like forever. My mouth would go dry, and my palms would become wet.

The path we six took was so winding and so poorly marked, I am amazed we did not get lost, traveling mostly at night as we did. By the time we found the man who was to be our transport into

Texas, we had been out of water and food for several hours. It was just after noon and the sun beat down on our heads. Thankfully, the man had something for us to eat and water for us to drink.

"Gentlemen, see these appliance boxes?"

The man was young. White. Maybe twenty-five. He had on new Reebok shoes. Very clean. White with black trim. I wondered then if they were real or fake.

"They're for you to hide in. We're twenty-five miles from the border. When you feel the truck stop, be very quiet. Stay absolutely still. We're crossing at a busy time. It's going to take us awhile to get through. Maybe a couple hours. Hopefully, the border patrol will be too busy to check inside. But if they do, if they find you, I'm letting you know right now that I will claim to have no knowledge of you. I will say you must have sneaked inside at my last stop. You'll be on your own."

He jingled his keys and looked over at me, I guess because I was so young.

"So, that's the deal. Everybody understand? If you're not up to it, now's the time to let me know. Otherwise, let's load up. Soon as we clear the border, I'll pull over and let you guys know we made it okay. Until then, once we get going, not a peep out of any of you."

I was the last one to climb into the back of the man's truck. Except for my desire to take care of my family, I do not know for sure that I would have had the courage to pull myself up. But I had told my mother not to worry about me. I had made her feel bad for trying to make me stay. The truth was I was scared. What if we got caught? And what if we did not? I knew no one in the U.S. I had no family waiting for me, no place to stay, no set job. Everything in me wanted to turn around and walk back through the desert, back to my home.

But I did not.

It was terribly hot inside the boxes, but the man had given each of us three bottles of water to keep with us. For the two hundred dollars, he was going to take us all the way to Dallas. He said there was much work there for men like us.

It did take a long time to get across. When we got to the border and it was finally our turn to go through customs, I could hear our driver talking to someone in English. My legs hurt from being cramped inside the box, but I did not move. I barely breathed. *Please, God,* I prayed. After what seemed like forever, I felt the weight in the truck shift as the man took his place behind the wheel. I heard him slam the door and start the engine. Finally, I felt motion.

We drove for several more minutes, then the other men and I came out of our boxes, smiling and glad. We were in Texas, and everything would work out just fine.

Once we got to Dallas, my traveling companions and I learned that what the man had told us about plenty of jobs was the truth.

For grown men. Yes. But not, I found, for a fifteen-year-old boy who looked more like twelve.

Five hungry days passed, and I got no work. I cannot describe to you my fear and despair. Day after day, I would show up early at the downtown location where people came to get workers, only to be passed over for men older and bigger than I. Every day that I did not get work, I became more afraid. What should I do? My family was depending on me. I had no money to return to my village. And even if I did, my job at the petrol station was no longer mine.

My first two nights, I paid three dollars for a place to sleep on the dirty floor in a house run by a skinny white woman who took in Mexican workers. But when two days and nights passed without me getting hired, I spent the next three nights on the street. I could not waste any more of the little bit of money I had brought with me.

Those nights on the street were some of the worst ones I have spent. They were even worse than the night I spent in the desert when I was twelve. No, there were no snakes, no scorpions, and no coyotes. But there were worse things. Men who were drunk and who were on drugs. Men who offered to pay me to do things so vile I will not speak of them here.

Finally, on my sixth day, a man took a chance on me. I do not know why he picked me, but I cannot tell you how grateful I was when he pointed me out and told me to get into his truck and come work for him. That day and every one for the next two weeks, I made four dollars an hour unloading pallets of bricks in a neighborhood where many nice houses were being built.

Four dollars an hour. I had money to buy food, money to pay for a place to stay, and money to take to the Western Union office to send to my family.

That was twenty-three years ago.

The needs of my family have never left my mind. I work hard, for them as well as for myself. No matter what my income, I have, from the beginning, sent half, sometimes more, of everything I make to my mother's address. My sisters help her manage the money. Some of it goes to them and some to my brother. Because of what I do, my nieces and nephews can go to school. My brother and sisters do not have to worry if they get sick.

We are all grown-up now. All of us married, except for me. My brother lives with his family in Mexico City. Because of the distance, I only get to see him about every three or four years.

Sophia lives with her husband in Progresso, a town close to the Texas border. It is an eight-hour drive from Eden Plain, which is where I live now. Sophia has one little girl. Her name is Veronica, but I call her Dulce, the Spanish word for candy, because she is so sweet.

I try to make it down to Progresso at least every three months. Family is everything, and Sophia and I are very close. We live nearer to each other than our other siblings, and so we are together the most. I love Sophia. Her husband is a good man. They live in a nice house, one that makes me feel welcome every time I cross its threshold. Sophia cooks a big meal when she knows I am coming, usually chicken with mole sauce, which she knows is my favorite. She prepares a comfortable bed for me in the extra room they normally use for storage.

I enjoy all of this special treatment, but Sophia's hospitality is not the only reason why I visit so often. No, I go for my little niece. My favorite part of the trip is when I drive up and Dulce runs out of the house to jump into my arms. Sophia says Dulce sits at the window and watches for me on the days I am expected to arrive.

When I think of her doing this, my throat gets tight.

"Uncle Manny! Uncle Manny!" She hugs my neck and kisses my face. "I'm so glad you came to see me! Why did you stay away for so long?"

I love all my nieces and nephews, but I must make this confession to you. Dulce is my favorite. You might think that is only because I see her more than the others, but that would not be the whole truth. Dulce is simply special. If you met her, I believe you would agree. She is three years old, with pretty brown curls, round pink cheeks, and teeth so white they look like two rows of little pearls when she smiles. I know what you are thinking. All little girls are pretty. I agree. But there is truly something special about Dulce. She moves like a little butterfly. She is smart and kind. Already, she wants to help her mother in the kitchen. And you should hear her sing! I have never heard a child as young as Dulce who can sing the way that she does. It is enough to make water come to the eyes of a man.

"She sounds like an angel," I tell her mother. "That Dulce can sing like an angel."

Someday, I may have a daughter of my own. But if I do, the moment I hold her in my arms, I know my heart will have one fear. Will I love her as much as I love Dulce?

At this moment I honestly do not know. Dulce is that dear to me.

Of the four of us children, only Maria still resides in our village, which is ten hours from Sophia's house, eighteen hours from Eden Plain. Maria's house is near our mother's. She looks out for her needs.

Every year at Christmas my mother sends me a box of doilies she has crocheted. Now a man does not want doilies in his house, but I love my mother, and the work of her hands is the way she shows her love to me. So every year I put those boxes on a certain shelf in the top of my closet. I have often wondered, if something happens to me and strangers or even people from my church come and go through my things, what they will think of a grown man with hundreds of doilies in his house?

Our mother is not rich, but according to Maria, who writes us letters every few months, she does not lack for anything. Our mother's home is in good repair. She can buy medicine for her arthritis, warm clothes for the winter, and she can purchase anything she wants to eat. She should have no worries about money or about ever having enough food.

Still, after all these years of living with all of her needs met and a little money tucked away, every night my mother lies down to sleep surrounded by the apples she harvests and stores under her bed. I think she should not bend to pick them up anymore. She should not reach to pull them from the tree. She could sell those apples to someone who would come and get them. She could even give them away. But Maria says no. Our mother insists on harvesting them herself. To her, those apples are like money in the bank, a hedge against hunger.

There is much talk in the news these days about immigration. That is a topic I think I had best leave alone, except to assure you that I am not illegal. In 1986, the U.S. government passed the Immigration Reform and Control Act. Those of us workers who could prove we had lived in the U.S. since 1982 and had worked in agriculture for more than ninety days between May 1, 1985, and May 1, 1986, were given green cards. We were granted lifelong legal residence in the U.S.

Because of my green card I can travel freely. I can work legally in any job made available to me. If I wanted to, I could even hold a government job. I have never left Texas, but I have lived all over the state, including the cities of Houston, Dallas, and Midland. I have spent much time in small towns, too. Apple Springs. Maypearl. Grand Saline. Those are only a few of the places where I have lived. Wherever I heard there was work, that is where I went.

Over the twenty-three years I have been in the U.S., I have done many jobs, worked for many different men. Most of my bosses have been fair. But some have treated me badly.

When I was seventeen, before I got my green card, I was part of a crew of Mexican men hired for two hot August weeks of clearing brush from a fence row.

It happened that among the group, I was the youngest worker. A man named Oligario was the oldest. He was past sixty and he looked out for me.

"Here, take this." On the first morning of the job, Oligario pulled an extra bandana from his satchel. "Tie it around your head so that it hangs down in the back. Like this. Then put your cap on over it. This way, you will keep the back of your neck from getting burned."

I did as he said. With the cloth hanging down the back of my head, I looked like a woman. But at the end of the day, Oligario was right. My neck was not red. But I did have terrible blisters on my hands.

"Your gloves are too thin," he said.

He was right. The gloves I had were not thick enough to hold up to this kind of work. They were already getting holes. "I don't have any others."

Oligario looked at his watch. It was seven o'clock in the evening. "Come on. We will catch a ride to town. You cannot work with those gloves. We must go to Wal-Mart and get you some better ones."

"Tonight?"

"You need them before tomorrow."

I knew Oligario was tired. I was tired and I was a much younger man. He had already taken off his boots. But his fatigue, nor mine, did not seem to be a concern. He put his boots back on and told me to come. Together, we walked to the highway, then turned toward town.

As we stepped together, I thought of the last time I'd traveled a path similar to this. Me and my father. Side by side. I swallow as I picture this, as I think of the cruelty of my father and of the kindness of this man, who was not even blood.

We didn't have to walk far. Within a few minutes, someone who was going right by Wal-Mart stopped and picked us up. Once we got there, Oligario helped me pick out the best gloves for the work we were doing. They cost five dollars, which would not leave me much to get by on until I got paid, but Oligario said the gloves were worth it, were necessary, and that I should get them. So I did. At the checkout, he opened the refrigerator case and pulled out two Cokes. After I paid for my gloves, he bought the Cokes and gave one to me.

I will never forget Oligario. He was kind to me during the whole time that we worked together, even shared his water with me when two days in a row I did not bring enough and ran out.

At the time, none of us on the crew were legal, but we were a group of good men. The only problem was Jorge, who drank whiskey at night. He enjoyed his drink, but the rest of us did not. Within minutes of lying down, Jorge would begin to snore so loudly it was almost impossible for the rest of us to sleep.

"Jorge! Turn over!" the other men would yell at him, but it did no good. I stuffed rags in my ears to try to get some sleep. Jorge sounded like a donkey calling for a mate. After three nights of this, the other men made Jorge sleep outside. He grumbled about this, but he did not give up his drink.

During the two weeks on that job, we worked hard with machetes, shovels, and hoes, starting early every day, working until the sun was low in the sky. The landowner had promised us good pay when the job was done.

"Do a good job for me, and I'll treat you right," he said.

He had a little blond boy who rode around with him in his truck. Oligario gave the boy candy. Every time he saw Oligario, he ran up to him for more. Once the child saw me with my sketchpad and pencil.

"Can you make me a picture?" He had blue eyes with very light lashes.

"Sure. What would you like a picture of?" I asked him.

"A dog." He leaned against my knee while I drew. I remember how warm he felt and how he smelled like soap.

"How about that?" I tore off the page and gave it to him.

"Papa, look!" He ran off to show his dad.

We saw the man's pretty wife. She had a kind face. The man let us sleep in his hay barn. There was no bathroom, but he had a water faucet we could use. At the end of every day, we took turns behind the barn, cleaning up with lukewarm well water that trickled from the end of a long green garden hose.

We pooled our money and prepared our food together over a cooking fire we built twice a day outside the barn. Eggs in the morning. Beans and rice at night. Always tortillas. Every few days, a stew made with ground beef or a chicken, tomatoes, onions, and garlic.

"That smells good." The five of us were eating our supper one night when the man came by to check on something at the barn.

"Would you like some?" Jorge was our cook.

"Sure. If you've got enough." He sat down with us and ate some stew.

I have never worked so hard in my life as I did those two weeks. My shoulders and my chest ached with soreness. Even inside my new and better gloves, my hands became rough and calloused. After only five days, I could tell that the muscles in my arms were getting harder and bigger from hour after hour of swinging at the brush and the weeds. Day after day we worked on that fence row. We transformed it from a snaky, overgrown mess into a tidy, clean border around the man's property.

There is a pleasure, a sense of pride, that comes from a difficult job well done. That pleasure is real and it is important, but I do not for a minute believe that pleasure is what drives a man to work hard.

At least not a poor man. Not a man who has seen hunger in a loved one's eyes. For men like that, for men like me, hard work is a means to an end. We work for one thing.

Money.

All that we can get.

Every blister, every sore back, every cut and scrape we five men endured during those hot two weeks was given willingly, offered in trade for anticipated wages and what they represented.

Food. Shelter. Security. For us. For those we loved.

We were glad for the work and eager for the pay.

At the end of the two weeks, we were not quite finished, so the man asked us if we could stay for another three days to get the job done. All of us agreed. Of course. We were actually glad. More days, more pay. In our heads we counted up how much more money we would make.

When it was done, when we had finished the job, we stood waiting for the landowner to give us our pay, the good wages we expected.

Instead, one by one, he handed each of us a twenty-dollar bill.

Twenty dollars? What was that? I looked at Oligario. At the other men. Their faces were hard. Their jaws were set.

"Get off my land." The man had a pistol in his hand. "Now.

I've already called the sheriff and told him I found a bunch of wetbacks hiding out in my barn. He's on his way. Gentlemen, if you don't want to be on a bus back to Mexico by tonight, I suggest you get off my land."

Twenty dollars for two and a half weeks' work.

Five of us. One of him. Yet the law was on the way. I saw Jorge move to step forward. I saw Oligario put his hand on his shoulder to stop him.

Other men would have gone back later and burned the man's barn. They would have poisoned his dogs or fouled his water well. God forgive me, I was so angry I wanted to do every one of those things to this man. How easy it would have been! But no. We simply picked up our satchels, put our hats back on, and disappeared from the property before the sheriff had time to arrive. Five different men. Five routes away from that bad man.

That was the last time I took a job clearing a fence row, the last time I saw any of those men. But it was not the last time I've been cheated. Not even nearly. One thing I want to make clear. I do not wish to start an argument about immigration. Even if I were inclined to do so, it would not be a productive discussion, because even though I am Mexican, I can see both sides.

But here is one fact: If he is treated unfairly, an undocumented worker has no recourse. No voice. He does his job, then takes whatever is given to him. If he is not paid, he will never call the police. If he is paid less than what he was promised, he will maybe look the man in the eye, but he will not challenge him. Rather he will put what he is given in his pocket and move on to someone who he hopes will treat him fairly.

You may feel that he has no right to expect anything else, no right to protection seeing how he, by his sweat, is breaking the law.

I understand.

You are entitled to your opinion.

As I am to mine.

Work is the one constant in my life. I've worked in cafés washing dishes, busing tables, peeling potatoes, and frying steaks and burgers and eggs. So I know how to cook. I've built fences, sheds, and barns. Once, I helped construct a bank. Some of my jobs have been in factories, including a hot, noisy one that made the kind of pipe they use on oil rigs, another where I learned to make delicate silver jewelry—earrings, pendants, and rings, most in the shape of the cross.

When I first came to the U.S., I knew no English. But being so young, I picked it up quickly. It wasn't so hard. Now, I am told, my English is good. Not only do I speak it, but I can read and write it too. I subscribe to the *Dallas Morning News* so I can read it every day. I'm not a citizen, but because I've made my home more years in the U.S. than in Mexico, in many ways I live as an American. When I eat at a restaurant, I prefer steak over enchiladas, though I always ask for a bowl of jalapeños on the side. I drive a Ford pickup. I like to watch CNN on TV. The Texas Rangers are my favorite baseball team.

When employers provide me with the W-4 form (not all of them do), I go to H&R Block to file my taxes. I shop at Wal-Mart. I give to the United Way, and I am a member of the Baptist Church. I pay my rent on time. I keep my duplex, which has two bedrooms and one bathroom, its own full-size washer and dryer, neat and clean.

I have kept my word to my mother. I have never gone back

to Mexico to live, nor do I believe I ever will. But every few years, when I can, I travel to her home to see her, to show her that I have my health. I am still her son. She is still my mother. She gave me life.

Over the years, I have had jobs that paid well and jobs that paid poorly. There have been a few times when I have not been able to find work where I was, which meant I had to travel to some new place. Some weeks and months I have done without things I needed in order to keep sending money to my family.

Please do not misunderstand. I am not complaining. My mother and my brother and my sisters are everything to me. I think about them when I get up in the morning. I pray for them when I lie down at night on my bed. I would do anything for them. As long as I am blessed with good health, they can count on my support.

chapter three

THE PAST FIVE YEARS, I'VE made my home in Eden Plain. It is a town with a population of just over thirty thousand, located in the eastern part of Texas, in the region they call the Piney Woods. Quite a few Mexicans live in Eden Plain, some of them legal, some of them not. Many live in apartments in the south part of town. You often hear of crimes that take place in that neighborhood. Fights. Robberies. Mostly among the youth. For while their parents work hard every day, many of the young people have too much time on their hands. With both the mother and the father working all the time, there is no one to teach the children how to behave.

This is a big problem.

I have no children, nor do I have a wife. What I have is my work. For the past two years I have had one employer, Owen Green. He is a rancher. A man who has always paid me a fair wage. Because of my good job, last year my brother built my mother a new house, one of concrete blocks instead of adobe. I sent the money for the materials. He provided the labor. You should see how proud my mother is of that house. It has a tile floor instead of one made of dirt, and an indoor bathroom.

Of the many jobs I have done in my life, ranch work is what I enjoy the most. Even in the summer, when the temperature can get up over one hundred degrees, I love being outdoors. I like the smell of the grass in the summer, of the earth in the spring, and of the air in the fall. Much of Eden Plain is covered in forest. The trees are beautiful, but they make it difficult to see the sky, impossible to view the horizon. There are times I feel too closed-in. But Mr. Green's land has been cleared. Banks of trees separate his meadows, and he lets trees grow around parts of his three ponds, but the rest of his property has been turned into pasture.

I like to see tomorrow coming, Mr. Green says when people ask why he has cut down the trees.

I like it too.

For the first few years I lived in Eden Plain, I worked for several different ranchers. None of them needed me full-time, but between those four or five men, I was able to earn the income I needed. When you're an experienced ranch hand, and that's what I had become, word gets around. You don't have to look for work. Work finds you.

Three years ago, Mr. Owen Green was one of those men. He got my name from somebody at the sale barn where he had gone to buy a load of cattle. I had not worked for him before, but he called me up.

"Who'm I speaking to?" he asked.

"Manuel Ortega. May I help you?"

"You a ranch hand?"

"Yes, sir."

"One what worked over on George Woodie's place?"

"Yes, sir. I have worked for Mr. Wood."

"My help just took off. Put me in a bind. Got a big load of cattle coming in tomorrow. You available next couple days?"

"Tomorrow?" I said. "Yes, I'm available. What time? Can you give me directions to your place?"

Unless you have had ranch experience, you may not understand that a lot goes into taking care of livestock. More than just putting out feed and making sure they have enough water. Depending on their age and the season, to keep them healthy, cows must be wormed, dehorned, and vaccinated. Unless you've got one you plan on using to breed, you castrate all your bull calves. And yes, that task is as unpleasant as it sounds.

All of this work is nearly impossible for one man to do alone, which explains why a rancher would need the help of someone like me.

"You Manny?"

The next day, Mr. Green came out of the door of his barn when I pulled up. He looked to be in his early sixties, a man of average height, probably five ten, of a solid build. Not fat, but big all around like a barrel. Broad shoulders, thick arms. His face was red rather than tan. He had the same hair as Billy Graham — gray, nearly white, wavy and over his collar in the back.

Mr. Green moved quickly to speak to me through the truck window. Like a man impatient with the world, already impatient with me even though it was twenty minutes earlier than the time he'd told me to come.

"Park your truck over there, then come on inside. Hope you've come ready to work because between the two of us, we got us a lot to do."

He did not wait to hear me say that I was.

I parked where I was told, and the familiar smell of fresh manure and the bawling of upset cattle hit me as soon as I was out of my truck.

Cattle are a bit like people in this way. They get stressed. Especially when they are moved from a familiar place to one they do not know. It is not unusual for a few to get sick. This load of young cattle, hauled in by truck, was not happy. They'd already traveled by truck more than ten hours. Now they were crammed together in unfamiliar corrals.

I grabbed my water jug, stuffed my work gloves into my back pocket, and pushed the automatic door lock button on my key. Then Mr. Green and I got to work. We moved the cattle from one pen to the next, drove them up into the shoot, tended to each one, then released them and brought more in. Because I'd done this type of work so many times, I knew what to expect. I knew what to do. But every rancher has his own ways. You just have to figure them out as you go along.

As the day went on, our biggest problem was communication. Mr. Green kept forgetting I spoke English. He would try to talk to me in Spanish, but he did not speak it well enough for me to understand.

"Sir?" I would try to figure out what he wanted. "This?" I would hold up a syringe or a rope or a vial of vaccine, trying to guess which one it was he was calling for.

"No!" Then he would repeat the same mixed-up words, only slower and louder this time.

So I would try again to get what he needed me to get or do what he wanted me to do, but it would not be the right thing, so he would say the same thing yet again, only this time louder than the two times before. Finally, he would either give up and ask me for what he wanted in English or he would stomp over to where I was and retrieve what he wanted himself.

You cannot imagine how frustrating it is for me when this happens.

But I have worked around Anglos enough to know when it is best not to say anything, so on that day, like many others, I went along. I let him believe that I was not smart. I let him treat me as one would a child who cannot understand even simple commands. You may not know, but this treatment is what a Mexican man grows accustomed to. I do not like it. But I expect it. As does every other man who is in my position. As one of my friends said, putting up with that kind of you know what is the cost of doing business.

At least it is so for a Mexican laborer, even one who reads the *Dallas Morning News* cover to cover every single day.

On that first day I worked for Mr. Green, more than once I wanted to say, *Sir, I mean no disrespect, but you're making this hard for both of us. Speak to me in English. Use regular words. Just tell me what it is you need me to do. I'll do it. Tell me what it is you want me to go get. I'll get it.*

But I did not. And we got through the day. We worked every cow, and by dark, we had it all done.

"Mucho key buena trah-bah-hairy," Mr. Green said to me at the end of the day when he handed me his pay. "Mucho dollars pork ustada ustedy."

I took that to mean I had done a good job, and so he was paying me good wages. Or something like that. He shook my hand and paid me in cash, what he had promised me plus a little bit more.

"Thank you, sir. Will you need me tomorrow?"

"No. Nada," he said. "No mucho workey mañana."

"Okay. Call me if you ever need me again."

"Adios," he said.

"Good-bye." I waved at him as I steered my truck toward his driveway.

At the time, I did not see anything out of the ordinary about that day, about Mr. Green's handshake, about any of it. What I saw was the end of a day like every other day. It had been yet another ten hours of hard work. Work that provided money for me and for my family. Work I was grateful for. Work that had made me tired.

I have changed my way of thinking since that day I first met Mr. Green. I no longer believe there is such a thing as an ordinary day. Every single minute of our lives has the potential to be the very one that marks a new beginning. Years later, I know this to be true.

My story bears witness to this.

It was six months before I heard from Mr. Green again. I returned home from church one Sunday night to a message from him on my answering machine. This time, to my great relief, he spoke in English.

"Manny. Owen Green here. Wondering. You come out the ranch tomorrow? Be needing some help regular for a while. Hope you're interested. If you can make it, come on up to the house tomorrow evening. 'Round six or seven. Let's you and me talk."

That Monday evening, I parked my truck in the driveway. Mr. Green's house was a shaded gray and white frame with a wide porch across the front. Pink crepe myrtle trees grew close up. Big live oaks a little farther out. I slammed the door of my truck. When I did, a couple of big yellow dogs came running from around the side of the house. Dogs can tell when you're afraid of them. They can also tell when you're not. All those two did was sniff at me, then hop up on the porch and lie down in the shade.

A sidewalk led to the front step. Seeing the flowers that grew on both sides of the walk and the ferns that hung from the eaves of the porch, I guessed Mr. Green had a wife. I climbed the steps, stood on the welcome mat, and rang the bell. Then I waited. It took Mr. Green so long to answer the door, I thought I had come on the wrong day. Finally, he swung the door open, stepped out onto the porch, and closed the door behind him. He was walking with a limp today, something I did not remember him doing when I worked for him six months before.

He sat down in one of the pair of white wooden rocking chairs.

But I continued to stand.

Mr. Green had two skinned places on his arm. Angry looking. Red. Only beginning to scab. I wondered if he had fallen or if he'd got tangled up with one of his cows. Accidents like that happen more often than you'd think. There is no predicting what a cow will do.

A limp. Wounds on his arms. Perhaps he was only stiff and sore, but maybe he was really injured, like with a pulled back or a sprained knee. That might be the reason he had called me for help.

"I'm needing more help around here," he said. "Got a few health problems. Nothing too bad, but giving me enough trouble I can't keep up my place by myself. I figure I'm needing some-body to put in about twenty, thirty hours a week. More during hay season. You available?"

"Yes, sir. I am available."

"Need a place to stay? 'Cause you do, I got a travel trailer you can live in. Can't see it from here. Back a ways behind the barn. Haven't been in it in a while. May be taken over with mice, but some them boys what have worked for me in the past stayed in it.

They were glad to get it, and you're welcome to it too."

I remembered the trailer he was speaking of from the day when I'd helped him work his cows. It was not more than twenty feet long. Rusted, no wheels, surrounded by tall weeds. No steps up to it, just rotted boards on stacked up blocks. Front door hanging by one hinge. It was not the kind of place you would expect a pig to live in. But it was exactly the kind of place some men would expect a Mexican to feel gratitude for.

"Thank you, sir. It's a generous offer, and I appreciate it, but I have a place in town."

He squinted up at me. "Sure you understand what I'm saying? You can stay in it for nothing."

"Yes, sir, I do understand. Thank you. But I have a duplex. It suits me well."

"All right then, suit yourself. I guess next question is can you start tomorrow?"

The first year I worked on his ranch, Mr. Green put in nearly as many hours as I. For a man his age, except for his limp, which was worse some days than others, he was limber and strong. I would be working on fences; he would be welding a gate. He would head out on a horse to check on his cattle; I would load up the ranch truck and put out hay. Mr. Green was a smart man. A good businessman. His herds were some of the best I have seen. His place was well planned and well maintained. He ran a good operation. Anyone who drove by his place could see that.

I had been wrong about him having a wife. The woman who stayed with him was actually his sister. Her name was Karen. She was a pretty, gray-haired lady who took great care of the flower beds around the house. Every time she happened to be out when I was up on the porch with Mr. Green, she said hello.

Mr. Green and I did not talk all that much either. Some days I would not see him at all except for on the porch, first thing in the morning when he told me what he wanted me to do. He wanted me there at seven. I was never late. Even though I only spoke English to him, about half of Mr. Green's words would be in English, the other half in what he thought was Spanish. After a few weeks, I grew to understand what he was saying, at least most of the time.

Some people speak only one language. Some people speak two. Working at the ranch for a year, I learned to speak three.

Spanish.

English.

And Owen Green.

After I had been with Mr. Green for maybe a year, I noticed him slowing down, not being able to put in as many hours as before. There is a lot of work to be done on a ranch. Fences need to be mended year-round, and in the summer, there is hay to cut, rake, and bale. Cattle need to be checked on every day because some will most always be sick and in need of medicine. You have to keep a watch on your cows ready to calve. Herds need to be moved from one pasture to the other, depending on the condition of the grass and the level of the ponds. In the winter, you have to put out extra feed.

I did not say anything, but to me it looked like Mr. Green's limp was getting worse. I believed he was losing some of his strength in his arms, and there were days he had trouble with his balance. He began to move more slowly and to have trouble getting in and out of his truck. There was not the same light in his eyes. His voice, which had been strong and deep, became softer and at times very weak.

He did not shave every day, which was a change.

As months passed, he began going in earlier for lunch and coming out later and later to begin his afternoon work. Instead of staying out on a horse or a tractor until supper time, he started calling it a day before time for the five o'clock news. There were more and more days he did not work at all. He would come out on the porch, give me my jobs, then go back inside and not come out the rest of the day.

And every week, when he handed me my pay, his right hand shook so badly that he would have to steady it with his left.

I had been working at the ranch for eighteen months when one morning my phone rang before I had gotten up. "Hello?"

"Honey, I am terribly sorry to bother you so early in the morning, but this is Karen Green. Owen's sister."

I sat on the edge of my bed and looked at the clock. Five a.m. I rubbed my eyes.

"Excuse me, ma'am," I said. "Who did you say this was?" My mouth was dry and my voice hoarse.

"Sugar, listen to me. This is Karen Green. Like I said, Owen's sister. I bet I woke you up. I'm sorry but I've got bad news. Owen's in the hospital. He asked me to call you. Not sure how long we'll be here, but Owen wants to know if you could take care of the place while he's gone."

She spoke quickly like a person does when they are nervous.

Which I guess anyone is when someone in their family is in the hospital.

"Yes, ma'am. Of course. Is Mr. Green all right?"

"Not really. Course Owen'd tell you different. Honey, he fell last night. Got up and went outside to see what those blame dogs were carrying on about. Probably nothing but a possum is what I figure. Anyway, I found him outside beside the back step when I got up this morning. I'll tell you, looking out that back door and seeing him laid out scared me so bad I nearly had to change my clothes."

"But do the doctors think he'll be all right?"

"Don't know yet. Doctor thought he might have broken his hip, but luckily, he didn't. He hates being here so bad, he's after them to let him go home today. But I told him nothing doing. Since he's already here, we're going to let them keep him a few days. Run some tests so they can try and get his Parkinson's medicines adjusted."

So that was it. Parkinson's disease. I knew what it could do to a person. A good man at my church had the same thing.

"Don't worry, ma'am. I can take care of everything that needs to be done at the ranch. Tell Mr. Green everything will be all right."

"I sure do appreciate it, sugar. You have no idea how much. Now put down every hour you work. Don't worry. Owen said to tell you he'll pay you for whatever extra hours you put in. He also said something about you might want to stay in that old trailer he's got parked out behind the barn, but between you and me, I wouldn't advise it. If you've seen that trailer, then you know it is not fit for a dog to live in. Best thing to do would be set a match to it in my opinion."

"Tell Mr. Green I appreciate it, but I've got my duplex in town, and it's no trouble for me to drive back and forth."

"That's what I told him. But you know how he is."

Mr. Green was in the hospital for five days. While he was gone, I came out and took care of the ranch every day. On the morning I knew he was coming home, a Monday, I planned my work so I would be at the barn at the time they expected to arrive. When I saw Miss Green's car, I stopped what I was doing and came up to the house.

I was surprised at how bad my boss looked. He was pale and had lost some weight. Miss Green had to help him out of the car. He used a cane to move up the walk, something I had not seen him do before. Even though I hurried, they were near the porch by the time I could get to the house.

"Hey there, Manny. Everything all right on the place?" He handed Miss Green his cane.

"Yes, sir. Everything is fine. Do you need some help?" The sun was beating down. I thought it was not good for him to get too hot. "Want me to bring in your bags?"

"Yes, Manny, that would be a really big help," Miss Green said.

I went to the car and got out the bags. A small suitcase, two shopping bags, and a limp bouquet of red roses. Carrying them inside, I got my first chance to see inside the house. I stood in the entryway and looked around. Tall ceilings with crown moldings. Shiny wood floors. Soft rugs. Comfortable-looking furniture. All of it nice, but what caught my eye was the art. Oil paintings on every wall. Landscapes. Still lifes. Flowers. Birds. It was difficult for me not to stop and stare.

"Manny, could you bring those things in here?" Miss Green said.

I put the flowers on the kitchen counter, set the bags on the floor where she showed me; then I went back to the living room, where Mr. Green had eased himself into a leather recliner.

He pulled the lever to raise his feet, but did not offer me a seat. "Give me a report. Tell me how everything is. Looks like we got some rain."

I stood on the edge of the rug, my hat in my hands. "It rained an inch and a half, according to the gauge."

"Those two cows we had up — they calve yet?"

"Yes, sir. Yesterday. Both of them. You've got one heifer calf and one bull."

"Good. Good."

Miss Green brought in a glass of water and four different pills.

"It's not time for these, is it?" Mr. Green looked up at her. "Already? We just got home." His hands shook when he took them from her.

"Sugar, it's past time. Go on. Take them. Then I'll make you some lunch. I bet you're hungry after that terrible hospital food."

"Darn right. Nurse wouldn't let me have nothing but chicken broth and red Jell-O for nearly three days. 'Bout starved me to death. And when they finally did bring me some food, couldn't tell what it was."

"Fish. They brought you baked fish, steamed cauliflower, and creamed potatoes," Miss Green said.

"All I know is everything on the plate was the same color. Tasted the same too. Every bite had a whang to it." He swallowed the pills, one at a time. All four of them. When he was done, Miss Green left the room.

"Glad you're feeling better, sir. Will you need me tomorrow?"

"We need to talk about that," Mr. Green said. "You reckon you could stay around full-time for a while? Till I get back up on my feet?"

"Yes, sir. I could."

"We're about to run into hay season. Don't know how long it'll be before I'm back to moving around. A couple weeks'd be my guess. Could run into a month. There's going to be more to be done around the place than what you can handle by yourself. You know any other Spanish boys needing work?"

"I know some men who might be available," I said.

"Good. Bring 'em here to talk to me. Tell 'em I got that trailer they can stay in for free. Like to see it put to good use."

"Yes, sir."

No way was I showing anybody that dump.

That was more than a year ago. Since being in the hospital, Mr. Green has not put in another day of work on his ranch. He isn't able. He is weak in his legs and his arms. His right hand shakes most of the time.

About a month after he was in the hospital, Karen got me off to the side one morning. "Do you know anything about construction, about building things?" she asked.

I told her I'd helped build some houses. What did she have in mind?

"A ramp." She wiped at her eyes and motioned toward the steps you had to climb up to get in the house. "For Owen's wheelchair. I know. He doesn't need it yet, but I want to be ready when the time comes."

From what I could see, that time was coming sooner rather than later.

"Go on down to the lumberyard and get whatever you need," she said. "Owen's not going to like it, but it's got to be done."

"Yes, ma'am."

I had that ramp built by the end of that week.

Soon after I finished the ramp, I moved into the position of ranch manager. It happened quickly. No one was more surprised than me about how it came about. Some days I still can't believe the position I'm in.

Karen, which is what Miss Green asked me to call her, asked me to sit down with her in Mr. Green's home office one afternoon. He was asleep in his recliner at the time.

"Manny, it's come time for you to take over the running of the place. I've called the feed store, and I've talked to Marvin down there. He's the manager, you know." Karen had a list of things she'd written on one of those yellow legal pads. Her pen had a pink butterfly on the end. Its wings wiggled when she wrote. "I told them you were authorized to order feed and any supplies we need for the ranch. Here's how all this is going to work. If you see that we need something, I want you to go right ahead and order it. Whatever you think. There'll be no questions asked, none by me, none by the feed store. I trust your judgment. Do you understand what I'm saying?"

She did not pause long enough for me to give an answer.

"Same goes at the sale barn. If some cows need to be sold, I want you to go ahead and sell them. If some need to be bought to keep up the herds, well, I want you to buy them. You know good livestock when you see it, so pick out what you think the ranch needs, as many as you see the need for. The bank knows about this. You'll have to have my authorization for anything over a thousand dollars, but all that'll take is a phone call from the banker to me."

A thousand dollars? I had never had such trust placed in me before.

"Is Mr. Green in agreement with this plan?"

"He doesn't know about it and he doesn't need to know. It's our job—yours and mine—to see to it that he thinks he's still running the place. The man's lost so much—his health, his dignity. I want him to feel like he's still got his pulse on things for as long as possible. The truth is, Owen'll still have input, of course, but without him really giving it over; he's going to be depending on you to keep the ranch up and running, to manage things."

I was not sure about this. Was it deception? Disrespect?

"Manny, you have to understand." She fiddled with the clicker on her pen. "Owen can't do this anymore. It's either you take over or we sell off the cows. It may come to that eventually, but for now, it's up to you. I know you'll be needing help off and on—hay season, to work calves. Hire whoever you know will do a good job. Let me know every week what we're going to owe in wages, and I'll have cash in an envelope ready for you to hand out on Fridays."

It occurred to me on that day, and has a few times since then, no one ever asked me if I wanted the job. It was assumed that I would.

And rightly so. I could never dream of owning my own ranch. To manage one is, I suppose, the next best thing.

Karen made it sound easy. The transition I mean.

It was not.

Two or three times a week, Mr. Green would be sitting on the porch when I pulled up first thing in the morning. He was out there waiting for me for one reason: to complain about how I was doing things.

"Feed store done delivered another load of feed. What are you thinking? We don't need it. Won't until next week. What is it? You getting some kind of kickback from the store? Making you a little on the side?"

He was the one who told me to order the feed.

"That load of heifers. Don't look like they're gaining like they should. You sure you're putting out enough feed?"

They were putting on weight at exactly the rate that they should.

"What do you mean you're planning on cutting hay today? That pasture's not nearly ready to be cut. Needs at least another two, maybe three days."

If I waited till the grass got any taller, it would be nearly impossible to cut.

"Yes, sir."

"No, sir."

"Okay, sir."

Whatever the man says, I try to do. After all, he is the one who built his ranch from the bottom up. There isn't anything wrong with his mind. He knows what he's doing, knows how to manage his place. He just isn't physically able.

I see it this way. I am his eyes, his ears, and his hands. Even when he tells me to do something I know isn't right, if it's not going to cause too much harm or inconvenience, whatever he says, I go along.

It kills Mr. Green not to be out working his land and his cattle. If I were him, it would kill me. On occasion, he hobbles out to his truck and drives himself around. He starts it, puts it in gear, and tears out down the driveway. At least he stays on the property.

"There he goes again."

Karen and I stand on the porch and watch him, both of us hoping, me praying, he doesn't hit a fence or a cow.

He grinds the gears.

"Is he going to hit that tree?" Karen stands on her tiptoes to see.

At the last minute, he steers the truck to the left and the little oak is safe. At least until the next time he decides to take his truck for a spin.

Ever so often, Mr. Green asks me to saddle him a horse so he can go out and check on a fence. "Worried about that back pasture. We may need to replace some of those posts."

When Mr. Green wants to ride, I always saddle a horse for me, too. What if he got off on the place and got thrown or something? We've got nearly four hundred acres here. It would be nearly impossible to find him.

"Care if I come along too?" I always ask.

"Suit yourself."

I feel terrible watching Mr. Green struggle to get his feet up into the stirrup, so I try to avert my eyes when he's trying to mount. He tries and tries before he is able to hoist himself up. But I know better than to offer to help. Every man's got pride, and no old cowboy is going to accept a hand getting on his own horse. He'll quit riding before he does that.

Parkinson's disease can affect you in a lot of different ways. The symptoms look like they come and go, with some days being worse than others. Mr. Green has trouble talking. Sometimes his voice is so low I can't understand what he is trying to tell me. It is frustrating for him when I keep asking him to repeat what he says. There are times he just gives up. Other times I pretend to understand. At least he has quit trying to speak Spanish to me.

I can't tell you what a relief that is.

chapter four

EDEN PLAIN IS ONE OF the best places I have lived. It is big enough to have the things you need. Not so big that traffic is a problem. I live inside the city limits, in a duplex. It's a fifteen-minute drive from Mr. Green's ranch.

Over the past few years, I've made good money. This has allowed me a comfortable life even while sending half of what I make to my family. My home is well furnished. It is not fancy, but comfortable. In my living room I have a brown leather couch, a coffee table, a recliner, and a TV. The couch is not real leather, but it is still comfortable. I have a table and chair set in my dining area, a double bed and a chest of drawers in my bedroom.

I have all the clothes that I need, a CD player, and books to read. My truck will be paid off in six months. Five thousand dollars are in my savings account in a downtown Eden Plain bank.

You would think that with all the things I have worked for and obtained, there would not be anything my heart would long for. You would not expect a man as materially blessed as I to feel lack.

But I do.

There is something I wish for every day of my life. A thing my eyes crave. But this object that my heart longs for is something I will never possess, something I cannot buy, no matter how much money I will make in my life.

This thing I long for is a photograph of my father. I would give everything I possess for one small snapshot of him. Black-and-white or color, I would not care which. As far as I know, not a single picture of him exists.

I have framed photos of my mother, of my sisters and brother and their families, many of Dulce, taken over the past few years. They hang on the wall next to my couch, and I look at them every day. Their smiles give me comfort and bring joy to my heart.

But the face I long for is my father's, the man I have not seen since I was twelve years old.

A person would suppose that after all this time—I am now thirty-nine years old—I would have left the memory of my father behind. You would think that I would have put him to rest, that I would look at him as someone who once was alive to me but is now dead. But that is not my truth. I think about him almost every day. I wonder if he is still alive. Does he have his health? Enough money? A place to lay his head?

His life is such a mystery. I wonder. After he left us, did my father make for himself another family? Did he take another wife? One younger? Prettier than my mother? Did he have more sons? Ones he loved more than me?

I see sons and fathers together at my church, at Wal-Mart. I watch them playing ball together. I see them together in the yards of the family homes across the street from my duplex. Sometimes I see them bent over the open hoods of cars. They smile. They speak. I study their faces. They are bound together. I can see it in their eyes. What has kept them together? What would it be like if I still had my father? Would I be a different sort of man?

Questions burn in my heart. Words I cannot escape. They echo in my ear when I operate noisy farm machinery. They interrupt the quiet when I pray. I hear them in my dreams.

Why did you leave? Was it something I did? Was I a bad son?

If I could see my father's eyes, perhaps I could find answers to my questions. Perhaps my heart would be still and my dreams would be sweet.

But I cannot. After all these years, his eyes have faded from my memory. I cannot get them back. And without him, without the memory of his eyes, it is like a hole exists in my heart.

My duplex has two bedrooms, which I admit is a luxury for someone who lives alone. In one of the rooms, I sleep. In the other, the one with a south window, I keep my paints. I have always loved art. I cannot remember a time when I did not have a hunger to draw, to capture what I saw around me and what I saw with my heart's eyes. When I was a little boy back in my village, I was always drawing with pencils, crayons, paints when I had them. Creating pictures is in my blood. It is something I have to do. Like I heard a man say, it feels to me like an itch that I must scratch. It is like a hunger in my soul.

When I was fourteen, living at the petrol station where I was working, I had no art supplies. So I scraped up soft, hot tar from the side of the road and used it for paint. When I did not find tar, I scooped up mud and clay, which I thinned with water. I used leaves and twigs instead of brushes. Because I had no canvas or paper, I made pictures on pieces of cardboard I found on the side of the road.

These days I have all the art supplies I need. Eden Plain has both a Hobby Lobby and a Michael's. I cannot tell you how much money I have spent at those two stores. There is no subject I have not tried to paint. Animals. Flowers. Buildings. Trees, lakes, and mountains. I have drawn them all. But no matter what other drawing or painting I am working on, I always have something else in progress at the same time—a portrait of my father. I have sketched him with charcoals and in colored pencil. I have painted him using watercolors, acrylics, and oils. If I had every picture I've tried to draw of my father, they would fill up the room in my duplex where I now paint.

But none of them hang in a frame.

I have not yet done one that has turned out right.

Over and over I try.

And in some ways my pictures look like him. His hair is easy. So is his chin. I've gotten better over the years, and I believe I can capture his nose, his ears, the shape of his head, and the way it sits on his neck.

But what I cannot capture, what I have been unable to recall, are my father's eyes. I change the angle, the brows, the size, the space between them, but I can never get them right. Unless you are an artist, you will not understand why the eyes are so important. But here is a fact every artist knows. A portrait can be perfect in every other way, but if the eyes are not right, it will not resemble the person.

It will appear to be someone else.

That I cannot get my father's eyes right is the heartbreak of my life.

Today is Sunday, my one day off. I do the same thing on this day every week. I go through my mail and pay my bills. I do my laundry. If I need anything, like deodorant or laundry soap or razors or shampoo, I make a trip to the store.

But always first, I go to church.

"Manny. Good to see you." The pastor, a man named Mitchell Case, greets me in the foyer just inside the double back doors. I am early. The church where I go to worship is near downtown. Grace Baptist Chapel. It is in a small, older brick building. There are two services every Sunday: one in English, one in Spanish. The church has two ministers. Pastor Case for the Anglos, and a young man named Juan Lopez for the Hispanics. While I have nothing against Pastor Lopez, I go to the English service because I am so fond of Pastor Case. Mitchell is what I call him because he has asked me to and because we are friends.

Only a few people have already arrived.

"How are you? Still working for Mr. Green? Everything going okay?"

Mitchell is the first person I met when I came to this church five years ago on a Tuesday night.

Why at church on Tuesday? you might ask.

The answer would not be because I was looking for God. Back then I thought I had all the God I needed. Instead, I came to the church because I read in the paper they were offering English as a Second Language classes. Even though I already spoke English well, I was hoping to become better at writing it.

But when I arrived, there were too many people in the class. Thirty-five showed up. Only a few of them knew a few English words. The room was small and stuffy. There weren't enough chairs. Mitchell was the only teacher. Anyone could see there was no way one instructor could take care of that many people. So I started to leave. But when I saw how nervous he was, how he had sweat stains on his blue denim shirt, I felt bad for him.

"Sir, if you'll tell me where to get more chairs, I'd be happy to set them up for you," I told him.

"That would be wonderful. Thank you. Oh, you speak English!" He looked at me as if I were his long lost brother.

After I arranged places for everyone to sit, I asked him if there was anything else I could do.

"Could you make copies? I don't have nearly enough. You know how to work a copier?"

I nodded.

"Great. It's in the office at the end of this hall. I think we need about twenty."

Then he started to cough, I guess because it was so hot. So before I went to make copies, I got him a cup of water from the cooler at the back of the room.

"Thank you." He gulped the water down. "I appreciate it. What did you say your name was again?"

That night, after class was over, Mitchell took me out for coffee. When he figured out I could speak English almost as well as he, he asked me if I would help him teach the class.

"I can't pay you, but we can go for coffee and pie after class. I'll even buy."

I already liked Mitchell. He was patient with the people in his class. He did not seem to mind that one woman had brought her three noisy children with her. He ignored the muddy boots of one man. He did not flirt back with the two young women who sat on the front row wearing short skirts and low-cut tops.

Not only that, it was more than obvious he needed some help. So I agreed to assist him. For the next sixteen weeks, I showed up and did what I could. And every night, after the last student was gone, we'd turn out the lights and head out for our coffee and pie.

Until I met Mitchell, I had not known anyone who was particularly religious. That first night, over peach cobbler at a little home-cooking café down the street from the church, he asked me, "What part does faith play in your life?"

I remember shrugging. "I try to be a good person. Is that what you mean?"

"Sure. That's exactly what I mean. But I'd like to hear more."

Two black men run the café. I think they are twins. One of them, who someone told me is a preacher on the side, came over to fill my coffee cup. "Need anything else, gentlemen?"

"We're fine," Mitchell told him. "Thanks, Pastor Roberts. Pie sure is good."

"I was baptized when I was a baby into the Catholic church," I said. "But the priest rarely came to our village — only a few times a year, so I did not grow up with my religion being a part of my life. We went to Mass only a few times a year. My mother always lit candles in our house, and I know she gave money when the priest came around. I am Catholic, but I don't think my Catholic beliefs are as strong for me as they are for some people who grow up going to church every week or who have the chance to go to Catholic schools."

"I can see how it could be like that."

That was all Mitchell said about religion that night. Instead, he asked me about my life. About where I had come from. About what had brought me to the place where I was then.

So during the weeks of that course I told him about where I had been born. All the places I'd traveled. I told him about my family. Even about my dad.

About halfway through the sixteen weeks, Mitchell invited me to come to his church. I decided to give it a try. It turned out that I liked what I found there. So after about a year had passed, I joined. If you are a good Catholic, you probably don't understand how I could become a Protestant just like that. I suppose I don't have a good explanation except that it felt right.

What we have at Grace Baptist are a lot of people who have gotten themselves in some messes, but who are struggling to get themselves out. We are a group of not-very-rich folks who care about the ones that are poorer than us. Believe me, there is no shortage of people in need. I can't tell you how many Sundays we pass the collection plate around for somebody who needs an operation or for somebody else whose furnace has just quit. We have classes and meetings at the church almost every night and sometimes during the day. Not just English classes either. We have AA and NA. Divorce recovery groups. Classes where they help dropouts get their GED.

Most people think of church as being someplace where you have to be cleaned up to fit it. Not so at Grace Baptist. People are welcome to come as they are.

You should see some of the clothing people show up in.

My faith is important to me. Without it, I would not feel like myself. Over the years I have come to understand that being a good person is a good thing but that it has little to do with God. Mitchell and I have spent many hours talking about God and grace and His love for man. What I believe is that love is what it is all about. Love for God. Love for His children. Which sounds very simple but is not.

What I try to do every day is love God more than I did the day before. But even so, there are many things about God I do not understand and many things that remain difficult for me. In both the Catholic church of my youth and the Baptist church where I now find a home, God is called *Father*. I will just tell you, this is not easy for me to hear. When a man has lost his father, when he has found him to be untrustworthy, hearing God spoken of as a father prompts feelings of confusion and contradiction. He feels as if his soul is being pulled in opposing directions.

I speak to Mitchell about this problem every few months. You would think that this question is one a person could settle in his mind and then move on, but for me it is one I return to again and again.

Mitchell is patient. "Manny, the way I see it, there are many ways to think about God. Many ways to pray. Many things to call Him. If Father doesn't feel right, then don't call Him that. I believe He understands."

I hope so.

Because when I pray, and I do every day, I don't think about God being my father. Rather I look at Him as my shepherd. My guide. My teacher. My king.

Those words mean something good to me. Something safe and worthy of honor.

Perhaps one day I will think about God as my father, and it will feel right, good, and true. But for now, that is not what I find in my heart.

Every day, Karen prepares lunch for me at the ranch. Not just a sandwich but a full meal. Usually fried steak or chicken, potatoes or rice, salad or vegetables, iced tea, hot rolls, always coffee with dessert. She is an excellent cook, and she has worked out a routine that we follow every day.

Mr. Green must eat at eleven because that is when his pills are due, and they must be taken with food. When someone takes medicine for Parkinson's disease, it is important that they take it at the right time. Karen prepares Mr. Green's plate. He eats and reads the newspaper. After lunch, she gives him his pills; then he goes to his recliner to sleep.

Just before noon, I come to the house. I take my boots off and leave them on the porch. Then I come inside, wash my hands in the bathroom by the back door, and sit down at the kitchen table. That is when I have my meal.

Me coming inside for my lunch is something that did not start until Mr. Green got home from the hospital, six months ago. It was Karen's idea. At first, when she offered me a meal, I thanked her but told her I had brought food from my house. I thought she was just being polite. But she persisted. She told me she enjoyed cooking and liked having company when she ate her own lunch. The food she served me could be part of my pay. She smiled and told me to consider it a small raise.

I enjoy lunch very much. During our meals, Karen and I talk. She tells me a bit about her life. She was married for a short time when she was young. Then she got divorced and took back her father's name.

"You have no children?" Today we are having smothered pork chops, a broccoli salad with raisons and nuts, which sounds strange but tastes good, and scalloped potatoes with cheese on the top.

"Oh yes. I had children. Hundreds of them." Her eyes shine. "No, not the way you think. I taught Sunday school. Third grade. For thirty-seven years. Long enough to have some of my students' children. I called them my grandstudents. In a small way, they were like my own children."

"I think you were a very good teacher." I stir my tea.

"I hope so. For sure I loved doing it. And the best thing about having those kinds of kids is I got to enjoy them for an hour, then send them home."

"What you did was a good thing. Where do you go to church now?"

"Nowhere very often. Every once in a while I make it to that little Bible church over on Fourth Street."

I am surprised someone who taught Sunday school all those years has stopped going to church. But it would be difficult for her to go now. She would have to find someone to stay with Mr. Green while she was gone.

"There's good people there. Everybody's real nice when I go. I don't know. I just never got back into the habit." She gets up to get us more tea.

"So you don't see your former husband? You don't hear from him?" I hope I am not asking too many questions.

"Not in forty years. I sort of thought at first I'd get remarried. But let me tell you, getting burned once makes you cautious about jumping back into the fire. I never came across a man I felt I could fully trust."

I have just put a piece of meat into my mouth.

"Goodness." Karen puts her hand on my arm. She turns a little bit red. "That wasn't very nice. Present company excluded. I'm sure you're very trustworthy, Manny."

"Was Mr. Green ever married?" I ask.

"Of course," Karen says.

I think she is surprised I don't know this, but I have almost no knowledge about Mr. Green other than how he wants his ranch run. Except for the weather, I do not remember us ever having a conversation about anything else.

"Her name was Eva. She died twelve years ago. Lung cancer. Woman loved her Camels. Smoked nearly two packs a day. Goodness, it was quick. Six months after we found out about the cancer, boom, she was gone." Karen gets up, puts on an oven mitt, and takes a pie out of the oven. Then she sits back down. "They say lung is one of the worst kinds you can get."

"It must have been very sad."

"It was. Eva was something else. Fun to be around. Talented, too." She looks up at the painting that hangs above the table where we are eating. Red poppies in a green vase positioned against a gold background that is flecked with shades of brown.

"So it was she who painted all the pictures."

Karen nodded. "Every one of them. Honey, the woman could paint anything. She gave art lessons sometimes at the library downtown." Karen wiped her mouth on her napkin. "I sure do miss her. Not only was Eva my sister-in-law, she was my best friend, too."

"I am sorry for your loss. For Mr. Green's loss too," I say.

"Thank you. It was terrible when she died, but you know it's been so many years. Time does make things easier."

"So you have always lived here. On the ranch," I say.

"Oh, no. I lived in Chicago. Oprah's hometown. But when Owen couldn't manage the ranch and taking care of Eva by himself, I took a leave of absence from my job and came down so I could help out. Somebody had to drive her to her treatments. Make sure she took her medicine and all that. At the time, everyone thought Eva would get better. We didn't intend for me to stay more than a couple of weeks, but as it ended up, she and Owen needed me till the end. Then there was the funeral and all that. After things settled down, Owen asked me if I wanted to just stay. There was plenty of room. I couldn't think of any reason why not, so here I still am. Twelve years later. I was a mortgage broker back when I worked, but I never enjoyed it. Facts. Figures. Everything on paper. Nothing real. The thing I like best is keeping a house—cooking, cleaning, taking care of people."

Karen makes me think of my mother.

"I love this ranch. Owen and I have always gotten along about as good as any brother and sister I know. He's a good man."

"It's good you're here now to care for him," I say.

"It is. Things have a way of working out." She reaches up and rubs the back of her neck. "Of course I never figured on Owen getting down like he is. I know this comes as big news, but I'm no spring chick myself. I'm actually older than Owen."

"Really?"

"Sixty-eight my next birthday. And Manny, I'm feeling every year. Owen can still do most everything for himself, but the time's coming he'll need help getting up and down. It's going to be hard."

Karen is a small woman. Five feet two. Perhaps one hundred and thirty pounds. "Anytime you need help, call me," I say. "I'll help you."

She begins stacking our plates. "Thanks. I appreciate that. I may take you up on your offer. You ready for pie?"

"Yes, thank you."

She cuts two big pieces.

"Mr. Green and his wife, they did not have children?"

"Oh, they did. One daughter. Chaney. She lives in Florida."

"So far away." If I knew where my father was and I knew he was sick, I would try to be there. To live and work close by.

"She calls once a week. Comes down a couple times a year. Never stays long. Chaney was close to her mother. She took it so hard when Eva died. I love Chaney like she was my own, but I'll just come out and say it—that girl is a prickly one. Gets her feelings hurt easy. Takes things the wrong way. I talk to her like she was mine, and I've told her over and over again that she needs to get over herself. Like you hear the kids say, chill. It's sad to say, but Chaney and Owen can't be in the same room more than an hour without getting into it with each other, and I'd say ninety percent of all that is her."

Mr. Green has a daughter. Who would have guessed?

From where we sit, I hear Mr. Green snort, then let out a snore. I look at my watch. Then I push my chair back and stand up. "Thank you for the meal." I say this every day. "It was very good. I appreciate it."

"You're welcome, Manny. Say, you like fish? Been thinking of frying up some catfish in a couple of days."

"I like fish," I say.

Karen gets up and begins clearing the table. "Mess of fish. Some fried potatoes and coleslaw. I'm stuffed, but that already sounds good." She's talking more to herself than to me.

"Thank you again."

Then I'm out the door, headed back to my work.

chapter five

"THE KEY IS TO GET close, bend your knees, and lift with your legs instead of your back." The nurse who comes to supervise Lori, the three-times-a-week home health aide, is teaching me how to lift without hurting myself. "Position yourself the same way every time so that you both know what to expect."

Mr. Green sits. I stand in front of him. I put my right foot parallel to his left foot, and my left foot sideways in front of his toes so if his feet start to slide my boot will stop him. He puts his arms around my neck, I put my hands under his arms. I lift. He stands. It takes him a minute, but I go slowly so he won't get dizzy. Once Mr. Green is on his feet, he can stand up. Then we pivot. To the left if it is morning and I am moving him from his bed to his chair. To the right if it is evening and I am helping him get back to his bed.

We started practicing this after one morning two weeks ago. It was terrible. Mr. Green could not get himself out of bed.

Like the beginning of any other day, I pulled up into the driveway. We had unloaded a new batch of calves the night before, and I could hear them bawling for their mothers as soon as I got out of the truck. I was about to head to the barn when Karen came out onto the porch and started waving at me to come inside.

"Is Mr. Green all right?" I could tell by the look on her face that something was wrong.

"I can't—I can't get him out of bed," she said. "I've been trying for an hour, but I can't do it. He needs to go to the bathroom. But no matter what I try, I can't get him up." Karen is a strong woman, but I could tell she was trying not to cry and that she had already shed a few tears.

This time, I did not wait to be asked inside. I did not take the time to pull off my work boots. "Which way?" I set my hat on the little table in the entryway.

Karen led me down a hall to a large room with blue flowered wallpaper and a king-size bed, which Mr. Green was lying across. He was still in his pajamas. He was half on the bed and half off.

"Sir," I said so he would know it was me. "Can I help you?"

"I need to get up," he said.

I leaned over and put my hands under his shoulders and helped him sit up. Karen pushed the wheelchair up close, and I lifted him over into it. He pointed toward the bathroom. His face was red. His feet were swollen. He was sweating.

"Yes, sir," I said. Then I motioned to Karen we were okay without her, and I wheeled him to the toilet.

Once we were in the bathroom, Mr. Green locked the wheelchair, held onto the grab bars on each side, and pulled himself up.

"I got it now."

I stepped back. Mr. Green started to lower his pajama bottoms. I was not sure what I should do.

"I said I got it. Go on. Close the door."

I did as he said, but just in case, I stood outside the door and listened. First a flush. Then the sink. A cabinet door opening, then closing. More water in the sink.

After he was finished in the bathroom, Mr. Green did not want to sit back down in his wheelchair. Instead, he wanted to walk to the kitchen. The good thing was he could still walk, slowly, with his walker. So he made his way down the hall. From what I could see, he did fairly well by himself once he was upright. It was the getting up and down that he could not manage by himself.

I followed behind him, not saying anything.

Mr. Green set his walker to the side, pulled out his chair, and sat down at the table. Karen brought him his eggs and his biscuits.

"You okay?" she asked him.

"I'm fine." He kept his eyes on his plate. His hand shook when he tried to put sugar in his coffee. More went on the table than in his cup, but Karen did not try to help.

"Good thing Manny was here." She stood beside Mr. Green's chair and patted him on the shoulder. "Don't know what we'd have done if he hadn't come along. Guess we'd have had to call the fire department."

"Karen," Mr. Green said, "we got any plum jelly?"

Karen's eyes met mine over his head. She got the jelly out of the fridge and set it on the table beside him.

"Thanks, Manny," she said. "Appreciate your help."

"No problem," I said. Then to Mr. Green, "Anything else you need, sir?" I put on my hat and reached for my leather work gloves, which I keep in my back pocket.

"You check on that load of heifers yet?"

"No, sir."

"Best do that first thing."

"Yes, sir."

"All right then." He did not take his eyes from his plate. He broke off a piece of biscuit and put it into his mouth.

Karen followed me outside onto the porch.

"I'm sorry," she said. "Owen—"

I raised my hand to stop her words. "It is all right."

"He could at least —"

"No, ma'am. He cannot."

She looked me straight in the eye, then shook her head.

I turned to go.

There is something about men no woman can fully understand. Above almost all else, a man values his independence and his strength. To not be able to get up and take yourself to the toilet in the morning is about the worse thing that could happen. To have to have your sister come and get you up? To have another man, a younger man, be called on to step in and help out?

For any man, that would be a cause of embarrassment and shame.

But *that* is exactly what I do every day since that first time Karen could not get Mr. Green up. When I get to the ranch, the first thing I do is go inside and lift Mr. Green out of his bed. Before I eat my lunch, I put him into his recliner, where he takes his naps. Since it has a motor in the seat that raises him up, when he's ready to get off it, he can get up with a little help from Karen. At the end of my day of work on the ranch, I go home and have my dinner, watch TV, go to the store, whatever I have to do. Then at nine thirty, I drive back out to the ranch so I can put him in his bed. The trip takes me ten minutes each way.

I know Karen appreciates it. She tells me she does.

And without him saying a word, I know Mr. Green hates it. I also know he hates me helping him less than he'd hate Karen helping him. I know for sure he hates me helping him less than he would hate being stuck flat in his bed all day.

Which does not make it any better at all.

"Karen says she's frying fish this evening." Every morning, when I am getting him up, I try to make conversation with Mr. Green.

"She is?" He sways. "You like to go fishing?"

"Sure." We stand there, breath to breath, until he gets his balance, then I ease back. "I haven't been in a long time, but yes, I like to catch fish."

"The pond down by the east meadow is stocked. Catfish. When I put them in, I expected I'd do a lot of fishing. Figured some of the neighbors would join me. But you know how it is. Everybody's busy. Got other things to do besides wasting that kind of time. Haven't dropped a hook in since I don't know when. Years I guess. No telling how big some of them boys have gotten."

"That's too bad."

He goes into the bathroom. I wait in the bedroom. From his spot in front of the toilet he calls. "You put out feed yet?"

"Yes, sir."

Karen has a doctor's appointment today. She had to leave a half hour before Lori gets here. I promised her I'd stay with Mr. Green during that gap in time. I came a little early today so I could put out feed before she left. When she gets back, I'll begin my day's work.

"Let's you and me drive down to the pond. See what we can catch. Surprise Karen when she gets back. Course she'll have to clean them. Unless you do it. Don't think I'm steady enough to fillet 'em, and that's the only way they're fit to eat." He flushes. "There's poles and a tackle box in the storage room. Figure Karen's got something in the freezer we can use for bait."

I'm not sure about this idea. "What about Lori? She'll be here in a few minutes."

"Ah, I don't know. Maybe she'd like to go with us."

"You think she's allowed to do that?" I don't believe fishing is on Mr. Green's Home Health Aide Plan of Care.

"Probably not. But if she wants to go, I won't tell on her." He comes out of the bathroom, zipping up his pants. "You?"

"No. Of course not."

"Why, I'd love to go fishing with you two boys!"

I wonder if Lori's supervisor, who always looks neat and professional the way a nurse is supposed to, is aware of how Lori dresses when she comes to provide Mr. Green's care. Lori, who says she is forty-two years old, but I think looks closer to fifty, wears low-rise scrub pants and tight T-shirts. She has a ring in her navel. I could tell you what kind of underpants she wears, but you can probably guess.

You would think they'd have some kind of rule about that.

"Long as I don't have to touch a worm or anything. Just got my nails done." She holds up her hands. "You like this color? You'll never guess the name of it. Okay, I'll tell you. They call it *Call Girl Red.*"

"That's real pretty, sugar." Mr. Green doesn't stop smiling when Lori is here.

Karen and I think Lori should work a little bit more. Talk a little bit less. Cut her fingernails. She's supposed to take Mr. Green's vital signs, help with his personal care, and do light housekeeping, such as changing his sheets and cleaning his bathroom. Karen says half the time Lori doesn't scrub the tub and that she never makes the bed up right.

"Only thing . . ." Lori is helping Mr. Green look in the freezer for something we can use for bait. The two of them are digging through some of the packages in the back. "You got a hat I can borrow? I can't take the sun. Gives me a headache." She pulls out a blood-stained white paper package. "What is this? Yuck! Chicken livers. Don't tell me y'all really eat those?"

"Sometimes Karen fries them up," Mr. Green says.

From the look of the package, Karen hasn't cooked any in a very long time.

"I don't know how anybody could eat something like that. Besides, they're full of cholesterol. Promise me." She gives Mr. Green a serious look; her voice is a whine. "Don't eat them ever again. They're not good for you."

"Scout's honor." Mr. Green salutes. "Won't touch another one. We'll feed 'em to the fish instead. Go on now, throw that package in the sack, honey. They make good bait. You two ready?"

"Should we wait until Karen gets back? Maybe she'd like to go with us," I say.

Lori looks at her watch. "I've only got two hours."

She's leaning over the kitchen counter, opposite Mr. Green. He is staring at her chest.

"Then I have to go. Got two more patients I have to see today. Esther Cook and Myra Martin." She slaps her hand over her mouth. "Sorry. I'm not supposed to say who I'm seeing. Confidentiality and all. Y'all aren't going to tell, are you?"

"Nah," Mr. Green says. "We don't know anybody to tell anyway. What's wrong with Myra? Didn't she have surgery? That's what I heard."

"Had half her colon cut out. Can't eat nothing but chocolate cake and buttermilk. All she does all day is watch the soaps and take her Vicodin." Lori reaches up to pick at something in her teeth.

"Since you've got to see some other patients, maybe you'd rather not go to the pond with us then," I say.

"No, I want to go. I just can't stay all day is all." Lori gives me an innocent smile.

Mr. Green is already at the back door. "Come on. No need to wait on Karen. Manny, write her a note. She knows how to get to the pond. She can come out there if she wants to." He is getting around pretty good today, using just his cane.

"Okay." I know when I am outnumbered. I write the note to Karen and leave it on the kitchen counter where I know she'll see it.

So we head to the pond, the three of us in the truck. Mr. Green insists on driving. It's only in the pasture, so I go along with him taking the wheel. It's so rough, he can't go all that fast. There's nobody for him to hit, so what will it hurt? We bump along. Lori sits in the middle. She's wearing one of Mr. Green's old cowboy hats. I'm on the passenger side, holding onto the door. I'll jump out if he runs the truck into a tree or something. With us, we've got the package of livers, three bottles of water, some beef jerky, and a package of Fig Newtons. In the back are a cooler to hold the fish we catch, if there are any. Four fishing poles and four lawn chairs so that Karen can fish with us if she comes out.

"Oh, my goodness. Would you look at how big they are."

Mr. Green has managed to park the truck close to the pond. We've gotten out. Lori is standing on the bank leaning over the water to get a good look.

When I get to the edge, I cannot believe the size of the catfish I see. Twenty or more of them, and they've all come up to the surface as if to say hello. I've never seen catfish do that. They don't appear to be the least bit afraid.

"How long since you said you fished this pond?" I say.

"Couple of years. I don't know. Maybe longer than that. These boys have gotten fat." He turns to Lori. "You ready to catch yourself a big one, honey?"

These catfish are so friendly they look like they're ready to jump on our hooks. I go back to the truck to get our stuff. We settle into lawn chairs and drop our hooks in the water. In less than thirty minutes we've each caught one or two apiece. As soon as we get them off our hooks, we drop them into the cooler, which I've filled up with pond water.

"Sure do like fried fish," Lori says. "If y'all are planning on a fish fry tonight, I may have to come back for supper." She's sitting close enough to Mr. Green that she reaches over and pats his knee. "Seems only right I should get to eat some of what I catch, don't you think?"

I see no need for Lori to come for supper. We can give her some fish. She can take them home and cook them herself.

"Why sure, Lori. You do that. Come on back after you see your other patients. We'll have us a big time."

Mr. Green pulls another fish from the water, takes it off the hook, reaches across Lori, and hands it to me to put in the cooler. Except that the fish is slippery and his hands are not strong. He drops the fish in Lori's lap.

She jumps up, and the poor fish goes to the ground, where it flops and flops until I pick it up. When I do, I feel so sorry for the fellow that instead of dropping it into the cooler with the others, I go to the edge of the water and put it back in. We already have more than enough.

"Look at this. I'm going to have to change clothes now. I've got fish poo on me. Pee-ew! I stink to high heaven."

I try not to laugh. Even Mr. Green lets out a chuckle.

"Sugar, sit back down. You're scaring the fish. You're all right," he says. "When we get back, Manny here'll get you something of Karen's to put on. She won't mind a bit."

I give him a look. He thinks I will go to Karen's closet and pick out some of her clothes to give to Lori to wear? We will have to see about that.

"Speaking of." Mr. Green looks over his shoulder. "Here Karen comes now. Lands, she's tearing out here like her rear end's on fire or something. She's gonna bottom out her car if she doesn't slow down."

He's right. Karen is going too fast.

She pulls up beside Mr. Green's truck, gets out, and slams the car door. "What do y'all think you're doing?"

"Fishing?" the three of us say together.

"Get those poles out of the water right now! You haven't caught any, have you?"

"What are you talking about? Of course we've caught some," Mr. Green says. "Manny, open up that cooler. Show her how much good we've done in less than an hour. Got a chair for you and a pole, too. We three's been having a great time. Don't know why we haven't been coming out here regular. Already done caught five of these big boys. We'll have us a feast tonight." He motions to me. "Manny, get a piece of liver and bait Karen a pole. I bet she'll catch the next one for sure."

Karen's face has gone pale, but her cheeks are flushed and she is breathing hard. I can see she's trying not to cry. "Are they still alive?"

"Of course," I say. "We'll keep them alive until we get them back to the house to clean them."

I am surprised someone who has fried fish before doesn't know that's how it's done.

"Let me see."

I lift the lid of the cooler.

"Oh no! It's Lucy. And Ethel. And Speedy." Karen is wiping at tears. "And . . . oh no, there's Paul. And Linda."

Just then Lori gets a bite. She yanks on her pole, and a big fat fish flies through the air and lands on Karen's shoe. She bends down and picks the fish up. "It's Raul! Let him go. Get this hook out of his mouth right now. You have to let them all go. Put them back in the water right now!"

"What are you talking about, woman?" Mr. Green is trying to get up. "Get hold of yourself. You're talking crazy."

"I am not." Karen is wiping her nose on a tissue she pulled from the pocket of her pants. "I know these fish. Every one of them. I come out here every morning when I take my walk, and I bring them scraps of food. They love cornbread."

Karen loves animals. You should see how the dogs listen to her. She tells them to sit, they sit. She tells them to leave a squirrel on a fence alone, they leave the squirrel alone. I have never seen anyone as good with animals as she. But someone who names catfish?

"You mean to tell me you come out here every day to visit these fish? You've given them names? You may be my sister, but you have done gone off the deep end with this one. How in the name of Pete can you tell them apart?"

"It's easy. Look at their faces. At their markings. They've all got different personalities."

I remove the hook from Raul's mouth. I look at Mr. Green to tell me what I should do. Cooler or pond? Which way do I toss?

"How would you like it if I cooked up one of your dogs? You wouldn't like it at all."

"A fish is not the same as a dog," Lori says.

"Says who?"

Karen wins. We let the fish go. But we do have catfish for supper that night. Lori comes back, and Karen asks me to stay. She cooks up a big platter full of fish. We also have fried potatoes and hushpuppies, sliced onions and coleslaw.

"What's the difference between eating catfish from the store and catfish from the pond?" I ask her after the meal.

She looks at me like I'm crazy. "Why, I don't know these fish. I never saw their faces. I don't know their names."

Now I understand. Completely.

chapter six

KAREN DOES NOT LEAVE MR. Green by himself in the house for even a little while. She saves her errands, such as the banking, getting her hair cut, and picking up things at Wal-Mart, for the three mornings a week when Lori comes. She tries not to make an issue of not leaving him alone, but Mr. Green is not dumb. He has the situation figured out. And he does not like it one bit.

"I'm hungry for some ice cream. And for some Nacho Cheese Doritos," I hear him say to her when I come in for lunch.

"Okay. I'll get them for you tomorrow when I go to the store."

"I'd really love some peppermint ice cream right now. Doesn't that sound good? Maybe some hot fudge sauce to pour over it? Why don't you run to town and get us some?" Mr. Green is standing in the kitchen, holding onto his walker, which he needs because his feet are dragging badly today.

Karen avoids his eyes. "Maybe tomorrow, Owen. I'm pretty tired. I just don't feel like getting out today."

"I'm not some kind of a child that needs a babysitter," he says. "I'm a grown man. I'd be fine. All I do is sleep in this chair. What do you think's going to happen to me?"

Should I offer to go get the ice cream? Or to stay with Mr. Green so that Karen can go? I have a lot to get done outside today.

I've been plowing all morning. I'll be at it all afternoon. Rain is predicted for later today.

"Owen, I said I'd go tomorrow." Karen turns her back to him to stir something on the stove.

I sit down at the table for my lunch, but I do not say a word.

"Fine." Mr. Green begins clomping his way out of the kitchen toward his recliner. "Forget about it. I didn't want any ice cream anyway."

Karen gives me a look. I lower my gaze.

I hope I never find myself in this situation. Mr. Green is accustomed to being in charge. He is the one who took care of things, who made decisions, who took credit when things went well, and who shouldered the blame when things went wrong. He took care of his family the way a man is supposed to.

He gets mad at his sister. Sometimes he wants to tell her off, but mostly he does not.

Because he needs her.

If she were not here, what would he do? If she got mad at him and left the ranch, how would he manage? The two of them walk a narrow line. She tries to treat him with respect, yet he knows she is in charge of him.

He hates it.

He loves her.

He would give anything not to need her so much.

Some days Mr. Green would be fine by himself for a few hours. But other times, he would not be able to get himself out of his chair and away from the house if there was a fire. Not only that, what if he got up to go to the bathroom or to the kitchen to make himself a snack and he fell? He probably wouldn't be able to get to the phone for help.

Some of the neighbors have offered to come in and stay with

Mr. Green so Karen can have a break. They tell her she should take a day off. But he says no. He does not want anyone else staying with him.

Mr. Green is modest. Any man would feel embarrassed about some of the things Karen has to do for him. But, as Karen says, family is supposed to take care of family. It is her job. Besides, with a small amount of help from me, she has worked out a pretty good system.

On this morning, Karen has been to the doctor. She did not get back until nearly noon, but Lori was here to stay with Mr. Green while Karen was gone. Lori even prepared and served Mr. Green his lunch. She is leaving as I come in at noon. Mr. Green is already asleep in his recliner. When I come inside, Karen is rushing around the kitchen, talking fast, pulling plates from the cupboard, stirring something in a bowl.

"Sorry. Nothing but cold sandwiches on the menu today. Tuna okay?"

"Yes, ma'am. Of course."

Karen is moving so fast that she cuts her little finger with the knife she is using to slice tomatoes. "Shoot," she says.

"Are you all right?"

"Just a little cut. But ouch, the acid from these tomatoes sure stings." She wraps a paper towel around her finger.

"You don't need to make anything for me to eat. I can go into town for food."

"Nonsense. I've got the tuna salad already mixed up. Sit down."

I do as she says; then she takes a seat too.

"Wait," she says. "I forgot. We've got a can of those ranch flavor Pringles. They would go good with these sandwiches. Can you get them? Top shelf of the pantry."

I always pray a blessing over our noon meal. After I did it once or twice, silently to myself, Karen asked me to start saying it out loud. She has grown to expect it and will not take a bite of her lunch until it is done. Today, as soon as I say my amen, she starts talking. Fast. Like nothing I'd ever heard her do before.

She tells me about the family of the plumber who is coming to put a new seal on the toilet. She talks about the size of the green beans she bought from the produce stand located on the left as you drive into town. These beans are bigger than the ones she bought last week. What if they are tough? Then she will have wasted her money. She tells me about the games she and Mr. Green played when they were young and about a dog they had whose name was Brown and who always stunk because he liked to swim in a stagnant pond.

All I do is nod. There is no call for me to speak. I have finished my sandwich, my chips, and two of Karen's excellent oatmeal raisin cookies before she has taken her third bite.

When I wipe my mouth on my napkin and stand up to go, she tells me what is really on her mind.

"I have some bad news," she says.

Her face is pale. Her eyes are serious. I sit back down. She puts her hand on my arm, and I can feel her cold fingers through the sleeve of my shirt. She swallows. I wait for her to speak. Karen took Mr. Green to the doctor for a visit two days ago; then she went back to the doctor's office today. Alone. Some of his test results must have come back bad.

"I need surgery. On my neck."

What?

She begins tearing her paper napkin into small pieces and placing them one by one on the table next to her barely touched plate of food.

"I've been in terrible pain for weeks. I kept thinking it would get better, that I'd just strained something. You know how I have to pull on Owen. I figured I'd got something out of whack and that it would get better on its own. But I've been popping those pain pills day and night. For a while they helped, but it's been getting to where I can't hardly turn my neck to the right. Last week I let them do some tests. Got the results this morning, and it's not good. The doctor says I don't have any choice. I've got to get this problem taken care of before it gets worse."

"This is something serious." I had no idea.

"Serious enough I have to stay a week in the hospital. Then I don't know how long in rehab."

"I will pray for you. And ask the people at my church to pray," I say. There is great fear in her eyes.

"I appreciate that. Lord knows I can use all the help I can get. The thing is, they don't do this kind of surgery here. I've got to go to Dallas to have it done."

Dallas. A three-hour drive from Eden Plain.

"The doctor's real positive. Says he thinks everything will go fine and that they can fix me right up. But the problem is, what am I going to do with Owen while I'm gone?"

"When will you have the operation?"

"They said I could wait a week, but no more than that."

"Perhaps his daughter can come," I say. If she hears her father needs her, surely she will come.

"I've thought of that. And I'm going to call her."

But when Karen tells Mr. Green about her plan, he says no. He does not want Chaney to come.

We are in the living room. It is night and I have come to help Mr. Green get to his bed. I stand beside his chair waiting for him to say he's ready. The two of them have been talking about the situation. About what he will do while Karen is in the hospital. They have been arguing I think.

I cough.

Mr. Green's voice is raised. "Chaney's got enough on her plate without taking time off her job to come babysit me. I'll be fine."

I do not understand this situation. At the end of his life, what does a man have except for his family? When he is old and he lies on his bed of death, will he care about his house or his land or his money? I think no. For none of those things will remember him when he is gone. None of those things will wail or weep for him at the moment he takes his last breath.

It is true, with no wife, no children, I am alone in Texas. But in Mexico, I have my brother and my sisters and their children. I have little Dulce. I have my mother. They are never far from my thoughts. If I were in need, they would help me as best as they could. And if any of them needed something, I would get it for them. If they called my name to come, I would drop everything and go to them. I would not wait.

"Owen," Karen says. "You're putting me in a terrible spot."

"I told you. We're not calling Chaney," Mr. Green says.

I do not know what is the correct thing for me to do. This is not a discussion for my ears. I move toward the front door. I can wait on the porch. When they are finished talking, I will come back in and help Mr. Green get to his bed.

"Hey! Where are you going?" Mr. Green says.

I stop. "Sir, I thought I would wait on the porch."

"Karen and I are done talking. I'm ready for bed."

Karen's cheeks are two spots of red. She has moisture above her lip.

"No, Owen. We need to settle this. I have to call the doctor in the morning and tell him when I'll be ready to have the surgery. After the operation's done, I'll have to stay in the hospital for five days. Then physical therapy rehab for a week. Which means me being gone nearly two weeks."

"I'll be fine," Mr. Green says.

What is he thinking? It is true, his disease has been under control for a month. He has not had to use his wheelchair at all, only his cane or his walker. But no one knows how long the good days will last. He may wake up tomorrow and be unable to move his legs.

"No, you won't be fine." Karen's voice is raised. "I'll be three hours away. Do you not want me to have the surgery? Is that it?"

"Don't be silly. Of course I want you to have the surgery."

"Well, you could have fooled me. Looks like you're doing everything to keep me from it. You're putting me in a terrible position."

"Dad blame it, Karen. You've always been one to overreact." Mr. Green starts to get up, as if he can stand by himself. I move to help him rise to his feet, but he motions at me to get away.

Karen throws up her hands.

Mr. Green won't look at her. I have never seen a more stubborn, more selfish man. At this moment I am so disgusted by him that if I didn't care so much about Karen and know that it would only make things harder on her, I would tell him that I quit tonight.

Mr. Green manages to get himself up out of his chair. When he nearly falls, my feet stay rooted where they are. Karen and I watch as he points his walker toward his room. He takes three steps, then turns around to face us.

"If you think I need somebody to be my nursemaid, I reckon Manny here would do," Mr. Green says.

My mouth flies open. Karen's does too.

He looks over at me. "Manny, can you cook?"

"Yes, sir."

"Can you read?"

Karen rolls her eyes. "Owen—"

"Yes, sir. I can read."

"Prescription bottles?"

"Yes."

"See there?" he says to Karen. "That's all I need. Somebody who can cook and somebody who can help me with my medicine. Me and Manny'll be fine. You go have your surgery. He can sleep in the guest room. Shoot," he says, "I don't know what kind of place he lives in, but he'd probably jump at the chance to spend a week in a nice air-conditioned house. Be sort of like a vacation, wouldn't it, kid? Tell you what—we'll even get somebody else over here to see after the ranch. Whole two weeks, only job Manny'll have is to be my nurse."

Taking care of Mr. Green sounds like something. That is for sure. What it does not sound like is a vacation.

Karen's face has turned red all over. "Manny, excuse him. I'm sorry. He didn't mean that the way it sounded."

"Mean what?" Mr. Green says. "I didn't say anything wrong. All I did was decide to give the boy a chance to live it up for a couple weeks."

I feel a familiar ache in my jaw, an old tightness between my shoulders. My lips do not move. I do not speak because I have learned when it is best to be silent. Mr. Green is an educated man. He is a good businessman, a rancher who understands how to manage his cattle and his land. He is a man who believes in honesty, a man who with his eyes sees that he has treated me with kindness and compassion. And in ways, he has. For two years he has paid me a fair wage. He provides me with whatever tools I need to do the work he gives me. He does not give me impossible tasks to do in impossibly short periods of time.

But Mr. Green is a man of ignorance, a man like many I have known in my life. Because of the color of my hair and my skin and the country of my birth, he believes that he knows me, that he understands me and all those like me. He believes all Mexicans are the same. And that we are nothing like him.

But this man does not know me. In all this time I have worked for him, not once has he asked about my life, my family, my home.

He does not even know my real name.

"Owen," Karen says, "Manny is not a boy. And he may work for you, but you have no right deciding what he will or won't do. He has his own life. His own responsibilities. And he has a decent place to live."

Mr. Green shakes his head. "You came up with a problem. I offered a solution. So sue me."

"Manny, I'm sorry. This is not your concern," Karen says to me. "You're doing an excellent job taking care of the ranch. And I—she puts her hand on Mr. Green's shoulder—"we appreciate it. I'm sorry you got dragged into this. It's a family matter. Owen, let Manny help you to bed. He's been here too long, listening to us carry on. Come on." She gives his shoulder a nudge. "The man's ready to go home."

"I'll do it," I say.

"What?" The two of them turn their heads toward me and speak with one voice.

"Mr. Green, I'll stay with you while Karen is gone. You'll need to find a man to do the outside work, but if you want me to stay inside with you while Karen is gone, I'll do it."

Someone might wonder why I would agree to take care of a man who does not respect me, someone who sees me as a stupid, uneducated person. But here is what I believe. Work is work, and I have never expected or looked for it to be easy. My family depends on me. They need every dollar I send to them. Having a job that pays well, no matter what that job requires of me, is not something to complain about. I can work on the outside or on the inside. I am willing to work for a man of wisdom or for a man with foolish thoughts. As long as I am paid a fair wage, and Mr. Green has proven himself to be a man who will do that, I will do whatever task is given to me.

And one more thing has helped me decide to do this task, to give up the outside work on the ranch to come inside to be a nurse and a maid: Karen will be gone for only two weeks. It is for her I will do this thing.

Two weeks.

What is fourteen days in the life of a man?

Nothing.

Nothing at all.

chapter seven

IT IS FIVE A.M. ON Wednesday, the day Karen is leaving for the hospital in Dallas. It is still completely dark outside, but we're in the kitchen. Everyone is dressed for the day.

"Remember, he has to take each pill at exactly the right time. A half hour early or a half hour late is okay, but no more than that."

"I'll give every pill at the correct time. You don't have to worry."

Karen shows me, yet again, where Mr. Green's medicine is kept. It is lined up on the counter. Eight bottles in a row. The directions are written plainly on the bottles. I see no problems with giving it correctly, but I listen to her instructions. She is nervous. The pills are not her true concern. Karen is afraid of what lies ahead for her today and of the danger she will face. The doctors have told her if the operation is successful, she will feel much better. If something goes wrong, she could be paralyzed.

The pot of coffee she made has finished brewing. The smell fills the kitchen. Karen fills two purple mugs. She hands one to me, the other to her best friend, Eddi. Eddi lives in Arkansas, but she has come to be with Karen during and after her surgery. Eddi will drive Karen to the hospital and will get a hotel nearby and stay until Karen comes home.

Like Eddi, I slept in this house last night. While Eddi has spent many nights at the ranch, it was my first time under Mr. Green's roof. I came last night so that Karen would not need to give a thought to his care on the night before her operation. Two times in the night I got out of my bed, put on my clothes, and walked down the hall to Mr. Green's room to make sure he did not need anything.

Eddi is a small woman, barely five feet tall, with short dark hair and long red fingernails. She laughs loudly, smokes many cigarettes out on the porch, and curses a great deal. I do not normally like women like Eddi, but I like her very much.

She smiles at Karen, then takes a sip from her mug. "Owen's not up yet?"

"He's still asleep." I have just come from looking in on him. "But he told me last night he wanted to be up when the two of you left. Should I wake him?"

Eddi looks at her watch. "You've got to be there at ten?"

Karen nods.

"You never know how Dallas traffic'll be. We should leave a little after six, don't you think?"

"That sounds about right," Karen says. "Owen's okay for now, Manny. Let's let him sleep a few more minutes."

The three of us sit down at the table. Eddi has made toast.

Karen wants to go over everything with me one more time. She has a long pad of paper and a padded brown envelope in front of her.

"There's cash in here. I think more than enough for anything you need, but in case something comes up, Owen's debit card is in there too. I've written the PIN right here."

"Okay."

"Some other things, too," she says. "Here's the number of the plumber, in case that toilet starts to leak again. Owen's doctor's name and number is right here. And if one of the dogs gets sick, I wrote down the vet."

She's going to be gone for two weeks. I do not believe much can happen during that time.

"And here's the numbers for two of the neighbors. They said for you to call if you need anything."

"I will," I say.

"Lori'll be here every morning to give you a couple of hours off. While I'm gone, the nurse said they could increase her hours. She said she'd come both Sundays so you can go to church."

"That will be good." We have already covered this. Twice.

"And you've got ranch help lined up," she says.

"Yes." We have been over and over this, too. Alejandro is coming to do my outside work.

"Good thing you're not going to be trying to take care of the cows and Owen, too," Eddi says. "That man's a full-time job all by himself. He's as demanding as a toddler. Manny, I don't know how much these folks are paying you, but I'm positive it's not enough."

"Seriously, he better behave," Karen says. "Just promise me you won't take him seriously. He doesn't realize how half the things he says come out sounding."

Karen often apologizes for Mr. Green. I think she is afraid he will say something so bad that I will quit and leave him alone while she is gone.

"I don't think the man's ever heard the term politically cor-rect." Eddi gets up to pour herself a second cup. "I told him last night he best treat you right."

I do not need these women to take care of me. "We'll be fine. I can take care of both Mr. Green and myself."

"So, when's the ranch hand coming?" Karen is looking again at her list.

We've been over this three times. "This morning at eight."

"What did you say his name was again?" Karen wants to write it down.

"Alejandro Santian. People call him Alex."

I was glad when Alex agreed to take care of the ranch this week. He has experience, and because he worked for Mr. Green during the last hay season, Alex is familiar with the place already. He is a young man with a family in Mexico. He does not speak much English, and he has no green card. But he is a hard worker. For the past five years, every spring he has come to Texas to work.

"Okay. His two weeks' pay is in the envelope too. Cash." Karen drums her fingers on the table. "There's something I'm forgetting. I know there is. Shoot, what is it?"

Eddi puts her hand on Karen's arm. "Honey, relax. Every detail's been taken care of. And Owen's not helpless. If Manny needs to know anything, he can ask Owen. Or if there's something neither one of them can figure out, he can call me at the hospital, and I can ask you. It's going to be fine."

Karen's face looks like she is not so sure.

At five thirty Mr. Green wakes up. I know he's awake because he has a bell he rings when he needs something. Over and over again he shakes the bell. It is loud enough to be heard anywhere in the house. You can even hear it out in the yard.

"Good morning, sir," I say when I come into his room.

"Where's Karen?"

"She's getting ready to go. She and Eddi are in the kitchen. Are you ready to get up?"

"Get me that blue shirt," he says, after I've helped him to the bathroom. "No, the other blue one."

I stand in front of him and button the blue shirt.

"I need my comb," he says.

With great care, he combs and smoothes his white hair.

When Mr. Green and I come out of his bedroom, Karen and Eddi are almost ready to go. Karen comes over and kisses him on the cheek.

"Take care of yourself," she says.

"Don't worry about me." His arm circles Karen's shoulders. Then to Eddi he says, "You look out for her. Make sure those nurses take good care of her. They should come when she calls. Get on the horn to the administrator if they don't treat her right."

Eddi salutes. "Yes, sir."

"Give me a call soon as she's out of surgery. And if anything happens—I mean if you need me to come up—"

Karen puts her fingers on his lips. "Don't even go there. I'll be fine. Sail through this like a piece of cake."

They have talked about Mr. Green coming to the hospital. Karen does not want him to visit. "If I see you, it'll make me worry about you," she told him early in the week. "If you see me, you'll worry about me. You've got Manny to help you. I've got Eddi to help me. We'll talk on the phone every day if we need to. When the two weeks are over, I'll be back home, and we'll be together enough to get sick of looking at each other's face. Agreed?"

Most men do not like hospitals. Mr. Green told Karen okay, if that was the way she wanted it, he would go along, as long as Eddi promised to call him if Karen changed her mind and wanted him to come. Even though I do not like driving in city traffic, I have told him I would take him to Dallas if he wanted to go.

"You got a driver's license?" he asked me.

"Yes, sir."

"Texas or Mexican?"

"Texas." Why would I have a Mexican driver's license? I haven't lived there in more than twenty years.

"Okay, then. I guess we're set."

From the porch, we watch Eddi and Karen get into Eddi's car. It is not light out yet, but the dogs are up. They follow the women to the car, sniffing at their calves as they walk. When Karen and Eddi are in and have slammed their doors, the dogs come back up onto the porch with us. The four of us stand there and watch as Eddi backs out, turns the car around, and eases down the driveway. When we can't see the taillights, the dogs stay where they are, but their tails droop.

I, too, feel a great loss once they are gone. I do not believe women understand the difference their presence makes. How the air in a place changes when they are gone. A home where there is a woman has a certain feel, a certain air. There is more life in a home where a woman lives. More color. More warmth.

I move my lips in a little prayer.

Mr. Green wipes at his eyes. For a moment his shoulders slump. Then he points his walker toward the house and heads to the kitchen. He calls to me over his shoulder.

"Breakfast. Two fried eggs. Two slices bacon. Three pieces of toast. Butter on both sides. Don't forget to feed the dogs. Garbage needs to be taken out. And when you make up my bed, well I don't know if Karen told you this, but I like the sheet to be tucked in extra tight at the foot."

"Yes, sir," I say. To breakfast, the dogs, the garbage, and the sheets. "Yes, sir" to all of it.

A man working for Mr. Green should know how to understand English, but being able to speak it is not something he would have to be able to do. As long as he knew how to say *yes, sir,* he would be able to get along without any problems.

After he has his breakfast, I shave Mr. Green and help him take a shower. I make his bed and cook his eleven o'clock lunch. After he eats I help him get to his recliner.

"Where're my glasses?" he asks after he has sat down.

They are on the table beside him. "Here, sir. Right here."

He looks at his watch. "Don't reckon we'll hear any news till late this afternoon."

"No, sir. I don't think we will."

He looks at his watch again. Then he reaches into his mouth. "Here's my teeth. Can't stand to wear them when I sleep. They rattle around too much."

He places them in my hand. They are wet and have bits of food on them.

"Clean them for me, will you? Then put them in that green plastic container. The one on the shelf next to my shaving cream."

While he naps, I clean his bathroom. Then I put his towels and his pajamas into the washing machine because he likes them to be cleaned every day. After that, I sweep the porch.

About every hour I look at my watch.

It is nearly three o'clock before Eddi calls. Mr. Green answers the cordless phone he keeps on the table next to his recliner.

I stop what I am doing.

"She's okay? The surgery's over? Good. Good. No, don't put her on. Let her rest. Tell her I'm glad she's all right. Yes, everything's fine here. Fine as frog hair now I know she's all right. You tell her I'll call her tomorrow." He hangs up the phone.

"So Karen's surgery is done. And she is fine," I say. "That is very good news. I am so happy to hear."

Mr. Green wipes at his eyes. "Yeah, it is good news. I'd like to keep the old girl around awhile longer. She's a keeper, if you know what I mean."

"Yes, sir. I do know. Karen is a good woman. Kind. Wise. A good cook."

"You can say that again," Mr. Green says. "Except for all them blame casseroles."

Karen has left fourteen casseroles in the freezer—one for every night—in throwaway foil pans. I have already taken one out to thaw. It is sitting on the counter.

"What have we got for tonight?"

"The label says it is chicken, rice, and broccoli."

"Put it back," Mr. Green says.

"Sir?"

"Put that mess back. We're not eating it. Karen's all right; let's celebrate. You like barbeque?"

"Of course." More than chicken casserole, that is for sure.

"You like beef or pork better?"

"Beef." So many years in Texas.

"Man after my own heart. Ever been to Big Uncle Buster's?"

"Uncle Buster's? No, I don't know that place."

"You don't? Well, we've got to remedy that. Big Uncle Buster's is a great little dive over on the east side. Couple of blacks run the place. Those people do know how to cook barbeque. They got the best ribs around. You're in for a treat, because you and me are loading up and going there for supper tonight."

Mr. Green and me. Going somewhere in his truck. I do not know what Karen would say about me taking him somewhere. She told me to call an ambulance if he needs to go to the hospital. She wrote on the pad of paper which neighbor I am to call if we need groceries or something else brought to us from town. Any errands that need to be done, I'm to do them while the home health aide takes care of Mr. Green.

We did not discuss what I'm to do if Mr. Green decides he wants to leave the house. From what I can see, he stays home except on days he must see the doctor. I don't believe Karen expected either of us to leave the ranch unless there was an emergency.

"I know what you're thinking." Mr. Green has lowered the footrest of his recliner. "Karen's out of the woods. That's great news. The other great news is that she's not going to be here fussing over me for a whole week and a half. The even better news is that what she doesn't know won't hurt her. I may not be able to put on my own socks, and the time's coming sooner than later when I won't be able to wash my own neck, but there is not a thing wrong with my mind, and my mind says we're not hanging around this house all week." He slaps his leg the way some people do when they hear a joke. "Like you Spanish boys say, 'No way, José.' Let's plan on leaving around six."

His words are not a request. What should I do? Rather than answer him, I go into the kitchen to prepare his pills. I get the right ones for this time out of their bottles. Okay, I believe I can safely accomplish this trip. I can understand his need to get away from this house. I, too, would feel a desire to do what I want to do without anyone telling me a reason why I should not. Without too much difficulty, I believe I can help him into the truck. I can take him to the restaurant. He can eat what his stomach craves. Then I can deliver him back home. No harm will come to him.

And tonight, he will sleep in his bed a contented man.

So at six o'clock, I help Mr. Green make his way down the ramp I built to where I have parked his truck close to the end of the sidewalk. I attempt to guide him around to the passenger side.

"Whoa, there Nellie," Mr. Green says. "What are you doing, Taco? You're riding shotgun. I'm driving."

"Sir, I can drive."

"Nope, that's my job. Go on now. You got the keys. I think I've done forgot my set."

Karen left the keys to Mr. Green's truck in the brown envelope. They are in my pocket now. "I'm sorry, sir, but it is not safe for you to drive. Let me help you around to the passenger side."

He curses. "I told you I'm driving. I'm not riding in the passenger seat."

In my whole life, I have never crossed the man who is my boss. It is not something I want to do now, but I have no choice.

"Sir, I will take you anywhere you want to go. I will turn where you tell me to turn. I will stop when you tell me to stop. I will stay as long as you want to stay and will drive you back home whenever you are ready. But no, I will not help you into the driver's seat."

"Give me the keys." His face is as red as if he had spent the day in the sun.

"No, sir. I will not."

We have locked eyes. Inside the house, the phone rings, which causes both of us to turn our eyes toward the front door.

"Shoot. That could be Eddi," Mr. Green says. "Something might be wrong with Karen. Run back in and try to catch it before they hang up."

I do as he says, and I do get to the phone on time. It is a wrong number.

I come back out and give Mr. Green the news.

He is standing in front of the truck, one hand on the hood to steady himself. "Whew. Scared me there for a minute. Not enough to scare off my appetite though. Tell you what—you're one hundred percent wrong about my driving. I can drive as good as anybody, but I figure you've been itching to drive this truck since you come to work here." Standing in one place for so long has made him tired. He is leaning heavily on his walker. "Don't blame you. It is a nice rig. So if you're set on getting behind the wheel, I'm not going to argue with it. Help me up and let's get going." He motions toward the passenger seat.

"Yes, sir," I say.

It takes a few tries, but we get him up into the seat. I move to fasten his seat belt.

"Nah." He pushes the belt away. "I don't wear them things. You put yours on if you want to, but I don't believe in them. Last thing I want to do is be in a wreck and get trapped inside."

Texas has a click it or ticket law. I hope we do not get stopped. I never go anywhere without buckling up, but tonight I leave the seat belt alone. Like I have heard said, some things are not worth going to the mat over.

"Careful now. Don't grind the gears."

We head down the driveway.

"There's a dip up here. Don't go too fast over that cattle guard. It's not as wide as it looks."

"Yes, sir," I say.

Yes, sir.

Yes, sir.

A million times, *Yes, sir.*

chapter eight

"SO," SAYS EDDI, WHO HAS called on the phone, "how're you two gentlemen this morning? Karen wants me to make sure y'all are doing okay."

I am not sure how to answer her question. Mr. Green is sitting at the kitchen table. It is the morning after our meal at Big Uncle Buster's. He has a partially eaten bowl of oatmeal and an empty juice glass in front of him. In his hand is a bottle of Maalox. He's been sipping from it since the moment he got up from his bed.

"Tell her we're fine," he mouths. He touches his index finger to his thumb. "Tell her everything is A-okay."

Then he burps, grimaces, and thumps himself on the chest with his fist.

"Everything is fine here," I say. "Mr. Green is fine. How is Karen? Is her condition improved?"

"I think so," Eddi says. "She's still hurting a lot, but she's got one of those pumps she can push for pain medicine. They sat her up on the side of the bed to eat her breakfast this morning. Later on, they say they'll have her up walking in the hall."

"So soon?" I say.

"Yep. That's how they do it these days. They get you up and moving quick. Say it cuts down on the risk of blood clots and pneumonia. Anyway, y'all are all right. Everything's going good.

Great. I'll tell Karen."

"Don't worry about Mr. Green," I say. "He is well. Tell Karen she is in my prayers."

"I'll do that. And Manny, Karen really does appreciate you staying with Owen. It means a lot to her to know he's in good hands."

"Yes, ma'am. Tell her not to worry about anything."

"Hope you don't go stir-crazy stuck out on that ranch, just the two of you."

"We'll be fine."

"You're a good man. Talk later. Call my cell if you need anything." Then Eddi hangs up.

"You want something else to eat?" I ask Mr. Green.

"Naw, this is fine. Have I taken my medicine yet?"

"Yes, sir. You took it when you first sat down."

"Good. Good." He burps again. "Man, am I paying the price for those ribs. Have to say, though, they sure were worth it." He sips again from the white plastic bottle, then looks at his watch. "That Spanish boy here yet?"

Alex has not been late yet. It is now seven thirty.

"He comes at eight," I say. "Would you like to rest in your recliner for a while?" This is what he usually does after breakfast.

"No. Let's go out on the porch and wait for that boy to get here. I want to be sure he knows what he's doing. What's his name again?"

"Alejandro. Alex," I say.

I help Mr. Green up from his chair. With his walker, he makes it out to the porch and sits down in one of the rocking chairs with very little assistance. Today he can lift his feet, and his hand did not tremble so badly while he was eating his breakfast. His voice is clear and strong. I have learned from looking it up on the Internet that Parkinson's disease has effects that a man cannot predict. Some days people who have it can barely walk. Their words are difficult to understand. Other days, they feel much better. They have more strength. Their words are clear.

He looks at his watch again. "You sure the guy's coming? 'Cause if he don't show up, I'm going to need you to put out feed and do some work on that fence."

I am standing near his chair, which means when he talks to me, Mr. Green must look up, something no man likes to do to another man. But in the three years I've spent working on this place, not once have I been offered a seat on this porch. Should I sit down in the rocking chair next to him or continue to stand? I shift from one foot to the other. I would squat, except that my right knee is bad and doing so causes me pain.

"Alex is a dependable man," I say. "He'll be here at eight o'clock. That's the time you said you wanted him to come. Remember?"

"How you know him?" He cranes his neck to look at me.

"He's a member of my church." I decide to take a seat, but on the steps, rather than in a chair.

"Y'all worship Mary, don't you." Mr. Green is rocking back and forth.

"Sir?"

"Catholics. They worship Mary. The pope too. Some them other saints too. Saint Francis, Mother Teresa. Isn't that right?"

"I was Catholic for a few years when I was a child, but I've been a Baptist all my adult life," I say. "I don't know much about the Catholic church."

"No kidding. I thought all you Spanish boys was Catholic."

"No, sir."

He rocks. Coughs and spits off the porch into Karen's flowerbed.

"You been in Texas long?" he asks.

"Since I was fifteen."

"Swim the river?"

"No. I rode with a man in the back of his truck."

Mr. Green pulls out his pocket knife and begins to clean his fingernails. "So, what are you, Manny? About twenty-eight? Thirty?"

"I am thirty-nine."

"No kidding. You don't look it." Mr. Green leans back in his chair and moves his eyes over me. "You got you a Mexican wife and some kids you send money back to?"

"Yes, I do send money to my family—to my mother, my sisters, my brother and his family."

"But no wife of your own?"

"No."

Mr. Green grins, then leans his chair back. "Well then, that explains why you look so young. Nobody to answer to. Nobody to nag you. Let me tell you, nothing like a nagging wife to put years on you." He laughs and rocks some more. "Not that my wife was bad about that. No, she wasn't one to nag much, but most women are."

He rocks some more, looking out at the yard while he does.

But then Mr. Green stops his rocking and looks straight into my face, as though he has suddenly remembered something he forgot. He leans forward in his chair. His eyes are set on me.

"Hey now, wait a minute. Something don't ring right. You're coming up on forty years old. No wife. No kids. You're not one of them homos are you?"

"No, sir. I am not." Before today, Mr. Green has never asked any personal questions of me. He is making up for lost time.

"You understand what I mean by the word homo? I don't know

what you call it in Spanish. Maybe—"

"The word is the same." I am embarrassed to be having this talk. "And I can assure you, I am not a homosexual. I hope some day to have a wife and children. It has simply not been the right time. For the past years I have been working. Providing for my mother. She is old and sometimes ill. She has many needs."

"So you do like women?" he says.

"Yes. I like women very much."

"Not men?"

"No, sir. Not men. Not in the way that you mean."

He rocks some more, is silent for a while, then, "Well then, glad we got that out of the way."

I am too.

Mr. Green's questions about my personal life insult me, but they do not surprise me. In these times people wonder about a single man. I am providing him with physical care. Helping him in and out of the shower. Up off the toilet when he is having a bad day. And into his pajamas every night.

Why have I not married yet is a question I am asked frequently by my mother, my sisters, and by friends at my church. Perhaps you wonder about my looks. There is nothing wrong with my appearance. I am of average height for a Mexican man. Five feet five. My teeth are straight. My hair is thick. I am not ugly. I am sometimes quiet, but I am not shy.

I have no problem going out on dates. Most Sundays I invite one of the many single women from my church to have lunch with me. When I ask, I am rarely told no. But if I am turned down, I invite someone else. It has been many months since I ate my Sunday lunch alone. Many Friday nights I am invited to a woman's house for dinner and to watch television or a DVD. Most Saturday nights I take a woman to a movie and out for coffee or ice cream afterward.

Though I do not have a serious girlfriend at the moment, twice in the past five years there has been a woman I considered asking to be my wife. First was Rita, a Mexican girl who was a labor and delivery room nurse. Ten years younger than I. She and I were a couple for almost a year. But she was ready to marry and have children of her own, and I was not. So after eight months together, she broke up with me and found someone else. A man ready to have her as his wife. The two of them now have twins. Cute boys with fat cheeks and full heads of dark hair.

After her, there was a girl named Tory, who I cared about a great deal. She was a music teacher, the same age as I am. Like Rita, Tory wanted to marry and have children. When I told her I was not ready to do that and did not know when I might be, she told me she loved me but could not wait. She now wears an engagement ring and is planning to be married in the spring to a divorced man who takes care of his three little girls.

Rita and Tory still go to my church. While they are friendly to me and appear to hold no ill will, it is hard for me to meet their eyes. It is not because I am angry, for I am not. They are good women and I wish them well. I find it hard to look at them because when I do, I see what I have missed out on.

With both of these women, I came close to making a commitment, to creating a family.

You wonder why I did not.

I am not afraid of spiders. I am not afraid of heights. But when it comes to marriage, I am a coward.

I am bone of my father's bone. Flesh of his flesh. The blood that flowed through his veins—that does still if he is alive somewhere—is the same blood that runs through mine. I am afraid of hurting someone else the way my father hurt my family. The way he hurt me.

But if I am honest, I know there is more. To love someone is to risk the pain of loss. The pain of losing my father, of him taking away his care and his love, is something I bring with me into every new day. Someday, I will lose my mother. She will pass away, and I'll not see or hear from her again on this earth. I know that time is coming, and I believe I will be able to bear it. For that is the way of life.

But to love someone and have her turn away as my father did is much worse. What if I married and she, like my father, became displeased with me? What if she left me, or asked me to leave her? Perhaps someday I will be a strong enough man to take such a risk. I hope so, because I do not want to grow to be an old man who is completely alone.

"That him?"

I see a blue pickup truck coming up the white gravel drive. "Yes, sir. It is Alex."

"Good. I'd about decided he wasn't coming."

I look at my watch. It is ten minutes until eight. This is Alex's fourth day to come to work on the ranch. Not once has he been late. Not once has he failed to do exactly what was expected of him.

"You say he's dependable? Knowledgeable?" Mr. Green struggles to get up out of his chair. He wants to meet Alex eye to eye.

I move to help him stand up. "Yes, he is a good worker. He has come every day. You do not need to worry. He'll do a good job."

"Is he good enough I can tell him what to do and know he'll do it?"

"Yes, of course."

"Will he work even if nobody's watching him?"

"He will."

"All right then. Let's get him lined up. Set his day's work out for him. Then me and you can get going." He is leaning on his walker, watching Alex.

Since Alex does not have a car, his friend Leonard has brought him. At the end of the day, Leonard will pick up Alex and take him back to the apartment Alex shares with four other Mexican men.

"Where are we going?" I ask.

"What do you mean where? You think we're going to sit around here all day and twiddle our thumbs?"

I had expected Mr. Green to do the same thing he has done the past three days. Eat. Nap. Take medicine. Eat again. Nap. Take more medicine. Watch the news. Eat again and go to bed.

"Nuh-uh. I've got some people I need to see. Business I need to take care of. And not to worry. I know how crazy you are to drive my truck. I'll let you take the wheel."

Mr. Green's business turns out to be a stop at the coffee shop in downtown Eden Plain. He is hungry? It has been only one hour since I served him his meal.

He tells me how to get there and exactly where he wants me to park.

When I have done this, I get out, go around, and help him out of the truck. "Your walker," I say. I reach to get it from the bed of the truck.

"Nah. I don't need it," he says.

He does need his walker. He may fall without it. But I leave it and stay close to his side.

I hold the café door open for him. We are still outside on the sidewalk, but the smells of coffee, grease, and cigarette smoke come at us like a wall of fog. Mr. Green stumbles when he steps over the threshold, but I grab his arm. When he gets his balance back, he jerks his arm away from my hand.

The place is small. A woman sits by herself at one table. She's got the classified ads spread out in front of her, and she's got a pen in her hand. At another table is a young family—a mother, a father, and two little girls. In the center of the café, at three tables pushed together, a group of old men are sitting, smoking cigarettes, and drinking coffee. Some of them are eating biscuits, pancakes, sausage, and eggs. I don't know how anyone could eat with all of this smoke.

"Hey there, CeCe." Mr. Green speaks to the short, blonde waitress who is standing behind the cash register. "How you been, honey?"

She says hello.

When they hear his voice, several of the men look up. They call out greetings. I realize now why we are at this place.

"Come on in here. Long time no see, mister." One man stands up to slap Mr. Green on the back.

"Where you been keeping yourself?" Another man stands to shake his hand.

"Looks like you're getting around pretty good."

Mr. Green takes the last seat at a table for six. I stand at his elbow for a moment. But when he does not address me, when he does not appear to remember I've come with him, I move to an empty table in the corner. I sit down by myself. One of the little girls waves at me. I wave back at her and nod to her father. When the waitress comes over, I order coffee and juice.

The place is so small that from where I sit, I can hear everything that's being said. From the old men's table comes the conversation of ranchers. Talk of the weather. Cow prices. Hay production and the rising costs of feed.

Someone has left a newspaper in the empty chair at my table. Everything but the sports. I start with the front section, and I do not stop until I have read the whole paper, even the classifieds.

The family finishes their meal and leaves. So does the woman who was sitting alone. A young couple comes in, orders, eats, and then is gone.

Four times, the waitress comes and fills my cup. Two hours pass. The café is empty except for me and the three tables of old men.

Finally, Mr. Green calls to me, "Manny. Let's get going."

The other men have stood up to go. They are putting dollar bills down beside their empty coffee cups. They have been here so long I am surprised the owner of the café has not come out to charge them rent.

Mr. Green needs me to help him rise to his feet. Sitting for so long, his joints become stiff. I move to help him.

"Who's this you've got with you?" asks an old man who, like the others, has put on a cowboy hat.

"Ah, this is my Spanish boy. Manny," Mr. Green says. "He's helping out some on the ranch. Likes to drive my truck, so I been letting him chauffeur me around."

"Yep. Never seen a Mexican boy didn't like to drive a nice truck. Better watch out, though. You look away, and he'll be settin' all your radio buttons to that blame Mexican cha-cha music."

The two of them laugh.

I do not.

"Don't let old Green here cheat you, now." The man puts his hand on my shoulder. "Shake him down for your wages every day. You hear me boy?"

"Yes, sir," I say.

The two of them laugh again. Then the old man starts

coughing. Mr. Green pats him on the back, but the man, who had smoked one cigarette after the other, says not to worry. A touch of emphysema. He is okay.

Outside on the sidewalk, Mr. Green stalls. But I have had enough. Enough waiting. Enough coffee. Enough smoke. Enough old men.

When finally we are back inside the truck, Mr. Green tells me to head east, which is the opposite direction of the ranch.

"Too long since I've been out this way," he says. "Keep on driving. I'll tell you where to go next."

I look at the time. As long as we are back home in time for his afternoon medicine, it will be okay. So I turn the truck in the direction he wants to go.

"What's the matter with you? Cat got your tongue?" he says, after we've gone a few miles, side by side, but with no words.

What does this man expect me to say? I am not his friend. I am not his family. I am the Mexican boy hired to drive him around, the butt of the jokes of him and his friends. I am expected to make conversation? My face grows hot.

"I am concentrating on the road, sir."

He rolls down the window and spits into the wind. "Whatever you say, Pancho."

Forgive me, but I cannot help but be glad when I look over and see he has a wad of spit on the side of his face.

We are only a few miles out of town when Mr. Green tells me to pull over.

"Too much coffee," he says. "I got to take a leak."

"I think there's a gas station a few miles up ahead."

"Can't wait. Pull over now. Like I told you."

I ease over to the side of the road. There isn't much shoulder, so I have to drive onto the grass. Before I have the truck completely stopped, Mr. Green is fumbling with the door. When he can't get it open, he curses.

"Hold on, sir. I'll help you."

I wait for three trucks and four cars to pass before I can get out. Finally, I go around to his side. He holds onto my arm, and we walk up the bank of the road to where there are some bushes.

Passing cars honk.

Mr. Green is sweating and pale, but we get the job done. When he is finished, I have to zip him up. Then I help him back into the truck. His breath is coming quick. His left shoe is wet. He has difficulty lifting his feet.

"Are you all right?" He is settled in and I am behind the wheel.

"Thought I was," he says. "Maybe not. Feeling a little rough all of the sudden."

"We should go back home."

"Yeah. Let's do that."

Mr. Green is asleep in his seat before we make it back to town. As I drive along, his mouth falls open. His chin keeps dropping toward his chest. When we arrive back at the ranch, I go inside and get his wheelchair. I help him into it. He is awake, but he is too tired and too weak to walk.

I push him up the ramp and across the porch. Should I put him in his chair or in his bed? I think the bed. I am wheeling him through the front door when the telephone rings.

"Don't answer it," he says.

It rings and rings.

"Shoot. Might be Karen," he says. "Hand me the thing." But he answers it too late. "Probably somebody trying to sell something. If it was important, they'll call back."

He sets the phone down. Then he tells me he thinks he will lie down. Not in his chair, but in his bed if I can help him get there.

"Of course, sir," I say.

Once he is settled, I ask, "Anything else?"

"No. That's all, Manny."

Before I am at the end of the hall, I hear him snoring.

chapter nine

THE NEXT MORNING I WAKE up and wonder what the day will bring. Will Mr. Green want to go somewhere in the truck again? Or will he be content to stay close to home?

After he is up and has had his breakfast, we go out again to the porch.

"What'd you say that boy's name is again?" He looks at his watch. "Ought to be here. You sure he's coming?"

I point to the end of the driveway. Alex's friend, Leonard's, blue truck has turned in.

We wait on the porch, me standing, Mr. Green sitting. Alex gets out of the truck. He is still a good ways from the house. We watch as he stands and talks to Leonard for several minutes before he finally closes the truck door and Leonard drives off. Then slowly, Alex makes his way toward the porch. His head is down. He barely picks up his feet.

Mr. Green squints. "Not exactly a spring in his step this morning, looks like. Must have stayed up too late. Looks like he's hungover. You didn't tell me he was a drinker."

Alex is not a drinker, but I, too, am surprised at the way he is moving this morning. Perhaps he is sick.

Mr. Green rocks back and forth in his chair. "Boy best get some life in him. I expect him to be ready to put in a day's work.

He can't expect to get paid moving no quicker than that."

I get up and go down the porch steps to meet Alex in the yard.

"Hold on. Where you going? You two in cahoots?"

I keep on going down the walk to where Alex is waiting at the edge of the yard.

"Hey you," Mr. Green calls from the porch. "I want to talk to you."

Neither Alex nor I turn around. With our backs to the porch, the two of us talk. When we are finished, Alex turns and heads toward the barn. He does not come up onto the porch like he has every other day.

Mr. Green's face is red when I return to him. "What's he think he's doing? I want to see him. He needs to come up here and face me."

"He is going to do his work."

"Not before he sees me, he's not." Mr. Green tries to rise from his chair. "Is he drunk? Has that boy been drinking all night?"

"No, sir. He has not been drinking."

"What's wrong with him then? Why didn't he come up here and talk to me?" Mr. Green's eyes are angry. "You and him are cooking something up. I wasn't born yesterday, you know. You're covering for him, and I won't have it. I'll send you both packing quicker than you can say go."

His breath is coming quick, and his right hand is trembling so badly that he tries to steady it with his left one.

I stand before this man, and I say words that choke me as they come out of my mouth. "Alex has a wife and two sons. They are four and five years old. This morning, his wife called him just before it was time for him to come here. She had to travel two hours on foot to get to a telephone. She walked so far because she had very bad news. Alex's oldest son, the one who is five, died yesterday."

Mr. Green stops rocking. His mouth drops open.

"The child drowned. His mother found him in a shallow pond not three hundred meters from where she was cooking their meal."

"Well, why in the world is he here? He should go and be with his wife."

"No, sir. He will go at the end of this month. For now, he must stay and work."

"He won't be there for his own child's funeral? That's crazy. Go get him. Tell him to take off and go right now."

From where we sit, Mr. Green and I can still see Alex. He is heading to the farm truck to put out feed. Every few steps his arm goes up to wipe at his eyes.

"Sir, you don't understand. Even if Alex left now, he would not make it home in time. His son will be buried this morning. His body may already be resting beneath the earth. In the part of Mexico where Alex lives, they do not wait to bury the dead. The funeral is often held the same day that a person dies."

"The same day? I never heard of such a thing."

It is the way of my village too.

The way of the poor.

"You sure he don't want to go home? Maybe he doesn't have money for the bus. Tell him I'll give it to him. Whatever he needs."

"The best thing he can do for his family is work. Work is what he wants to do."

"You're sure."

Alex needs the money. And he needs to be busy, not at his apartment with no one around and nothing to do.

Mr. Green's hand is trembling. His face is red. "All right then. He's a grown man. But you go out and check on him in a few hours. Make sure he don't change his mind."

"I will do that."

"He got water with him?"

"He brings it every day."

"Make sure he's got enough."

About every hour, Mr. Green tells me to go out and make sure Alex is okay. When he tells me to do this, I walk far enough off the porch and toward the barn that I can see Alex, but not so close to him that we talk. I know, though Mr. Green does not, that he must work through his grief unobserved. Alex is busy, working more quickly than he would on a normal day. The only way you can tell something is wrong is that, over and over again, he pulls a rag from his back pocket, pauses long enough to wipe at his eyes and his nose, then puts the rag back, lowers his head, and goes on with his work.

At noon, Mr. Green insists the two of us get in the truck and take some lunch to Alex, who has now gone out to mend the fence that runs along the back side of one of the far pastures. We have never taken Alex lunch before, but today Mr. Green has told me to pack food enough for three workers. Ham and cheese sandwiches. A package of cookies. A can of Pringles. Two apples and a banana. Driving up, we see Alex before he sees us. When we get close, we can see his swollen face and the red in his eyes.

"Give him his lunch and tell him how sorry I am about his boy."

I do.

"Ask him if there's anything I can do."

I speak to Alex, then turn to tell Mr. Green what Alex has said back to me.

"He says thank you, but there is nothing. He only wants to work. He says to tell you he is thankful to you for giving him this job. And for you not to worry. He will put in a full day."

"Ain't right." Mr. Green is wiping his eyes as we drive back to the house. "Losing a child like that . . . just ain't right."

When Alex comes up to the house to wait for his ride, Mr. Green asks me to help him out onto the porch. "Call him. Tell him to come up here."

Alex climbs the steps to the porch.

He gets paid on Friday. His wages are in the envelope Karen left. Today is Wednesday, but Mr. Green pulls out a wad of bills and holds them out to Alex.

Alex looks at me. He does not raise his hand to take the cash.

Mr. Green tries to say something to Alex, but his voice cracks and nothing comes out.

I motion to Alex he should take the money.

"Thank you," he says in English.

Mr. Green lowers his gaze and shakes his head slowly back and forth. Finally, he raises his hand to pat Alex on the shoulder. Then he turns his walker around to go back inside.

And for the rest of the night, neither of us speak.

Karen has been gone a week. We have both talked to her on the phone. Her voice is a little bit hoarse, but she says she is doing fine. According to Eddi, the doctors say Karen is doing great. Hopefully she will be home in another week. When Eddi asks how things are going with me and Mr. Green, I tell her everything is all right.

And it is. So far there have really been no problems.

We are sitting at the breakfast table. I have made pancakes.

"Shoot, would you look at that." Mr. Green has dripped syrup onto his shirt.

This morning, instead of putting on one of his regular blue shirts that he wears every day, he chose a white one with sharp creases on the sleeves. Not only that, after his shower, before he got dressed, Mr. Green put on cologne, something I have never seen him do.

He dips his napkin in his water glass, then wipes at the spot. "Can you still see it?"

"No. Only the wet spot."

"You don't think it'll show when it dries?"

"No." Why all this worry about a small spot on a shirt?

"I've got a little business to attend to today. Somebody I want to go see over in Green Hill. You know where that is?"

"About an hour from here? East?"

"Yep. Let's plan on leaving in a half hour. You be ready by then?"

"Yes. How long will we be gone?"

"Most of the day is what I'm figuring."

I pack a bag. In it I put water, fruit, crackers, and his plastic pill planner, which I have loaded for the day. He has said not to pack a lunch. We will stop somewhere, maybe Dairy Queen, for our meal.

We are on our way before Mr. Green tells me the purpose of our trip.

"Couple of years after my wife died, I took up with a lady friend name of Lillian McDonald. Her husband, Marshall, was a friend of mine. When he died, me and her started seeing each other. Kept company a good two years. Woman was a peach. Good-looking, red hair, green eyes. Figure like Sophia Loren."

I turn my head to look at him.

"What? You think I'm already dead? There may be snow on the mountain, boy, but there's still a fire in the oven. Hey, look out!" He points to a car up ahead. "He's slowing down."

"I see it."

I am glad for the distraction because I have no desire to hear about any fire. In Mr. Green's oven or anywhere else.

"Lillian was always full of fun. We'd go out to dinner. She loved me to take her to the Chinese buffet. You would not believe how many of those fried wontons that little thing could put away. Sometimes I'd take her to a movie. Three or four nights a week, we'd play dominos. Chickenfoot mostly. That was her favorite game."

"She sounds like a nice woman," I say.

"After a couple of years her kids started talking about moving her off to Arizona. I don't know what got into me. She wanted to stay in Eden Plain and get married, but I drug my feet. She got tired of waiting. Next thing I knew, off she went."

I know something about that.

"So she still lives in Arizona?" Why are we headed to Green Hill?

"Nope. Not anymore. Three years ago Lillian moved back to Texas. To Green Hill. Soon as she got settled in, she called me up. Wanted to get together. Pick up where we left off. But at the time, I'd taken up with another widow woman, so I told her no, I didn't think I wanted to see her."

"But you have kept in touch."

"Not exactly. After that phone call, she sent me a card with her address on it. Said she wanted me to have it in case I ever changed my mind." He reaches into his shirt pocket and pulls out a card. "This is it right here. 1253 Mountain View Drive."

"So she knows we're coming?"

He shakes his head. "Nope. I'm going to surprise her."

"But you've talked to her recently."

"Not since that day she called me right after she moved back."

"Three years ago?"

"Believe so." He puts the card back into his pocket. "Then again, it might be closer to four. I lose track."

A sign up ahead says we are twelve miles from Green Hill.

"When we get into town, be on the lookout for a florist. Lillian loves yellow roses, and I'd like to take her some."

"Slow down." Mr. Green slaps the dashboard.

I am going fifteen.

"Should be right up ahead. Shoot, I can't read the street numbers. You're going too fast." Between his knees, Mr. Green is holding the arrangement of yellow roses we stopped and bought. "Does that say 1500? I think you've gone too far."

We are in the 1200 block of Mountain View. It is a nice neighborhood of older one-story brick homes. I spot house number 1253.

"Sir, this is it. You want me to pull up in the driveway or park on the street?"

"This is it?" He stares out the window, squinting. "You sure?"

"1253 Mountain View."

He pulls out the card and looks again at the address. "I guess on the street's okay. Don't block the mailbox is all. Lillian's got her flag up. Don't want her to miss her mail."

I park the truck. The house is cream-colored brick with green shutters and a black front door. The yard is green. The hedges are well-trimmed. An American flag is stuck in the ground next to the sidewalk that runs from the street to the house.

Mr. Green hands me the roses to hold, then pulls down the sun visor so he can use the mirror. He digs in his pocket for his comb, runs it through his hair, then through his thick brows.

"You got any breath mints?"

"No, sir."

"Gum?"

"Sorry. No."

"Okay. How about some water."

I pull a bottle from the bag.

He takes a sip, swishes, then swallows. Again and again. He does this four times.

"You reckon she'll be glad to see me?"

"I believe she will be surprised."

I help him out of the truck. He insists on leaving the walker in the back. I offer to carry the flowers for him, but he tells me no, he is all right. After the long ride, he is stiff. His feet drag. We move slowly up the walk. When we get to the front door, a woman opens it before we have a chance to ring the doorbell. She is young and pretty, and she has a baby in her arms. In times like these, it is not good for a young woman to open the door to a pair of men she does not know. Is her husband aware that she does this?

"May I help you?" she says.

Mr. Green hesitates. Perhaps this young woman is Lillian's daughter. Even her granddaughter.

"Lillian. I'm looking for Lillian McDonald. Is she here?"

The young woman squints in the bright sunlight. Her baby raises its head to look at us, then lays it back down on her shoulder. She rubs its back. "I'm sorry. Lillian doesn't live here."

"But you know her?"

"Sure. Well, not exactly. She sold us this house."

"How long ago was that?" Mr. Green has put his hand on the brick wall next to the front door to steady himself. He is out of breath.

"Two years."

"So she moved to another house," he says.

"Oh, no." The young woman moves the baby to her other hip. "She couldn't live in a house anymore. After that stroke, her kids put her in the nursing home. Last I heard she was still there."

"A home? You sure?"

From inside the house, we hear a phone ring.

"Sorry, I've got to go."

Mr. Green tries to say something, but he can't get his words out.

"I've really got to go."

"Ma'am, do you know which nursing home she is in?" I speak quickly.

"Uh . . . Park Lane." The phone is still ringing. She has her hand on the door. "No, not Park Lane. Lane Park. Something like that. Bye now."

We stop at a convenience store to ask for directions to the nursing home.

"Lillian's girls never did do right by her," Mr. Green says. "Sticking her off in some home. Ain't right. I bet she's got a thing or two to say about those ungrateful little heifers."

Once we find the home, we park and go inside. There is the smell of urine. Of cooked fish. Of pine cleaner. People in wheelchairs are lined up against the wall near the front desk. Someone from one of the nearby rooms calls over and over again for someone to come help. A very fat nurse is talking on the phone. When she hangs up, Mr. Green asks where Lillian's room is.

"Twenty-three," she says. "Down about halfway, on your right. Them sure are some pretty roses you got there."

We head down the hall.

"What number did she say?" Mr. Green looks at the doors.

"Here it is." I know we are at the right room because Lillian's name is written on a card that sits in a little slot next to the door. It is halfway open.

"Should I knock?"

He doesn't get a chance. From the other side of that door, someone calls out, "Who's there?"

Mr. Green hesitates.

"Who's there? Come on in here so I can see who it is."

Lillian is in bed, but she is not asleep. She is lying on top of the bedspread, propped up on her elbows. She's wearing purple pants and a purple blouse. The head of the bed is raised to an almost forty-five degree angle. There are metal side rails on the bed, but they are down.

"Lillian, darlin', it's me." Mr. Green moves close to the bed and touches her hand.

I stand beside him, nearer to the foot of the bed. How long has it been since Mr. Green saw Lillian? This woman does not have red hair. It is gray, a little bit blue. Her eyes may be green, but they are so cloudy a person would have a hard time telling what color they are. As for her figure? The one Mr. Green described with the light in his eyes? This woman is plump. She has the round stomach and low chest of a great-grandmother.

"How are you feeling?"

Her eyes lock with his. "Better now. I thought you'd never come."

He bends and places a kiss on her lips. Then he straightens up.

I look away.

"I brought you some flowers. Your favorite. Yellow roses."

Her face shines.

Mr. Green's arm trembles from the weight of the heavy vase, but he holds them so that Lillian can take in their smell.

There is a chair in the corner of the room. I move it close and position it behind his knees so all he has to do is sit down.

"I am going to step outside for a little while," I tell him. "I am going to take a short walk."

Mr. Green eases himself down into the chair, but he does not answer me. He is only seeing and hearing Lillian.

"I'll come back in a little while."

This time he nods.

I head down the hall toward the outdoors. I move past the people lined up in their chairs. Past the fat nurse behind the counter, past a gray-haired black man in the lobby who is trying to play Joplin on an old upright piano with too many stuck keys. I leave through the door we came in.

There is a bench outside under a shady oak tree. I take a seat. The weather is warm. Across the street is a school. Children are playing on the playground. It is a good place to wait. I have a tiny sketchpad in my shirt pocket and a drawing pencil. I look across the way to a little girl who is standing near the fenced playground. She has dark hair and eyes. She reminds me a little bit of Dulce. I do a small drawing of her. Then the bell rings, and she and the other children all go inside.

Soon cars begin to pull into the parking lot alongside the

nursing home. Nurses begin to come up the walk, one or two at a time. They carry tote bags and they wear scrub suits. I suppose they have come to begin their shifts.

I keep a close watch on the time. In one hour, I go back to check on Mr. Green. I stand outside the door. Neither he nor Lillian sees me. They are talking, laughing, remembering past times. He is holding her hand. Everything is all right. Since it is not time for his medicine, I get a Dr. Pepper out of the pop machine in the lobby and go back outside to my bench.

The next time I come in, an hour later, Lillian has fallen asleep. Mr. Green is sitting beside her, keeping watch. This time, Mr. Green sees me.

"I'm ready to go." His nose is red.

"Okay." I wonder if he should wake Lillian up and tell her good-bye.

I help him stand up. He bends and kisses her forehead. She reaches up and scratches her nose, but she does not wake up.

"Let's go." He pulls out his handkerchief and blows his nose.

We are ten miles down the road before Mr. Green speaks. "She didn't know me."

How can that be? I cannot see Mr. Green's face. He is turned to look out the window.

"She thought I was her husband. Thought I was Marshall. Man's been dead nearly ten years."

"But you could not make her understand it was you?"

Only then does he turn to look at me.

"I didn't even try. She was so happy to see Marshall, I let her think I was him."

chapter ten

IN THE KITCHEN, I GO to the freezer. The label on today's foil-covered pan says Chicken Enchiladas, something I hope Mr. Green will like. Most of the meals Karen left for us have been good. Only a few of them not so good. This week we had Hamburger Stroganoff, Taco Pie, Sloppy Joe Casserole, and Chicken Divan. Taco Pie was not the favorite of either Mr. Green or me. Too much cumin. Not enough chili powder.

I set the pan of enchiladas on the counter to thaw for supper. When Mr. Green wakes up, I will prepare his lunch. Now, I put the water on to make iced tea. Once it is brewed, I add the sugar. I have learned from eating lunch with Karen the secret to making good iced tea: stir in the sugar while the tea is still hot.

Once I'm finished in the kitchen, I put a load of clothes in the washer. I sweep the porch. While I am outside, I feed the dogs and check them for ticks. From the porch, I can see Alex in the pasture on the tractor putting out fertilizer. The cows have been fed. Early this morning he repaired some fence. The weather is as close to perfect as weather can be. Blue sky. A light breeze. Around seventy degrees. I stand on the porch and watch Alex as he makes a few back and forth loops. Then I go back inside. What else is there for me to do? The carpet needs to be vacuumed, but the machine will wake Mr. Green up. He does not feel well unless he has a long afternoon nap. The carpet will have to wait until later in the day.

I move from room to room without any purpose. This has become my habit. With every passing day, the walls of this house close in on me a little bit more, making my joints feel stiff and my head ache. The tasks expected of me do not occupy enough of my time. I am accustomed to harder work than this.

Today is the worst. Maybe because the end is in sight. The time is coming soon when I, not Alex, will be out spreading fertilizer, repairing fences, putting out feed. Probably in about a week or a week and a half at the most. You would think that would make it easier, but at this moment it does not. I am so restless I feel irritable and not like my normal self. There is nothing I care to watch on TV. No one I want to call. I do not feel I can be still enough to read. I suppose I could work on a painting, but even that does not interest me today.

What I need to do, what I long to do, is saddle a horse and head out across the pasture. Except for Mr. Green needing me when he wakes up, except for it not being safe to leave him alone for even a little while, that is exactly what I would do.

I am ready to return to the easy sleep a man earns when he works with his muscles a good part of the day. Alex has done a good job, but I am eager to check on the cows every day, to be the man they watch for to give them their meals. There is great satis-faction in providing for an animal's needs.

But I must stop this.

Stop this ungrateful attitude.

Stop allowing myself to feel discontent, to find fault with this good position, this well-paying job. In two days they will release Karen from the hospital and she will come home. Her surgery was a success, which makes me glad. In her daily calls, she is cheerful and her voice is strong. She says she feels better than she has in years. Her back does not hurt. Her legs are not numb. The physical therapists say she is doing well.

"That is wonderful," I tell her. Our plan is that as soon as she is able to resume her care of the house and of Mr. Green, I will return to my work outside. "Just wonderful. Stay as long as the doctors tell you to. We are fine here. I will take care of Mr. Green for as long as you need me to do so."

When I say these words to Karen, do not think that I am telling a lie. When I look back on these last couple of weeks, it is not that taking care of Mr. Green has been so difficult.

Not at all.

And it is not that his treatment of me has been so terrible.

It has not.

Mr. Green is not a bad man, only one who has had little understanding of people who are different from him. In the past two weeks, I have seen his better side. In truth, I have grown fond of the old man. I cannot believe I am saying this, but even on a day like today, a day when I would give anything not to be stuck inside, I can honestly tell you that when I return to my care of the ranch, I will miss spending time with the old man who is my boss.

I stand in the living room. The fireplace has floor to ceiling windows on each side of the hearth. Those windows open up onto the front porch. The bright red coat of a male cardinal dipping into one of the front yard bird feeders catches my eye. The bird eats carefully, without greed. After every bite, he raises his head to listen. He turns from side to side, then lowers his head for another taste. When he has enough, he flies away.

Yes, soon I will return to my routine. But today, everything I can think of to do is already done. So I stretch myself out on the couch for a short nap.

The barking of the dogs wakes me up. When I open my eyes, I cannot tell how long I have slept. Thirty minutes? An hour? I go out onto the porch. What is this? I am shocked to see Karen's car coming up the driveway. What a great surprise! The doctors have released her early. I am surprised that she didn't call to let us know. She must not have wanted Mr. Green to know. Should I go and wake him up for this? No, I should let Karen get settled inside, then go and wake him up so that he can come into the kitchen and find her sitting at the table as though she was never gone.

He will be so happy to open his eyes and find Karen back home in this house.

But then what I see changes. Only Eddi is getting out of Karen's car. Eddi alone. Crying. Barely able to walk.

I go down the steps to meet her on the sidewalk. My pulse is quick but my steps are slow. "Eddi? What's wrong? Where is Karen?"

Eddi comes close. She leans into my chest and puts her hands on my arms. Her breath comes fast. I can smell the odor of the cigarettes she has smoked.

"It's bad. Really bad. I can't believe it. I just won't, but it's true." Her words shoot out like water from a high pressure hose. "Oh, my God. It's true." She is shaking. "Something happened. Karen was feeling great. She ate her breakfast. We took a walk down the hall because the doctor told her she needed to get up and move around more today. But when we got back to her room, she couldn't catch her breath. So I helped her get back into bed, and then I called the nurse."

The dogs keep running around us. They are barking and barking. Stop, I want to say to them. Shut up. I want to say the same thing to Eddi. I want to tell her to stop talking. To hush her mouth.

To please not say anything else. But I don't speak. I wait for Eddi to finish her words.

She takes a step back from me, but she keeps her hands on my arms. I feel the heat from her palms through the fabric of my shirt.

"The nurse didn't seem all that concerned, but she put this mask on her. It was attached to this bag. She told Karen to relax and take slow, deep breaths. She put the oxygen monitor on her finger. It showed the mask wasn't helping. I thought the nurse knew what she was doing, but Karen got worse instead of better. She couldn't catch her breath no matter how much she tried to relax and breathe slow. Finally, the nurse called for more help. Two people came. They made me wait out in the hall. Then while I was waiting, wondering what was going on, I heard them call a code blue to Karen's room. It was terrible. People came running from everywhere. They pushed this big cart into her room. Nobody would tell me anything."

No.

Please, God.

No.

"She didn't make it," Eddi says. Her forehead is pressed against my chest. She shakes her gray head back and forth. "The doctor said they did everything they could but she didn't . . . she didn't make it."

Only twenty-four hours have passed, but how life can change in the course of a day.

They said it was probably a blood clot that went to Karen's lung. A complication of surgery. Something that could not have been predicted. An event that happened so quickly there was nothing they could do.

I do not understand. I do not expect I ever will. How can someone be doing well? How can they be almost ready to go home, then suddenly die? I understand God has a plan for every life. I believe we are all in His hands. But that does not mean my heart can understand or accept something like this.

Everything is in a state of confusion.

No one is really in charge.

I am worried about Mr. Green. He looks like he has aged ten years since we got the news. His face is red. He keeps wiping at his eyes. We called the home health nurse. She got the doctor to authorize some pills to help with his nerves, but Mr. Green will not take them. He can barely walk, so we are using his wheelchair even inside the house. The tremor in his hand is worse, and his voice is low and weak.

"I can't believe she's gone. First Eva. Now Karen. There's no one left. What am I going to do?" Over and over he says the same thing. To me, to Eddi, to the neighbors who have brought food. His grief is like a great weight on his shoulders that is causing his body to bend toward the earth.

He is scared. Confused. Full of fears. I knew he loved Karen, that he cared about her a great deal. What I did not know until now is how dependent upon her he was.

I can see it now. Karen loved her brother. She did not want to take away his dignity. She let him and she let me believe Mr. Green was much more in charge of things than he really was. She stayed in the background, quietly going about doing so many things that I never knew.

When I look at Mr. Green today, I see nothing in him of the hard-working man who built this ranch. He looks like what he is:

a sick, old man who must have someone else take care of his every need.

The past twenty-four hours he has not wanted me out of his sight.

I do not know what to say, only what to do. Which is stay beside him. When Mr. Green is awake, I sit by his chair. When he is asleep, I rest on a cot next to his bed so that he can see me when he opens his eyes. When he goes to the bathroom, I talk to him through the door so he knows I am still there. When he sits at the table for his meals, I take a seat too. My presence comforts him the way the sight of a parent can comfort a child.

Eddi must decide what to do. Tasks and decisions that do not belong on her shoulders have landed there because there is no one else. Such a small family. Only Karen, Mr. Green, and his daughter, Chaney, who Eddi has not been able to reach.

"Owen, they're holding Karen's body in the morgue. We have to tell them what to do."

The hospital has called twice already.

But Mr. Green will not talk about it. He says he wants no say in the matter. Eddi should do whatever she thinks best.

So Eddi decides on cremation. She tells me that many years ago Karen told her that was what she would want when her time came. There is to be no service. Eddi says except for a few neighbors and perhaps a handful of members from Karen's church—which is not very big and mostly elderly people—who would come?

If they are paid extra, the funeral home says they will deliver Karen's ashes to the ranch. Eddi has to decide. Should they bring them in a box or an urn?

This is something I do not care to discuss.

But my desires go unnoticed, and Eddi talks to me about everything. I can see she is in a difficult position. She is not a member of this family. She has no obligation to Mr. Green. Soon, she must return to her home in Arkansas.

"Manny," she says to me, "we've got to go over your plans. It's obvious that Owen can't be left alone." Eddi has a pencil in her hand and a yellow legal pad in her lap. "Especially now. I'm telling you, Chaney's got no choice but to come. And she will. I'd say sooner rather than later, but the truth is, I don't know exactly when she'll get here. I'm not putting any pressure on you. I realize this is not your problem, but I need to know. How long can you stay?"

Mr. Green has fallen asleep in his recliner.

"As long as I am needed," I tell her.

I am filled with dread at what lies ahead. Caring for a sick man, washing his clothes, cleaning his house, and cooking his food is not what I expected to be doing at this time in my life. But what choice do I have? This man is not able to take care of himself. I cannot leave.

It does not matter that at least four ranchers I know would hire me full-time if I approached them. Almost once a week I turn down requests for my help. I cannot think about how much I was looking forward to returning to my work outdoors. My hope is that Chaney will get here soon.

"No, really. I need to know," Eddi says. "Spell it out for me in black and white, Manny. You've got your own life. Your apartment in town. How much past this week can you stay?"

"Mr. Green is in need. I will stay and care for him. I will not leave. I promised Karen I would take care of her brother while she was gone. I will not break my word."

"Karen was crazy about you." Eddi's voice chokes. "Before I got here, she told me on the phone about you. Said that you were a good, good man and that Owen was lucky to have hired you. I know if she could, she would tell you thank you for doing this.

As for Owen—you know better than to expect any appreciation from him. He can be the crankiest, most ungrateful man I have ever been around."

She is right, though the past few days I have seen none of that side of him.

"Thing is, losing Karen, he is just pitiful right now." She wipes at her eyes. "One thing you don't have to worry about. This family has money. More than you know."

This news is not a surprise to me.

"Owen's turned his checkbook over to me for now. Karen had taken care of most everything ahead of time, but he signed a bunch of checks and told me to pay any bills that need paying. I'll make sure you get your wages." She shuffles some papers. "Now about the ranch. Can Alex stay on?"

I have already discussed this with him. "Yes, he will stay. It is good for him to have this work."

"Great." Eddi writes on the pad. "I appreciate you talking to him." She writes more. "I'm leaving notes for Chaney so she'll at least have some idea what she's dealing with when she gets here. You think of anything else I should tell her?"

Five days later, I help Mr. Green into his pickup. Before I get in, Eddi slides in on the driver's side to sit shoulder to shoulder between Mr. Green and me. Her left knee rests against the gear shift. She holds the box containing Karen's ashes on her lap.

She is leaving in the morning. Going back to her home. Chaney has plans to arrive in three days.

My window is down. The smell of cow manure is in the air. I steer the truck through a gate, over a cattle guard, and into the pasture. We are headed to Mr. Green's pond, which is located on the back side of the ranch. I drive slowly because the ruts are deep and rough. We bounce up and down. The shocks on the truck should be replaced.

Except for our sad task, this would be my favorite kind of day. The sky is blue with only a few clouds. We have had a lot of good rains this spring, so the grass, to be harvested later for hay, is tall and thick and green.

When we get to the pond, Eddi and I get out, then I go around to help Mr. Green. We have brought folding chairs. Eddi gets them out of the back of the truck. She sets them up on the bank of the pond, then goes back and gets the box of Karen's ashes out of the cab.

I had thought we would wait for Mr. Green's daughter to do this, but Chaney told Eddi to go ahead without her.

I have been to many funerals, both in Mexico and in Texas. At every funeral I have attended, there has been dignity. A coffin. Flowers. And prayers.

Because I am not family, I had no say in Karen's final arrangements. But the thought of cremation is disturbing to me. I understand—ashes to ashes, dust to dust. It is the same. But had Karen been my family, she would have had a nice funeral. I would have put pink roses on top of her casket. A pastor would have come to say the last words. I would have had her buried in a peaceful cemetery, and I would have bought her a stone marker.

The three of us sit close to the bank, side by side in our folding chairs, facing the water. I do not know what is coming next.

"Beautiful day," Eddi says.

I nod. We are here to talk about the weather?

"Sunshine. No clouds. Karen would have enjoyed a day like today."

I look to Mr. Green. I am not sure he has heard.

He pulls his handkerchief from his pocket and wipes first at his eyes and then at his nose. His eyes go to the edge of the pond where more than a dozen fish have come to the edge.

"Karen's catfish," he says.

Looking for their cornbread.

I wipe at my eyes.

Eddi gets up out of her chair. She stands near the water to have a close look.

"Owen, there's some big boys in here. How long since you dropped a hook in this water?"

"Been two years."

"That doesn't make sense," Eddi says. "Why'd you stock this pond if you didn't plan on fishing it?"

"I did fish it. Regular until Karen came."

"I never heard Karen talk about going fishing," Eddi says.

"She didn't," Mr. Green says.

I shoo a dragonfly away from my face. Mr. Green tells Eddi about how Karen made pets of the fish.

"I'm not surprised," Eddi says. "Dogs, cats, I guess even fish. Nothing Karen liked better than seeing something enjoy one of her good meals."

I remember the big lunches Karen prepared for me. How she watched me eat and how she always offered me more. How, many times, in the afternoon when I got ready to go home, I would find part of a cake or a pie on the seat of my truck.

"She was a kind woman," I say.

"The best," Eddi says.

"No telling how big these fish'll get," Mr. Green says. "Catfish can live to be old. They don't ever stop growing as far as I know. No matter. Don't reckon I'll be eating any of them."

The three of us sit in silence for perhaps half an hour. The sun moves low. It shines red and orange starburst rays through the trees. A cloud of gnats hovers over the water. And across the pond, a bunch of cattle come up to drink. From somewhere a bit east of where we sit, a mourning dove's voice signals the coming of the end of the day.

After a while the mosquitoes start to bite.

Eddi rubs her hand over the box. She fingers the lid and looks over at Mr. Green.

He nods. "Go on." His voice is thick. "You do it. I can't."

Eddi looks then to me.

I lower my eyes. I should help her, but like Mr. Green, I cannot.

So Eddi gets up. She has the box in her hands. Mr. Green and I watch, but we don't move. The cattle have worn a path near the edge of the pond. Eddi follows it, picking her way around cow pies and stepping over small bushes and branches until she is about halfway around.

From our seats, we see Eddi stop. She bends. Then she sets the box on the ground and removes the top. When she does, she pauses for a minute, looking at what is inside. Finally, she straightens up and carries the box to the edge of the pond.

The cows raise their heads.

She lifts the box high.

The birds stop their songs.

She stretches her arms and holds the box out over the pond.

The fish, in the water at our feet, become still.

She gives the box a little shake, and Karen's ashes spill out. They hang in the air for a long moment. Then they fall, to spread across the water. To scatter. Moved by the wind. Some on the bank. Some on Eddi's shoes, which she wipes off with her hand.

When she is done, Eddi puts the cover back on the box. She stands looking out at the water for a long minute. Then she makes her way back to where we are.

"I suppose that's done," she says. Eddi has wiped her hands on her jeans. You can see ashy handprints. One on each side.

My eyes become wet.

"You two ready to head back?"

Mr. Green nods.

If I could, I would stay in this spot until dark.

Instead, I help Mr. Green up and to the truck. Eddi folds up the chairs and loads them in the back. None of us says anything when I start the engine. I put the truck in gear and point it back toward the house.

In my rearview mirror, I see the pond, and I know Eddi was right in what she chose to do.

True, there is no cemetery. No grave. No headstone.

But I was wrong.

We have shown Karen our greatest respects.

chapter eleven

EDDI LEFT A WEEK AFTER Karen's death. That was one month ago.

Since then, it has been only Mr. Green, the dogs, and me. Together out here on the ranch. Chaney did not come when she said she would. She only called and talked to Mr. Green. Some kind of problems with her work is the only explanation he would give me for why his daughter did not come when he was in such desperate need. Thankfully, nothing has come up that the two of us could not handle. The bills have been paid. Alex and I have received our wages. Nothing has broken down on the ranch. Mr. Green has not gotten sick.

For all of this I am more grateful than I can explain.

I try not to judge, but you should know that it is very difficult for me not to do so. What kind of a daughter . . .

See? There I go again.

Since I have lived either alone or with men all of my adult life, I did not understand until Karen died the difference a woman's presence makes in a place. It is not that we have let household tasks go. It is not like that at all. Don't think that we have turned the place into a bachelor's pad because we have not. Believe me, I have lived in some untidy places. I have shared quarters with some men who were sloppy housekeepers.

Here at the ranch, there is no moldy food in the sink, no saddle or engine parts in the living room, no beer cans in the bathroom. I keep the house clean. I do the laundry. I keep up the yard. Everything is as it should be. Rather it is the spirit, the light, the energy of Mr. Green's home that has changed since Karen, and after her, Eddi, left. The house is too quiet, even though Mr. Green leaves the TV on much of the day. It has a feeling of dullness. Of not enough light.

Yesterday I cleaned all the windows, thinking perhaps that would help. It did not.

Mr. Green misses his sister.

I miss my friend.

We need a woman in this house is what I think.

Chaney says she is coming on Saturday. Flying in to Dallas. Renting a car. I tell Mr. Green we could go to the airport to pick her up. Even though it would be many hours in the car, we could do it. I thought it was the least we could do.

But when Mr. Green offers, Chaney says no. There is no need for us to meet her flight. We should stay home and wait. She will come on her own in a rental car.

I am in the room when he has this conversation with her. "Manny," he says after he hangs up, "you and me need to talk."

One important thing has changed between Mr. Green and me. Since Karen died, I no longer wait to be invited to sit. I have my own living room chair. Not one that I own, but a comfortable chair I sit in all the time. I also have a rocker on the porch that I relax in when the two of us sit outside. The same one every time.

Mr. Green picks up a pen from the table beside him. He turns it over in his hand and begins clicking it. Again and again.

I wait for his words.

"You've been good to me," he says. "Better than I deserve.

Don't know what I'd have done if you hadn't been here to take care of me. It's been hard." He pulls out his handkerchief and blows his nose, something he has done many times each day since Karen died. "But you have done more than any hired hand should be called upon to do. You been a friend. More'n that. You done for me what a son would do for his dad."

My throat gets tight. "I'm glad I was able to help."

I wonder. Who takes care of my father when he is ill?

"I always wanted a son. Greatest disappointment me and Eva ever had was that we only had the one child."

What answer does my father give when he is asked if he has any sons? Does he tell others he has none? Or does he say that he had two boys at one time but that he has them no more. Are we dead to him, my brother and I? What about my sisters? Does he remember them?

"Don't get me wrong. Me wanting a son doesn't take nothing away from Chaney. She's my daughter, and I'm real proud of her. It's just that—" His voice chokes.

I should help him by saying something, but I cannot speak either. If I try, I am sure my voice, like his, will break.

I try to stop myself from going to these hard places in my heart. I try not to think about the most important man in my life, who has been lost to me for so many years. I try, but I fail. Why, God? Why must every mention of a father, of a son, send me down this same road? I would like to feel some relief. I would like not to feel this pain that burns my throat, that wets my eyes, that feels like an acid ache in my stomach.

"Been thinking." Mr. Green taps the pen against his palm. "You still got that apartment in town?"

"Yes, sir, I have my duplex."

I have not slept there since the night before Karen went to the hospital for her surgery. Once a week, while Lori is here with Mr. Green, I drive into Eden Plain to purchase groceries and to do whatever errands he has asked me to do. While I am in town, I go by to check on my place. I collect my mail. I pay my bills. I get whatever I need and make sure everything is all right.

"How long you plan on staying with me?" Mr. Green says.

"I don't know."

My answer is honest. I have turned this question over and over in my mind. I have never been sure what was expected of me. I do not know what I am supposed to do, and there is really no one to ask. Since Eddi left, every day is the same. I get up, I take care of Mr. Green. At night I go to sleep under his roof.

Until Chaney gets here, there is no one else but me. Once she arrives, I do not know what will change. Mr. Green will still need someone to provide his care, to help him to the bathroom, to assist him in and out of bed.

Truthfully I see no end ahead.

You may wonder at me. Why am I doing this? I am under no obligation to this man or to his family. Why am I staying when this is not the work I want to do? What holds me to this place and to this old man? Am I such a good person? Such a loyal man?

I only wish that were true.

But it is not because of anything good in me, for I am a selfish man. Rather, what holds me to this place and to this task are words from the Bible. Words I learned many years ago, words that have become so deeply carved upon my heart that I am unable to shake them, even when that is what I wish to do.

Love the Lord your God with all your heart, mind, and soul.

Love your neighbor as yourself.

Tell me, do you see any loophole in those words? Any way out? Try as I might, I cannot find any such thing. Mr. Green is my neighbor. I have grown to love him. I cannot leave him at a time like this.

"You've been here over a month. Helping me out," he says. "Taking real good care of the house. That boy Alex's doing a good job outside too. Been thinking you might want to let your place in town go." Mr. Green now thumps the pen against his leg. "Nothing but costing you money. You may as well move your stuff out here. We can clear out one of the bedrooms. Two of 'em if you want. Take however much room you need for your belongings."

This comes to me as a surprise. I do not know what to say. I can see in his face, he very much wants me to say yes.

"I'm offering to let you move in here permanent. Make the ranch your home."

Does he mean forever?

"But your daughter," I say, "she may not agree with this plan. Perhaps she will want to stay here."

"Chaney? Nah. This is between the two of us. None of her concern."

He is wrong. This is very much his daughter's concern. He is seventy-three years old. He takes ten different kinds of pills. He owns large herds of cattle. His ranch has miles of fences to maintain. Four hundred acres of ranch land that need constant attention. All of this, and some days he is so stiff and weak, he does not get up from his bed until it is time to eat lunch. I must help him button his shirts and zip his pants after he uses the toilet. At times his speech is so soft and weak he cannot talk on the phone. So far his mind is mostly clear, but how long will that be? People with Parkinson's disease may someday become confused.

"So," Mr. Green says, "you going to take me up on my offer? Let your place go? You got much furniture? 'Cause if you do, you can sell it and use what's already set up. Course that'd be up to you.

I got that flatbed trailer out there under the shed. Be just the thing for you to use to move your belongings."

"I appreciate the offer," I say. "But this plan is something I must think about." I do not meet his eyes. "I want to pray about this before I make a decision."

Mr. Green is surprised. But he does not want me to know how badly he wants this thing.

When his daughter comes, she will understand there are many decisions she must make. Suppose she asks me what I think she should do?

I have given this a great deal of thought, and here is what I will tell her. Look, this is not a good situation. Your father needs help. The help of his family, not the assistance of a paid stranger like me. I am an honest man. I have not taken nor would I take advantage of him. But other people would not be so honorable. You should move here and take care of your father.

That night, after Mr. Green is in bed, I make myself a cup of instant coffee—Nescafé, with canned milk and sugar, the same drink my father enjoyed when I was a child. In my socks, I take my mug and go out onto the porch. When they hear me, the dogs wake up and come around the house to first sniff at my knees, then fall asleep at my feet. The moon, one day away from full, is so bright it casts gray green shadows on the ground. Tonight there is no wind.

I take a seat on the steps and lean my back against a column. Nice house. Good pay. Work that is not hard. Do I want to stay here? For how long? Will I—do I—have a choice?

I have had many different jobs in my life, most much more

tiring than this one. The good thing about indoor work is that you never have to worry about a job getting cancelled or delayed because of the weather. No matter what, your job is there. You will get paid.

That is something to be grateful for. Something I never take for granted. I cannot tell you how often I thank God that I am able to work. I thank Him for my strong body and for the good health that allows me to provide for my family. Recently a storm damaged the roof of my brother's house. He did not have the money for repairs, but I did. Two months ago, Dulce had to go into the hospital because of her appendix. The bill from the hospital was more than my sister and her husband make in one month. But it was less than I make in a week. Because of my job, I was able to help.

So please do not think I am complaining when I keep returning to how much I long for the outdoors. That is where my heart feels most at ease. I miss riding a horse. When I am frying meat at the stove or putting sheets on a bed, I hunger for the feeling of the sun on my back and the wind in my face. I prefer the kind of work that makes my muscles ache at the end of a day rather than the tasks of caring for a sick and lonely man.

Mr. Green's care is work that makes my heart, my mind, and my soul tired in a way that delays my sleep when I lay my head down at night.

Yet nothing is simple. I have come to like Mr. Green, to feel an attachment to him. The affection I feel for him is more than obligation, more than obedience to the Word of God, though truthfully it started with that.

And this surprises me. Many things the man does and says are harsh, unkind. When he begins to talk to me about immigration, I try to change the subject. If that does not work, I find some excuse to leave the room. To him, his words make perfect sense. To me, they echo with ignorance and hate.

Some days I spend a good portion of my time keeping my tongue from saying out loud what my mind wants to say. Yet, still, I care about him. I don't want him to be alone. He has begun to feel, in a small way, like family. I feel bad for him. For the loss of his wife, then his sister . . . for a daughter who so seldom comes.

"We need to go to the store."

Mr. Green is standing in front of the refrigerator. The door is open. He does not stand up straight. His back and shoulders are round. I see his body bending toward the earth a bit more every day.

"Why?" I ask. "What do you need?"

I am wiping down the countertops. It has been only three days since I shopped for groceries. We have plenty of everything, I think.

"A cake, some strawberries, and a carton of Cool Whip."

"You want strawberry shortcake?"

"I want it for Chaney. It's her favorite."

Chaney is flying from Orlando to Dallas late tonight. Since she will not arrive until nearly midnight, she plans to spend the night in a hotel, then drive to the ranch in the morning.

"Okay," I say. "I'll go as soon as Lori gets here."

"Get a bag of Snickers," he says. "Chaney likes those too. When you get them home, put them in the freezer. That's how she likes to eat them."

"All right."

"Some cookies 'n cream ice cream too. And a bunch of green grapes. Make sure you get the kind without seeds."

"Okay."

Chaney must have a sweet tooth. Maybe I should make a list.

We have spent the past three days getting ready for Mr. Green's daughter's visit. At his instruction, I have deep cleaned the house, washing all the curtains, wiping the walls and ceilings with damp rags. There are fresh sheets on Chaney's old bed. And fresh pillowcases, which I have sprayed with starch and ironed with steam. New towels hang in the guest bathroom, and I have moved my things from it to the mudroom bathroom near the back door. Both dogs have had baths. I have dipped them for fleas. I have washed the front porch. And I have planted three flats of pansies along the front walk.

"Wake me up early tomorrow," he says, later, when I help him into bed. "If Chaney gets an early start, she could be here by ten."

"Okay. Around seven?" He usually sleeps until nearly eight.

"Make it six."

"Six. Okay."

"Is my new blue shirt clean?"

"It's hanging in your closet."

"Good. Good. Remember . . . six. In case she gets here early. Don't want you and me to still be in bed."

The next day Mr. Green is awake before six. He calls to me, and so I get up, get dressed, and go to him. I see him look at the digital clock on the table beside his bed. I help him shower and shave. When he puts on his watch, he checks it, makes sure it is set correctly. Then he puts on his new blue shirt. I button it for him and tie his shoes. In the kitchen, while I am cooking our eggs, I see him check the clock on the wall.

After breakfast we go out on the porch. Even though it is only eight thirty, Mr. Green thinks it best we sit outside and keep watch. Chaney could be early. He wants to see her drive up. So we sit and we rock and we wait.

Nine. Nine thirty. Ten. Ten thirty.

At eleven, Mr. Green must have his pills. With food. I urge him to go inside.

"The dogs will let us know when she gets here," I tell him. "We'll hear them barking as soon as she turns off the highway."

With great reluctance Mr. Green agrees. We go in, and I prepare our lunch. After we eat, I convince him to rest for a while in his recliner.

"I'll keep watch. I'll wake you when I first see her turn in," I say.

"I'm thinking about calling the highway patrol." He looks at his watch for about the two hundredth time today. "She could have had a wreck. Something worse. Woman traveling alone, anything can happen."

"No," I say, "I do not believe anything is wrong. She probably got off to a late start. She may have become stuck in traffic. You know how bad the roads are in Dallas."

What I do not say, but what I am thinking is, *Why is she putting her father through this? Why does she not call?*

Finally, at six o'clock, we hear the dogs barking. Mr. Green and I look at each other. We are in the living room, watching the news to see if we can hear anything about a bad wreck. I get up and go to the window.

"That her?" Mr. Green asks.

"Yes, sir. I believe that it is."

chapter twelve

A BLACK FORD EASES UP the drive. The dogs are barking like crazy. They run out to meet the car. When it stops, they sniff at the front bumper, then make their rounds of the tires, lifting their legs.

I stand beside Mr. Green, a half step behind him. His eyes are fixed on the figure inside the car. His left hand is on the railing of the porch. His right hand holds his cane. Today is one of those days when he needs his walker, but all day he has refused to use it. His chin is trembling and his eyes are wet. I know he would like to go down the steps to meet his daughter, but he cannot. He is too weak and too shaky to take the steps. To go around the side to where the ramp is would mean taking his eyes off the woman in the car. Something he cannot bear to do for even a moment.

So we wait. From where we stand, we can see the woman put the car into park and turn off the key. But she does not get out. I can make out a little of what she is doing inside the car. First she adjusts her cell phone. Probably she is turning it off or setting it to silent. Then it looks like she is attending to things in the passenger seat—putting items into her purse is what I believe. Or getting something out. I cannot tell which. Finally, she lowers the visor to check herself in the mirror. Doing all of this takes only a few seconds, but it feels like hours.

Finally, the driver's side door opens and a woman gets out.

Chaney is tall. I think nearly six feet. She has dark blonde hair, halfway down her back. A slender build. She is wearing jeans and a gray sweater. No jacket, though today's October afternoon has turned gray and windy. For a moment, I see her pause and gaze up at the house. For the smallest moment, she hesitates. Then she opens the back door of the car and pulls out a tote bag.

"She needs some help, Manny," Mr. Green says.

I go down the porch steps and out to the car. "Go on," I shoo the dogs back up onto the porch. Chaney has gone around to the trunk. She is tugging on one of two very large bags. This is good. She plans on an extended stay. The bag she is pulling on is wedged inside the trunk in such a way that it is not moving.

"Hello. I'm Manny," I say. "I'll get those for you."

"Thank you. I'm Chaney Green. Nice to meet you. If you get this one, I can handle the other one."

"I'll get them both. You go on. Your dad is anxious to see you."

She nods. Her eyes dart toward where he is standing, waiting; then they flit back to me. In them, I see two things. One of them I expected. One I did not. In Chaney's eyes, I see love for her father, but I also see great anxiety, even dread. Her skin is pale. Small drops of sweat, like little tears, rest on her upper lip.

I want to put my hand on Chaney's arm. I want to ask, what is wrong? Why are you afraid? Why have you waited so long to come? And most of all, why are you standing here in the driveway, worrying with your bags instead of running as fast as you can into your father's arms?

What I would give to see my father waiting for me the way Chaney's is for her.

"Thank you." She pushes her hair away from her eyes and lifts the strap of her purse up onto her shoulder.

By the time I get the bags unloaded and the trunk closed, Chaney is climbing the steps toward Mr. Green. Slowly, but with her eyes fixed on him. He has dropped his cane and let go of the rail. His arms are outstretched. She steps closer, and he takes her in his arms. They stand on the porch, both of them crying. Chaney's thin shoulders shake within the circle of her father's arms.

My eyes do not linger.

The sight is too much for me.

I carry Chaney's bags around to the side, up the ramp, and inside through the side door. I take them down the hall and place them on the floor in her old room. Two tall, west-facing windows look out onto Mr. Green's back pasture. I have raised the shades. I stop for a moment and look out. The sun is setting. There are a few clouds. The sun's rays extend up, out, and to the sides in a starburst design that is one of the most beautiful sights you will ever see. People around here call a sunset like this God light. I suppose every light is of God, but no matter how many times I see this sight, it always turns my heart toward Him.

Be with them, Lord. Be with Chaney. With Mr. Green.

She has been away a long time.

Bless them.

Is something broken between this father and this daughter?

Heal them.

He looked for her all day. And now she is here. All should be well.

You know their hearts. Please provide what they need.

A wing chair sits between the two windows. Next to it is a small table that holds a lamp and the vase of late-blooming zinnias I cut this morning. A soft, rose-colored rug covers the floor. The queen-size bed is made up with sky blue sheets.

Not so many years ago, I worked at a fancy Houston hotel. There, I learned to pay attention to small details. I hope Chaney will find the room comfortable. I have done my best to make it so.

I hear Chaney's and Mr. Green's voices in the living room. It is nearly six thirty. I go into the kitchen. The beef stew I made for supper has been ready for more than an hour. It is still hot, simmering on the stove. Cornbread, wrapped in foil, waits in the oven. We have everything needed for strawberry shortcake. I've sliced the berries and stirred sugar into them. They wait in the refrigerator, next to the Cool Whip. Yesterday, when I went to the store, I bought a Sarah Lee pound cake. I have sliced and placed it on the counter under a glass dome to keep it fresh.

The table has been set since four o'clock. Three plates. Three forks. Three knives. Three spoons. Napkins. A pitcher of sweet tea. A saucer of sliced lemon. Butter for the cornbread. A dish of Karen's homemade pickles to have with the stew.

Mr. Green and Chaney are making their way toward the kitchen. Something comes to me. What was I thinking? Quickly, I remove one of the place settings. I am closing the cabinet door, where I have put back one of the plates, when the two of them come into the kitchen. I drop the third set of silverware into the drawer.

"What smells so good?" Chaney moves to the stove.

"Beef stew." I lift the pot lid. Steam rises. It is just right.

"Manny's a great cook. He and I've been getting along just fine in the grocery department." Mr. Green hooks his cane over the back of one of the chairs, then moves to sit down.

"Need any help?" Chaney asks.

"No, thank you. Please. Sit down. Everything is ready." I ladle up two bowls of stew. I get the cornbread out of the oven, cut it into squares, and stack the pieces into a basket I've lined with a clean dishtowel. Then I put ice in the glasses, place them on the table, and pour the tea.

Only then does Mr. Green realize there is not a place set for me. "Aren't you going to eat?"

"If it's all right with you, I need to go into town for a couple of hours. There are some things I need to check on at my duplex." I wipe my hands on a paper towel.

"This time of night? Can't it wait until morning?"

"No, sir. I need to go now."

"Well, at least eat a bite first." Mr. Green picks up his three evening meal pills, which, like always, I have placed on his plate. "You got to eat."

"Yes. Please, have some stew first." Chaney's hands rest in her lap. She sits very straight in her chair.

"I'm sorry. I have to go. I'll eat when I get back."

"Good as this looks, may not be any left." Mr. Green squeezes lemon into his tea.

"Enjoy your dinner." I turn off the burner under the stew. "Leave everything on the table. I'll take care of the dishes when I get back. There is cake on the counter. Strawberries and Cool Whip in the refrigerator. The dessert plates are right here. Is there anything else you need before I go?"

"We're fine, Manny. Thanks for making this nice meal." Chaney unfolds her napkin.

"You are welcome. I hope you like it." I move into the mudroom, which is just off the kitchen.

Mr. Green stirs his stew. "Where's the salt?" He is looking for the shaker, which I have forgotten to put on the table.

My jacket hangs on a hook near the back door. I've already put it on and zipped it up when Mr. Green asks, but I step back toward the kitchen to get it for him.

Chaney gets up. "Tell me where it is. I'll get it."

"Right there. On the counter next to the sugar bowl."

"Got it." She hands Mr. Green the salt and sits back down.

"What about the pepper?"

I pause. My hand is on the door.

Chaney motions for me to go on. She gets back up to get the pepper.

Okay, I nod, then head out the back door toward my truck.

I return a little after nine. Mr. Green has an appointment with the doctor in the morning, so instead of pulling around to the back of the house as I sometimes do, I park my truck in front of the house, near the end of the ramp. The sky is so full of clouds only a few faint stars are visible.

"Hi there."

I jump at the sound of her voice. "I didn't see you."

"Sorry. Didn't mean to startle you."

I don't see Chaney sitting on the porch steps until I am standing right in front of her. The house is still lit up, but she has not turned on the porch light. Behind her, through the open blinds, I can see Mr. Green, asleep in his recliner, in front of the TV.

"You made it back." Chaney has an afghan draped around her shoulders. She is smoking a cigarette.

"Everything is okay?"

"I think so. He's asleep." She motions to a spot on the step beside her. "Join me. Want a smoke?"

"No thank you." I hesitate. I should go in and clean up the kitchen. Soon it will be time to help Mr. Green get ready for bed.

"Come on. I want to hear your take on how my dad's doing."

I ease down beside her. One of the dogs comes up. I rub his head and scratch behind his ears.

"You've been here how long?"

"Almost two months."

"But before that, you worked for dad."

"Yes. I managed his ranch for more than three years."

"Three years." She puts her cigarette to her lips, inhales, then flicks ashes into the dirt beside the steps. "You've stuck it out with Owen Green for a whole three years. Not let him run you off or drive you crazy. Outside of his immediate family, and we're a small family, not many people can say that. I'm thinking you ought to get some kind of an award. At least a good raise."

Is she making a joke? There is no laughter in her voice. I sense she would like for me to tell her I find her dad to be a difficult man. But I cannot. What she implies may be, and on many days is, true. But I will not speak disrespectfully about my employer. He is asleep not twenty feet from where I sit.

"I love the ranch. I enjoy my work. Your father has never tried to cheat me. He pays me a fair wage."

"Good for you. I'm glad."

But her words do not sound glad. Did something bad happen while I was gone? Did the two of them have a disagreement? We sit in silence for several minutes. Chaney tugs on the blanket so that it covers her knees. It is cool out tonight, but there is no wind.

"So. How is he?"

She has spent the past few hours alone with her father. Surely she has seen the ways he has declined since she last saw him.

"Some days are better than others. Today he can walk with his cane. Tomorrow he may need his wheelchair. One day his voice is strong. Another, it is soft and slurred and he is difficult to understand."

"His mind seems okay."

"So far, yes. He is forgetful, but I think in the ways normal for a person his age."

"Do the doctors think he's getting better or worse?"

I am surprised she seems not to know much about Parkinson's disease. "They do not really put it that way. They prescribe new medicines that must be taken at exactly the same time every day. They give exercises for him to do. They say he should eat healthy food, avoid stress, and get plenty of rest."

"But they don't say exactly how he's doing." Chaney pulls a leaf from the gardenia bush within her reach and begins picking at it, breaking the waxy leaf into tiny pieces and letting them fall. "They don't give any indication how long he'll be able to get around or if they think he's getting worse."

"No. They do not say anything like that. He sees the doctor tomorrow. Perhaps you can ask."

Silence. Again.

"Mr. Green tells me you are very busy. You must have an important job."

"I sell real estate."

"Houses?"

"Some. Lately, more commercial property than residential."

"You like your work?"

"Most days."

Her cigarette is finished, so she puts it out. I watch her grind it into the gray wood of the steps I painted just last week.

"How about you? You said you like working on the ranch. How about being my dad's nurse? You like that too?"

"It is not so bad except for one thing."

"I can only imagine what that is."

"I miss the outdoors. I like working outside more than in the house."

Chaney turns her head to look at me. I do not return her look. I stare straight ahead.

"Dad says you're planning on moving in here."

"No. He asked me to, but I have not given him an answer."

"Are you thinking about it?"

"I would like to stay on as ranch manager, but how much longer will I be needed to take care of Mr. Green? I can look after the cattle and the ranch without living in this house."

"What do you mean? Dad can't take care of himself. Of course he needs you. Not only that, he's crazy about you. He hasn't stopped talking about you since I got here. Manny this and Manny that. All through dinner. He talked about what you do for him, where you take him. He told me about your family in Mexico, where you go to church, all the jobs you had before you came to work for him. I feel like I know more about you than I do about my own best friend, and he told me all that in less than two hours."

Chaney's words are without displeasure, but her voice has a sharp edge. What I hear is not anger. But neither is it approval. I am confused. I have done my best to take care of her father. Does she feel I have overstepped my place?

"Perhaps I have told your father too much about my life," I say. "But since Karen died, it has been only the two of us here in this house. Your father likes to talk. Since he lost his sister there has been no one but me. I have tried to ease his loneliness."

She raises her hands. The afghan slips off her shoulders. "Hey, don't get me wrong. I'm not complaining."

If she is not complaining, what do her words mean?

"It's all good. Anything to keep Pop happy. I want you to stay on. I hope you will. I don't see any need to change this arrangement. You're doing a good job."

"But now you have come. You are family. I cared for him only because you were not here."

"But he still needs you. Now more than ever. Goodness, me and Dad here alone? Just the two of us? That's not going to work. We'd kill each other by the end of the week. And yes, I'm here for a while. For how long, I'm not sure. I've taken a six-month leave from work. After that, I'll play it by ear. I may not even stay the full six months. But truth is, unless he goes to a nursing home, Dad's going to need help from here on out. That's not going to change, as you well know. I really hope you'll move in permanently."

So this is what she wants.

"Dad likes you. He told me you take care of him the way a son would care for his father. Already, the way he talks about you, you would think you two were father and son."

She means to flatter me, to convince me to stay. I look over my shoulder. Mr. Green is starting to wake.

"I should go help him get to bed."

I move to get up, but Chaney puts her hand on my arm.

"Think about it. Consider it. Please. I can't tell you how much of a load it would take off my mind to know you're staying."

"I will think about it."

"Good. Because I can tell. Dad considers you almost a member of the family. He'd hate it if you moved out."

I stand up. "I have done my best to care for him. If I stay, I will continue to do the same. I am fond of your father. His comfort and happiness are important to me. But you must know, I have not forgotten you are his family."

She looks at me with a question in her eyes.

"I am the hired help."

I get up and go inside.

"Ready for bed, Mr. Green?"

"Where you been?"

"Out on the porch. Getting a little fresh air."

"'Bout time you came in. I been needing to go to the toilet. Help me up."

No, Chaney does not need to worry. I know my place. As long as Mr. Green is able to speak, she can be sure I will not forget.

chapter thirteen

MR. GREEN HAS TO WAIT until after they draw his blood to eat, which means he is starving by the time we get to the doctor's office. They come first and take him back to the lab. Then they bring him back to the waiting room to sit until the doctor is ready to see him.

While he is with the lab girl, I tell Chaney she should be the one to go back to the exam room with her dad. I will stay in the waiting room.

"He's not going to have to, uh . . . undress or anything, is he?" She is chewing on her bottom lip.

"They ask him to take off his shirt."

"That's all?"

"He can't do it by himself. You'll need to help him with the buttons."

"I can handle that. But he keeps his pants on?"

"He did before."

After they take his blood, Mr. Green comes back to the waiting room, where he takes a seat. He checks his watch. It has been only ten minutes since we arrived. It is still fifteen more before his scheduled appointment time.

"What's taking them so blame long? I'm about to starve to death."

Chaney pulls a little bag of granola from her purse. "Here, Dad. This might tide you over. You want me to get you a drink of water?"

"What is that? Cereal? What d'you mean trying to give me that? You know I don't eat that stuff."

His voice is loud enough to cause a young woman, also waiting to see the doctor, to look up from the *National Geographic* she is reading.

"Fine. Whatever."

Chaney puts the little bag back into her purse. Her face is pink. She gets up and crosses the room to get a magazine for herself. When she comes back, she leaves two empty chairs between her and her dad.

"Mr. Green?" It is the nurse. "How are you feeling today? Good to see you. Ready to come on back?"

I help Mr. Green rise to his feet. Today he is using his walker. Slowly he makes his way toward the doorway that leads to the exam room hall. Chaney follows behind.

"This your daughter?" the nurse asks.

Mr. Green doesn't answer.

"Chaney Green." She holds out her hand.

"Nice to meet you, Chaney. Your dad's one of our favorites. Second room on the right."

When they come out, I see Chaney has some pamphlets and booklets on Parkinson's disease in her hands. She is smiling. And so is Mr. Green.

"See you in a month." The receptionist waves from behind the glass.

"Let's go to the Cracker Barrel," Mr. Green says.

We are barely out the clinic door.

"They got a good breakfast."

"I like that idea," Chaney says.

She is on one side of her dad, her arm on his elbow. I move ahead to unlock the truck. Neither of us have had breakfast, but at least we got coffee, which Mr. Green could not have. Like him, I am more than ready to eat. Cracker Barrel is just up the road. A comfortable place for a meal.

We are at our table but have not been seated when Mr. Green tells the hostess to bring him coffee and some packets of cream.

"Sir, your waitress will be with you shortly." The hostess is a young girl, perhaps seventeen. It says on her name tag that she is in training.

"What? Something wrong with your legs where you can't just go and get the pot?" He grabs hold of his walker. "Tell me where it is and I'll get it myself."

"Dad, stop it. Sit down. You'll get your coffee."

"Don't be telling me what to do. I want a cup of coffee. That too much to ask?"

People at the next table are looking. This is the worst I have seen Mr. Green act in public.

"Mr. Green," I speak quietly into his ear. "Our waitress is on her way over. She'll bring coffee. How many creams do you need?"

"Three."

"You want to sit here or on the other side?"

"Here's all right."

I pull out his chair.

"Where'd Chaney go?"

"To the restroom."

"Don't know what the heck's wrong with her. She's as prickly as a horse with a bee under its blanket."

By the time Chaney gets back, Mr. Green is on his second cup.

"You all right, sugar?" He is like a pot on the stove. Boiling over one minute. Cooled down the next.

"I'm fine, Dad."

"Not getting sick are you? Easy to pick up something at the doctor's office. If you're not sick when you go in, you may be when you come out."

"I feel fine."

"You ready to order, then?"

I catch her eye. "The pecan pancakes are good here. That's what I'm having."

She nods.

"Y'all order what you want. Three fried eggs, sausage, biscuits and gravy are what I'm having."

"Remember?" From across the table, Chaney leans forward. "The doctor said you should watch your cholesterol. I don't think eggs and pork are what you should be having. What about these whole grain waffles with fruit. Doesn't that sound good?"

Mr. Green slaps the menu down on the table to glare at her.

I lock eyes with Chaney. Let it go. Please, let it go.

"Then again, I guess this time won't hurt." She speaks to the waitress. "I think I'll have a side of bacon with my pancakes. Manny, you want some too?"

Eating breakfast gives Mr. Green his second wind. While we are paying the bill, he decides he needs a haircut. After that, a trip to the hardware store.

We are making trips into town about every third day. Chaney being here at the ranch, Mr. Green has a shorter temper, but he also has more energy, more interest in things outside himself. He has not said this, but I know he wants to prove to her he is still independent, still in charge, able to do things for himself. Since she has come, he has been pushing himself to do more, trying to use his cane instead of his walker, avoiding his wheelchair as much as he can.

"Turn left at the stop sign. Barber shop's down about a block and a half," he says.

I see the sign: J & A Family Haircuts. It is in the middle of a little strip mall. There is a gift shop one side. An ice cream place on the other.

Chaney decides to leave the haircut to me. She will be in the gift shop until we get through.

J & A's is a small place. Only three chairs. Two men, one black, one white, are both cutting hair. A middle-aged woman is sweeping up clippings from under the third chair. When we open the door and step in, the white man, tall, in his early thirties, does not stop what he is doing, but he says hello.

"Hey there, Joel," Mr. Green says. "You got time to give me a trim?"

"Sure do. If you don't mind waiting on me. Won't be long. Maybe ten minutes. You got that much time?"

"I don't have nowhere to go. Not one thing I need to do. Take your time. Finish up what you're doing."

Mr. Green has patience. With me. With Joel, the barber. But not with the hostess. Not much with the nurse. None with Chaney.

"Sure sorry to hear about Karen passing," says the black man. His customer is a woman with short gray hair. I guess at this place they do both men and women.

"Thank you, son, I appreciate it." Mr. Green eases himself onto a soft couch, one so low I know he is going to need help getting up.

"Every time she came in for a cut, she brought us something she baked."

"You and every business in town. Woman didn't go pay the water bill without taking cookies or a pie." Mr. Green looks up at me. He motions to the couch. "Sit down. Take a load off. Fellers, want y'all to meet Manny here. He's been staying with me out on the ranch. Helping me out with the place. Manny, this here's Joel. That's Abe."

Both of them say hello.

In the past he has spoken to me the way he does to one of the dogs. But today I am introduced as if I were an old friend.

Mr. Green looks at the woman. "Hon', I done forgot your name."

The woman, who has finished sweeping, looks up and smiles. "Emily."

"She hasn't been here long." He says this to me behind his hand.

"So, Mr. Green. How you been getting along?" Joel has his scissors in one hand, a comb in the other. His customer is a man getting a cut.

"Can't complain. How's that boy of yours? What's his name?"

"Colton. He's growing. Getting a mouth on him too. Driving his mother and his sisters crazy."

There is a photo taped to the mirror above the counter. It is of a family: this man, a blonde woman, two teenaged girls, and a younger boy. All of them smiling. All of them dressed in blue.

"How old's he now?"

"Ten next month."

"Be grown 'fore you know it."

"You got that right."

Mr. Green is in the chair when Chaney comes into the shop. A half hour has passed.

"Just checking on you two."

"My daughter, Chaney," Mr. Green says.

"Nice to meet you," Joel says. "Just finishing up here."

Joel takes off the cape. Mr. Green starts to get up.

"Hold on just a second. Let's get some of these hairs off your neck." Joel whisks a big soft brush back and forth over Mr. Green's shoulders.

I help Mr. Green ease out of the chair. He reaches into his back pocket, gets out his wallet, and begins thumbing through it for the correct bills. His hands are shaking so badly this task is difficult for him. He could use my help, but offering it would embarrass him here in front of this man.

"Where you from?" Joel is talking to Chaney, making polite conversation, doing his best not to notice the trouble Mr. Green is having with his wallet.

"Florida. Orlando."

"You've come a long way. Here to visit your dad?"

Mr. Green looks up. In that moment, I realize she has not told him what her plans are.

Chaney's eyes meet mine, but then she turns toward Joel so that she is facing him instead of her father.

"Yes, I came to visit. Sort of. I'm not sure how long I'll be here. Haven't exactly decided."

"However long you're in Eden Plain, hope you have a good time. If you stay long enough to need a haircut, stop in. I do color too. You ever had highlights? I think a few around your face would be really pretty." Joel hands her a card. "Just to let you know, most of the time I stay booked. Good idea to call ahead for an appointment."

At the hardware store, Mr. Green picks out a bird feeder and looks for a part for his chain saw, which he says has not been working right.

"He's been cutting wood?" Chaney asks me while Mr. Green is talking to the salesman.

"Not in the past couple of years."

"You think he's planning on actually *using* his saw?"

I do not have a chance to answer her because Mr. Green, who has found what he needed, is coming toward us, clomping down the aisle on his walker.

A man on a walker cutting down a tree with a chain saw? What is he thinking? And how am I ever going to talk him out of this?

chapter fourteen

MR. GREEN IS ASLEEP IN his recliner. We have eaten our lunch, and I am finishing up cleaning the kitchen.

"You ever get lonely? Just the two of you by yourselves out here on the ranch?"

Chaney is sitting at the kitchen table. She has been here for a week, and we have eased into a routine. Meals. Medicine. Mr. Green's naps. Conversations over coffee while he sleeps.

"Of course," I say. "But I am accustomed to solitude. I have spent much of my life alone."

"Dad says you're not married. That you've never been."

"No."

"Me either."

This I already knew. Mr. Green told me he thinks Chaney has not married because she is too tall.

"You miss having a family?"

She is arranging items on the table—the salt and pepper shakers, the sugar bowl, the container of napkins. She lines them up in a row.

"At times."

"Me too."

I bring over the pot and refill our cups. "Do you wish you had children?"

"That's a hard question. I never wanted to have a baby without a husband, and since I haven't gotten married . . . well, I make it a habit not to want what I don't have. I'm thirty-four years old. Past my prime baby-making years." She takes a sip of her coffee. "I'm making it sound like I've had no control over any of this, which is not true. I've had chances to get married. Couple of times to good men who wanted children and who would have made great dads."

"What stopped you? From marrying these men?"

"I don't really know. It just wasn't right. What about you?"

"The same, I think. Like you, I have had my chances at a life with someone. But something stopped me. I always thought I would marry. I hoped to have children. But like you, I have perhaps waited too long."

"How old are you?"

"Thirty-nine."

"You don't look it. And when it comes to having a family, men don't have the same time constraints women do. You don't have to worry about stale eggs and biological clocks winding down."

I am not comfortable discussing things such as this with Chaney. I would not be at ease discussing them with any woman.

Chaney gets up and goes to the pantry. She returns with a package of Oreo cookies, one of her favorite snacks. I like them, but what I really miss is Karen's home-baked sweets. I can cook, but I don't bake.

"You know, coming back and staying with my dad, sleeping in my old room—it stirs things up. It brings back lots of memories."

"Good ones?"

"Some. More than anything it makes me miss my mother."

"The artist." I enjoy her work every day.

"Yes. She loved to paint. I wish I had some of her talent."

"Your father does not talk about her very often. You two were close?"

"Of course. I loved Mom a lot. And I miss her terribly. Some days I can't believe she's really gone. But actually, growing up, I was closer to Dad than I was to her. At least until I got to be a teenager. When I hit fourteen, neither one of them knew what to do with me, which is no big surprise because I didn't know what to do with myself. It felt like everything with me went haywire right about then. I went from being the obedient daughter who was just like my parents to being an independent kid, a free spirit who questioned everything they did, everything they said."

I can see how a man like Mr. Green would have had a problem with that.

"My mom and I made peace before she died, which I'm grateful for, but it feels like Dad and I have been at each other for about the past twenty years. We irritate each other. We misunderstand each other. He makes me so mad sometimes. About all he has to do to hurt my feelings is open his mouth. It's not supposed to be like this."

Mr. Green loves her very much. I have no doubts about that. But since Chaney has arrived, I have often felt like a referee. Chaney says things that set him off. He makes comments to her that are unkind. They argue about every little thing. I can see both sides, but too often, Mr. Green turns the situation so that it feels as if it is he and I against his own daughter. He wants me to be an ally. Someone who will take his side. My standing in his eyes, my position in this house, has risen because she is here.

Isn't that right, Manny? he'll say about something they have disagreed on. *Have you ever heard of anything so crazy in your cotton-picking life?* Even if he does not say anything, he will look at me and roll his eyes. Or he will lift his hands to the heavens to show how exasperated she has made him.

This puts me in a terrible position. Mr. Green is my employer, but his daughter has become a friend. She may end up staying permanently. That is my hope. And if she does, we must get along. I do not want Chaney to feel like she is on the outside.

When Mr. Green tries to get me to take his side, and when Chaney looks at me to do the same, I do my best not to say a word, not to allow my thoughts to show on my face. It is not my place to give either of them advice. Mr. Green would not take it from me anyway, but I would like to tell him to stop acting this way. He should treat his daughter with respect. I want to tell him, both of them, how lucky they are to have each other. They should speak with kindness and love.

They will not always have each other. Every day should count for something good.

"Did something happen when you were a teenager?" I ask. "Was there one big thing that caused this divide between the two of you?"

"Not really. Compared to stuff my friends did, I was a pretty good kid. What happened is I think he's never forgiven me for having a mind of my own. This really got to be an issue about the time I became a teenager. Dad believed in the death penalty, so I wrote articles for the school paper against it. He loved to hunt. Well, the way I saw it, I had no choice but to rally for gun control. Here he was a rancher who made his living and fed his family by raising beef cattle. I became vegetarian. Every night at the dinner table I made a big deal about how I was never going to eat anything with a face."

"But you eat meat now."

"Of course I do." She grinned. "I outgrew sprouts and tofu

about the time I went to college and discovered Pizza Hut's three-meat combo with extra cheese. I haven't been vegetarian for years, but I still hold to a lot of beliefs different from Dad. Take politics for instance. He's still got that Bush/Chaney bumper sticker on his truck."

"You are a Democrat?"

"Independent. But yes, I have Democratic leanings."

Mr. Green spends hours and hours watching FOX news.

"When I was growing up, Mom and Dad and I went to the Baptist church. As soon as I turned fifteen, I joined the Church of Christ. You'd have thought I'd become a Buddhist. Dad had a fit. He told me the Church of Christ believed all the other churches were going to hell because they played pianos."

"I do not think that is true anymore."

"It wasn't true then."

"So your dad is a Christian?"

Mr. Green and I have never talked about religion, but every Friday he reminds the home health aide what time to come on Sunday because he knows of my desire to go to church.

Chaney looks like she does not know how to answer this. "I think so. As far as I know. It's been years since he and I discussed religion. That's something you should probably ask him."

I don't know why I haven't already. She is right. I should have asked him long before now.

"And you?"

"I believe in God. In Jesus. I read the Bible."

She meets my eyes, but then looks away.

"Sometimes."

I nod.

"And I pray. Sometimes."

I dip my cookie into my coffee. I do not mean to make her uncomfortable.

"A cold front is expected today," I say. "I should put out bird seed."

Chaney breaks her cookie into small pieces. "I try to be a good person, but I don't go to church as much as I should. Working in real estate, you have to be willing to show houses on Sundays because that's when people are off and free to look. I know that's an excuse. Not a very good one."

"I do not believe going to church is what makes you a good Christian."

"But people should go, don't you think?"

"Of course."

"How many times have you missed in the past year?"

"Twice." Once, the Sunday after Karen died, the other on a morning the home health aide arrived late.

"Yep. That's what I thought. You're a good Christian, Manny. A better one than me."

"What y'all doing in there?" It is Mr. Green, calling from the living room. "Both y'all come here. I been thinking about something. Want to run it by you."

Chaney and I look at each other.

"Here we go again." She gets up and takes our cups to the sink. "I'm afraid to guess what he's come up with now."

Mr. Green has turned on the TV. He is watching the local news, and the sports is on. First they cover the national teams; then the announcer moves on to high school football. Eden Plain's claim to fame is the fighting Wildcats. I have read in the newspaper that this year's team may make the state playoffs.

"Chaney, remember how we used to go to all the home

football games? Me and you and your mother?"

"I remember. You and Mom had season tickets in the reserved section. I sat with my friends in the student section next to the band so we could make fun of the cheerleaders."

"Been thinking about getting tickets for this season. Three of them. One for each of us. You like football, Manny?"

"He probably likes it better than I do," Chaney says.

"Yes, sir. I like watching good teams play."

"Ever sat in the high-dollar seats?"

"No. I've only been to a couple of games, and I sat in general admission."

"What I thought. Down there with all the kids running up and down. I'll get us good seats. Be good for you to have a chance to see how the rest of the world watches a game."

"Dad!"

I give her a look. *Let it go.*

"What?" he looks at me, then at her.

Chaney shakes her head. She sits down on the couch, picks up her magazine, and begins studying it as though it were the most interesting thing in the world. Still standing, I look over her shoulder. "Ten Steps to Younger Skin."

"How much are the tickets?" I expect to pay my own way.

"Not for you to worry about, Manny. This'll be my treat. We'll all go together. First game's this Friday night."

Lately, Mr. Green has been having more and more trouble lifting his feet. His legs are stiff. He has almost fallen twice in the past three days. I picture the football stadium. Getting him up the bleachers may be a problem. Do they have a ramp?

"I'm gonna call up the school." Mr. Green grabs the phone. "Manny, go find the number for me, will you? You know, I'm gonna tell them to send us tickets for the rest of the season. We been spending too much time at the house. This'll be something good to do on Friday nights."

"I don't know, Dad. I'm not as crazy about football as you are." Chaney still has her face in the magazine. "Maybe you should just get two tickets. You and Manny could go."

A cold front has come in and the room is chilly. Chaney pulls an afghan up over her legs. "I wouldn't mind a few nights to myself."

"What is it? You too good to be seen with your old dad and with Manny here? Small-town football not exciting enough for you? Your social calendar too full to fit in a few Friday night games?"

I think Mr. Green is teasing, but there is an edge in his voice. I go to the kitchen, where the phone book is in the drawer. I write the number down, return to the living room, and hand the paper to Mr. Green.

"This is the number?"

"Yes, sir. The main number for the high school."

"Decide right now." Mr. Green looks over at Chaney. "What do you want me to do? Order you a ticket or not?" His voice makes it obvious what he wants her to say.

"All right, all right. Get me tickets. If it's that big a deal, I'll go."

"You're sure?"

Chaney turns the page. He dials. Twice he gets the wrong number.

"Something the matter with this blame phone." He waves it at me. "You forget to put it on the charger again last night?"

I offer to dial the number for him, but Mr. Green tells me no, he'll do it himself.

This morning, I built the first fire of the season. While he tries yet again to call the school, I go to the fireplace, pick up the poker, and give the coals a stir.

"Three season passes." He has finally reached the school. "Yes. Fifty yard line."

Chaney lets out a loud sigh. She rolls her eyes at me.

Mr. Green hangs up. His face is pink. He rubs his hands together, then pulls his handkerchief out of his pocket and wipes at his forehead.

"Okay, we're all set. They'll mail us our tickets. Ought to be here in a couple of days. I'm looking forward to this. If Eden Plain wins like they say they will, we may have to get playoff tickets too."

Chaney doesn't look up from her page. "Go team. Rah, rah, rah." She says it too low for her father to hear.

"What'd you say?"

"Nothing, Dad. I didn't say anything."

I called ahead to check and learned that yes, they have a ramp leading up to the reserved seats. We are in the parking lot, which is filling up fast. I look for a space in the handicapped section, but they are all filled.

"You want me to let you two out at the gate?"

"Nah. I'll be all right."

"Dad, are you sure you're up to this?"

"Paid good money for these tickets. I came to see this game. We should have got here earlier is all."

He says this to Chaney, who had argued that we did not need to leave the house when Mr. Green wanted to.

The closest parking place I can find is a block away. Chaney and I get out, then go around to help Mr. Green. He fumbles with trying to lift his feet onto the footrest of the wheelchair I have taken out of the back of the truck. We can hear the band warming up and the announcer over the loudspeaker, though we cannot understand what is being said. People carrying stadium cushions, blankets, and tote bags pass us by.

"Come on you two, hurry up. Don't want to miss the kickoff. Got your tickets?"

When we get inside the gate, fans are lined up four deep along the chain-link fence that runs alongside the field. This makes it hard to see the field, but according to the clock we have five minutes to go before kickoff. A huge crowd has shown. It has been a few years since I have been to a game. They have done construction on the stadium since I was last here. I'm not even sure which is the home side and which one is for visitors. I stop and try to get my bearings.

"This way. Over there." From the low position in his chair, there is no way Mr. Green can see better than I which way we should go.

Chaney figures it out. "Home side is over here."

As we move closer, I see that the cheerleaders, mascot, and drill team have formed parallel lines for the team to run between when they come on the field. Four Boy Scouts are marching down the sidelines, making their way over to the flagpole.

Chaney checks her ticket to see which way we need to go. "Section D. Seats six, seven, and eight. This way I think." It is so loud she has to shout. "I think the ramp's over this way."

I turn Mr. Green's chair in the direction she says. It is not a straight path. Not only must we maneuver our way around the long lines in front of the concession stand, but various school organizations have set up tables to sell things. T-shirts. Cupholders. Candy.

"Excuse me. Excuse me. Sorry. Could we get through please?"

Finally, we make it to the ramp.

"Stop. Hold on. I didn't get a program."

"Dad, please. Let's find our seats."

"I don't know these kids. I need a program."

Chaney gives up and darts back down the ramp to buy one for him. I start to go on without her, but Mr. Green says no, he wants to wait right where we are for her to get back. So we stop, even though his wheelchair is partially blocking the aisle.

Chaney's mouth is set in a tight line when she gets back with the program. "Could we please just find our seats?"

When we find the right row, Chaney helps Mr. Green stand up even though he says he does not need any help. I fold his wheelchair and set it near the rail as much out of the way as I can manage. People stand up to let us pass. With difficulty, Mr. Green is able to sidestep his way to his correct seat. Chaney goes next, and I follow.

"Excuse me," I say. "Sorry. Excuse us."

"No problem." People are polite, but I do see a woman wince when Mr. Green steps on her foot.

Finally, we get settled into our chairs. Mr. Green is sweating. His face is red and he is breathing hard. He was telling the truth about paying for high-dollar seats. This is not the usual tennis shoe and sweatshirt crowd you expect to see at a high school football game. Everyone around us is dressed up. It is mostly men with gray hair and their wives. No one is wearing jeans, which are what Chaney and I both have on. Rather I see slacks, sport coats, leather jackets. All the women are dressed in nice clothes and have on lots of jewelry. This must be the section reserved for rich white people. In the whole section where we are seated, I do not see a single black person. And except for me, no Mexicans.

"That's three school board members behind us," I hear Mr.

Green tell Chaney. "Bank president on the other side of you." He catches the man's eye and waves.

The man waves back. "Good to see you, Owen."

Other people tell Mr. Green hello. No one looks surprised to see him. Everyone appears pleased to greet Chaney.

No one acknowledges that they see me. It is not that anyone is rude. No one checks my ticket to make sure I am in the right seat, though the woman sitting beside me looked startled when she first saw me. Rather, it is as though my presence doesn't register. I am invisible, the way a waiter or someone who mows the yard is unseen and forgotten.

I have experienced this many times before in my life, and over the years my skin has grown thick. I have more to concern me than how I am reflected in an ignorant stranger's eyes.

"What are we doing sitting with this bunch of snobs?" Chaney whispers in my ear. "I'd rather be down there with the kids. Or at least in the general admission section. Those people look like they're having fun."

I wonder the same thing, but I stare straight ahead and do not answer her.

The three rows directly in front of us are marked with a sign that says Reserved for Coaches' Wives. They, too, are filled with well-dressed women, all but one of them white. From where we sit, I can smell their perfume.

Finally, the game is ready to start. A young voice comes on the loudspeaker to pray in Jesus' name.

"They let them do that? Pray at school-sponsored events?" Chaney says.

"Well of course," Mr. Green answers.

Recent editorials in the local newspaper have proclaimed Eden Plain a Christian town, one that does not care that prayer is no longer allowed in schools. After the prayer, the band plays the National Anthem. We all stand, but no one around us sings. Then the school bands take turns playing their fight songs.

Chaney looks at her watch. "I think we're in for a long night." She says this where Mr. Green does not hear.

The opening kickoff finally takes place, and the game begins. I like football, and this turns out to be an exciting game. Eden Plain has a talented quarterback. I look over and see that Mr. Green is enjoying the game. I am too in spite of where we sit.

Chaney notices none of this. Her eyes are on the field, but she's not paying attention except for how many minutes are left on the clock. Over and over again, she checks her watch. Then she pulls a file from her purse and works on her nails.

Points are scored on both sides. The game is tied at halftime. People in the stands yell words of encouragement to the Eden Plain team as they head for the locker room.

The last two quarters of the game, neither team scores a point. Then the Eden Plain Wildcats score on a long pass play with just under a minute to go to pull out the win.

"Now that was a good game," Mr. Green says once we have gotten back to the truck. "Those kids can play."

"They sure can," I say. "Good running game."

"They've got some speed."

Chaney yawns. She has nothing to add.

"Next week we got to get here a little earlier," he says.

Next week I will wear slacks instead of jeans.

chapter fifteen

WHEN CHANEY KNOCKS ON THE outside frame of my open bedroom door, I am so intent on my work that my head jerks up at the sound. When I am painting, I often lose track of time.

"Didn't mean to startle you."

"No problem."

How many minutes have passed since I checked on Mr. Green? I left him asleep in his chair after lunch. I check my watch. Only twenty. Good. When I passed by the den, down the hall on the way to my room, I saw Chaney sitting in front of the computer screen, a place where I have seen she, too, loses track of time.

I set the paint pallet down on the little table where I keep my oil supplies. My easel is set up in the corner of the bedroom where I sleep, in front of a south and southeast window because that is the best source of light. Under my feet is a drop cloth I laid down to protect the room's hardwood floor from stray paint and the possibility of a turpentine spill.

"Is your dad okay? Do you need something?"

"Dad's fine. He's still asleep. I just checked on him. I don't need anything."

Chaney is dressed in faded jeans and a tan sweater. She wears no shoes, only thick white socks, which explains why I did not hear her come down the hall. She leans against the frame of the door.

"I got off the computer, and the house was quiet. Just wondering what you were doing."

I hold up my brush. From her spot in the doorway, she can't see what I'm working on. Only the back of my canvas.

"So you paint."

"When I have time. Sometimes in the afternoon, but mostly early in the morning before your dad gets up."

I do not have a set routine. It has been only a few weeks since I brought supplies here from my duplex in town. Anytime I have a few minutes alone, I pull out a pencil and paper. Sketchbooks come in many sizes, from lap-size and larger down to small ones that will fit in a shirt pocket. A good drawing pencil takes up no space. I am rarely without those two items. I carry pencil and paper the way old men take along reading glasses and nitroglycerin pills.

Chaney breathes deeply. "I'd recognize that smell anywhere. Nothing like the scent of oil paints. Makes me think of my mom. She usually set up in the mudroom. I'd come home from school, and there'd be the smell of chocolate chip slice-and-bake cookies mixed with fumes from her turpentine. When I had friends over, they thought our house stunk. Not me. In my mind, that was what home and my mom were supposed to smell like."

Like Chaney, I love the smells of an art room. But they say inhaling paint fumes is not healthy. It may even cause brain damage. Which is why I always crack a window when I'm working.

"Can I see what you're doing?" She is still standing in the doorway. I have not invited her in.

"Sure. It is not complete, but you can have a look."

Chaney comes into my room, moves past the nightstand, the bed, and the dresser, and steps around to stand in front of the easel. She crosses her arms over her chest. For a long minute she does not speak.

"This is really good." She steps back a few inches. "My mom never did people. She said they were too hard."

Chaney has recently applied lotion. Over the fumes, I can smell it on her hands.

She motions toward the painting. "Who is this? The man in the picture?"

"My father."

I have tried, in this portrait, to capture his likeness from a different angle. But like all the others, the painting is a disappointment. He is looking down. The upper portion of his face is obscured by shadows. While the composition is good, I have not painted his likeness.

Once again, the problem is with the eyes.

"Manny, you're very talented. I had no idea. Have you ever sold your work?"

Her words please me. I wipe my hands on a rag.

"No, I paint for myself. I've been drawing pictures since I was a child. Making art is an addiction. Like your cigarettes are to you." I smile at her. She has told me many times how she wishes she could quit. "I try to stop drawing, but I can't."

"Ha. Like you try real hard."

"No. I suppose I do not."

"Maybe you should try the patch. I quit once for three months."

We laugh at her joke.

"Do you get to see your dad often?"

There is an L-shaped window seat built into the corner where we stand. The curtains are pulled back. Chaney takes a seat in front of one of the windows and leans back against the glass.

"No."

"Where does he live? Texas or Mexico?"

I begin cleaning my brushes. It is easy, while doing this, to avoid her eyes.

"He moves around. I am not sure where he's living right now."

"You're close?"

Her voice is soft, and I think that somehow she *knows*. *Something.*

"No. Not so close. It has been a while since I saw him."

"I bet you miss him."

My brushes are clean. I smooth and mold the bristles with my fingers, then stand them upside down in a jar. A good brush, if taken care of properly, can last nearly the lifetime of its owner. I look to make sure I have no paint on my pants, then sit down on the other leg of the window seat.

Chaney is still leaning back. She has curled one foot up under her and pulled one knee up close to her chin. Her hand pushes her hair back behind her ears, behind the heavy silver hoops she wears every day. In the light from the window, it is easy to see the tiny lines at the corner of her eyes, and the ones women who smoke get around the mouth.

There is a cushion on the window seat. It is a comfortable place to sit. An easy place for two people to face each other and talk. I rub at some burnt umber paint I have on my thumb.

"Before you came," I say, "you went two years without seeing your dad. Did you miss him?"

Chaney turns her head to look out the window. "That's a hard question. I thought about him, sure. I worried about him and hoped he was all right. And it's not like I didn't check on him. I called every weekend. When we talked he always said he was fine. But did I miss him? I don't know. Parents. What can I say? Mostly I felt guilty. I knew I should come for a visit. And I meant to. Over and over I'd plan to come, but something would come up with work and I'd postpone my trip. Before I knew it, two years had passed. Time just got away from me."

I want to tell her how she should not waste the hours she has with her father. She should never allow time and distance to separate the two of them again. Those who have contact with their parents cannot understand the feelings of longing a person can have for someone they have lost.

I would think Chaney would know this having lost her mother. Yet the woman has been gone for so long, I suppose Chaney's grief has become less. Chaney has told me she and her mother were close at the very end. They saw each other every day and were able to tell each other good-bye before her death. Chaney was not left with the hunger I have for the sight of my father. She has never felt the craving that is never satisfied.

When a parent disappears yet is still alive on the earth, where does a child put his grief? How can his heart heal? There are questions a child, even a grown-up child, wants to ask but never has the chance.

"It's not that I don't love my dad. I do."

"I can see that. He loves you too."

With the back of her hand, Chaney wipes at her eyes. "I always expect it to get easier, being his daughter. Years go by. You'd think it would, wouldn't you? But it doesn't. I always wanted a dad who doted on me. I wanted him to be protective and affectionate, and that just wasn't him. He was always working. Work was the most important thing. And it's like he kept up this wall between the two of us. I wanted to be close to him, to be his darling little girl. The apple of his eye, as they say. But it was never like that between the two of us. That closeness wasn't there. You see how things are? How he and I rub each other so wrong? It's been like that for as long as I remember."

The passion and pain of her words surprise me. Yes, she and Mr. Green argue and disagree, but it appeared that Chaney did not take any of it to heart. Mostly I have seen her walk away or appear to ignore the irritations between the two of them. She has done a good job of hiding what is inside, of holding back her words.

"Your dad was so excited when he found out you were coming. The day you flew in, he could not wait for you to get here."

"And when I got here, he didn't know what to do with me."

"You believe that is true?"

I wish Chaney could have seen Mr. Green's face when her rental car pulled into the driveway. She does not know how much her father wants her to be here. She does not realize how much it will hurt him if she decides not to stay. It is true, Mr. Green should tell her himself. But he has not. I am not sure he can.

"What are you doing? Taking up for the old man?" She smiles.

"He is a good man."

"I know. You're right. I can tell he's glad I'm here. And all this is silly." She pulls a tissue from the pocket of her jeans and wipes at her nose. "I'm a grown woman. He's an old man. I should be over all this. Usually I am. It's just that he'll say something to me or give me a certain look, and it's like I'm back to being that fourteen-year-old girl who's disappointed him. Again. You know, he's not the dad I wanted, but what's worse than that is I'm not the daughter he wanted either. I never married. I didn't give him grandchildren. I have all these crazy ideas and causes he can't begin to understand. I'm the first to admit it. The stuff between Dad and me is not all his fault. It goes both ways."

I look at my watch. A half hour has passed.

"I should go check on your dad."

"Ah, he's all right. If he was awake we'd be hearing that bell."
She's correct. Mr. Green is very good with his bell.

Chaney looks around. "This is a cozy spot. I think you've got the best room in the house. My room doesn't have nearly as good a vibe as this one. I think I should make you trade."

"It is a comfortable place. The light is good for painting." I lean back against the window. I am enjoying this time.

"So tell me" — Chaney pushes the sleeves of her sweater up to her elbows — "about you and your dad. All the Mexican families I've known have been very close. What's it like with you two?"

The way Chaney speaks, the way she looks at me with deep interest and the desire to understand, causes something in me to tip. To open up. I did not intend it, but from my mouth pours truth, a truth I seldom speak, one she does not expect.

I motion to the painting. "The last time I saw this man was when I was twelve years old. That was the day he left my family forever. He got on a bus and never came back. He left me to take care of my mother, my brother, and my two sisters. Do I miss him? Yes. I miss him every day that I live."

"You haven't seen him in how long?" Chaney has put her feet on the floor. She is leaning toward me. He hands are beside her, pressing into the cushion.

"Twenty-seven years."

"Why did he leave?"

"I do not know."

"He hasn't contacted you in all that time? He never called?"

"There is no telephone at my mother's house."

"He never wrote a letter?"

"No."

My mother thought he might. She watched for a letter. But one never came.

"Manny, I'm so sorry. It must have been terrible growing up without a dad. Twenty-seven years? No word from him? All that time?"

I shake my head.

"Do you even know if he's still alive?"

"No, I do not know for sure. But most days I believe he is."

"After my mom died, sometimes I would think I saw her. Walking down the street, in line at the bank. Is it like that?"

"No. When I see my father, it is more in my mind. I picture him, and I believe that he is happy, that he has a good life. Perhaps a new wife. A new family. Other children."

Chaney's eyes are locked onto my face.

"Then there are other times when I think he is probably dead, that he has been dead for many years. There are times when I cannot imagine that my father, apart from my mother, my brother, my sisters, and me, still has breath."

"Have you tried to find him?"

I shake my head. "I would not know how to start. But even if I did, I do not believe I would look. When he left, my father made it plain he did not want to be followed. He did not want to be found."

"So you've given up on ever seeing him again."

I nod my head, but then I say, "That is not completely true. When I pick up a pencil or a brush, it is with the hope they will lead me to him."

The question in Chaney's eyes tells me she does not understand.

"Let me show you."

I hand her a sketchbook. She lifts the cover and begins to turn the pages. Every one is filled. When she has looked through that book, I hand her a stack of three more. She thumbs through them.

Slowly. Finally, when she has looked at every page, I reach for the three unframed canvases that are beside me, leaned up against the wall. I hold the paintings up, one at a time, for her to see.

"Your dad."

I nod.

"This is how you look for him."

I nod yes again.

"The pictures are amazing. He's very handsome." She looks and for a long moment does not speak. Finally, her voice is a whisper. "You've found him this way, haven't you?"

"No." I shake my head. "I try and I try, but I cannot capture his likeness. In some of the pictures I have come close, but in none of them can I see his eyes."

Chaney sits very still.

I put the last painting back. I take the stack of sketchbooks from her lap. I lay them on the floor near my feet.

"But I cannot stop trying. No matter how many times I decide to give up and let the memory of my father go, I do not stop. I cannot."

I look at Chaney. She looks at me. A great silence sits between us. After a long moment, I stand up.

"I should go check on your dad."

She nods. We leave my room. Her first, then me. We walk down the hall, and my eyes rest on the back of Chaney's head. I study her shoulders, the curve of her back, her slim hips, her flat bottom, and her silent sock feet. It occurs to me that I have just shared with this woman three private things.

My hope.

My desire.

My prayers.

And for the first time since she arrived, I find myself wondering and caring about what she thinks of me.

chapter sixteen

TODAY IS THURSDAY. GROCERY SHOPPING day. Chaney and I go together while Lori is taking care of Mr. Green. It takes us ten minutes to drive from the ranch into town.

Eden Plain has several grocery stores. Even though the prices are higher, we always shop at Brookshire's. It is a clean store, locally owned. The produce is fresh, and the people who work there are friendly. No matter who you are, a strong young man or a weak old woman, they insist on carrying your groceries out and putting them in your car.

"Find everything you need?" the cashier asks.

"Could I get two packs of Marlboro Lights, please?"

While the woman is getting the cigarettes, Chaney gives me a look. "I know. I'm cutting back."

"Did I say anything?"

"No. But you were thinking it."

I raise my hands as if to cover my head. "What? A man cannot have his thoughts?"

"Young man, better watch this woman." The cashier is smiling. She has a gold tooth. "Sounds like she's trying to put you on a short rope. Are y'all married or what?"

I feel my face get hot. Chaney does not look embarrassed at all. She laughs.

"Nope, we're not married. But I don't have to tell you how it is with the men in your life. Got to keep an eye on them. Can't be letting them get the upper hand. I'm doing my best. What can I say?"

The cashier rolls her eyes. "Don't I know it, honey. Been married forty-two years." She holds up her left hand so we can see her ring. "You hear about people getting divorced, leaving their husbands for somebody else. Now why in the world would I go and do that? Took me this long to get Harvey trained. No way I'd be up to starting over with somebody else."

"I'm with you," Chaney says.

I would like to know exactly when did she get to be the expert on marriage and men.

We pay and the cashier puts the receipt in one of the bags.

Lee is our carry-out person. "Hi, Miz Chaney. How you doing?" He is a fifty-year-old man with the mind of a boy about ten. I think it is good that the people at this store give him a job. Not many businesses would hire someone like him. Lee dresses neatly and in clean clothes, but he smells. Someone should tell him about deodorant. I think it would help. But maybe they have and it doesn't work, or he forgets to put it on. Lee is also very fat. About the same size around his stomach as he is tall. I don't know if it is because of his weight or a problem with his sinuses, but Lee always breathes through his mouth. Just pushing a cart of groceries makes him breathe hard. He is very friendly. Once he meets a person he does not ever forget their name. Even having trouble catching his breath does not keep Lee from talking and talking.

Chaney is always kind to him. She tells him she likes his shirt, and she always asks him about his dog, Pepper.

You can tell Lee is very fond of her.

"You going to the big game Friday night, Miz Chaney? I

love football. I think we're going to win state this year, don't you? Johnny D. is a good quarterback. He's the best one we've ever had. I think we should throw the ball more. That's what everybody says. Do you think we should throw it more? Some people say our receivers are not all that good, but I think they're good."

Lee is looking at Chaney instead of both ways when he pushes the cart out the door of the store. It is only me guiding the front of the cart and telling him to wait that keeps him from walking out in front of a car.

"Do you like my hat? I got it yesterday. It says Eden Plain Wildcats. You can adjust it. See this thing right here? You put the little buttons in the holes to make it as big as you need. I'm going to wear my new hat Friday night to the game if I get to go. I have to buy me a ticket. I think I have enough money, but I don't know for sure. If I can I'm going to go. I want those Wildcats to whip the other team's a—" Lee slaps his hand over his mouth. "Sorry, I mean I want them to whip the other team's tail."

Lee is so excited talking to Chaney about football he has forgotten about putting the groceries into the truck. The day is overcast and windy. Probably in the low fifties. But Chaney stands there shivering, listening to every word he says, as though she has all day. I catch her eye over Lee's head. She nods. Then while Lee keeps talking, I unload the groceries from the cart and put them into the back of the truck.

When I am done, I motion to the empty cart. "Lee, here you go. Thanks for your help. Chaney and I need to get home so we can check on Mr. Green."

"Oh. Okay."

Lee looks a bit startled, as if he's not sure what I said, but then from the look on his face I can see he has heard. He takes the cart from me. When he has his hands on it, he stands up as straight as a soldier.

"Thank you for shopping at Brookshire's. Have a good day. Please come back soon."

"Bye, Lee."

"See you next time."

The two of us go around to our opposite sides of the truck to get in. We're both inside, and I have slammed my door. Chaney grabs her door handle, but instead of pulling it closed, she tells me to wait a minute. She grabs her purse, gets back out of the truck, and chases Lee down.

He has stopped in the middle of where cars are trying to pull in. He does not seem to realize that he could get hit. Neither does Chaney, from what I can see. Inside the truck, I can see she is digging in her purse for something. I can't tell for sure what it is, but I can guess. She puts something in Lee's hands. His looks at it, but he doesn't smile. He looks confused. Chaney says something to him and points to what she's given him. She says something else. Then Lee gets the biggest smile on his face you've ever seen. Chaney pats him on the arm. He grabs her up and hugs her. Then she turns and runs back to the truck.

"Sorry. Thanks for waiting."

Her cheeks are pink from standing out in the cold wind. I put the truck into gear and pull forward out of the parking space.

"I think it is against the rules for Lee to take tips."

"I know."

"I hope he doesn't get in trouble."

"You planning on telling the manager?"

"Of course not."

"Then it shouldn't be a problem. You think?" She rubs her hands on the top of her legs. "I'm freezing. Care if I turn up the heater?"

"What took you so long? Did you get my medicine?"

Chaney and I carry in the groceries through the back door. Mr. Green is sitting at the table.

"We got it, Dad. What's the problem? We've been gone less than two hours. Where's Lori?"

"Back there." He motions to the other part of the house. "She's making up the bed. What about my eggs? You get eggs?"

"Two dozen. Just like you said."

Chaney and I go into the kitchen and start putting things away. We work together. I hand her items out of the sacks. She places them on the pantry shelves.

"I hate putting groceries away," Chaney says. "I don't know why. I just do."

"Me too. Working together makes it go quicker."

"Yep. It does."

"What are y'all talking about in there?" Mr. Green calls. "Hey, where's the mail? Did anybody get the mail yet?"

"We got it on the way in, Dad. I'll bring it to you in a sec."

Chaney stands in front of the refrigerator. I hand her milk, juice, canned biscuits.

"Freezer or fridge?" She holds up a package of ground beef.

"Fridge. I'm making chili for supper."

"Sounds good. I never met a man as good a cook as you." She opens the meat drawer and puts it inside. "How'd you learn?"

"I had no choice. If a man wants to eat and he has no wife,

he must learn to do for himself."

Chaney laughs. "If I was anybody's wife, they'd still have to know how to cook. I'm terrible at it."

Mr. Green yells out again. "Hey. I need my glasses cleaned. Bring me a paper towel."

"Okay, Dad. Be right there."

"So if you don't cook, what do you eat?"

"Cereal. Lots of cereal. And yogurt. Fruit. Salads. I can make salad. And I get takeout sometimes."

"Sounds delicious."

She shrugs. "I don't like to eat by myself. So living alone, I don't eat all that much."

I gather up all the empty grocery sacks and put them in the pantry and close the pantry door.

"Will you drink some coffee?" Chaney is putting on a fresh pot. "I'm still cold. I need something to warm me up."

"Hey, what's all this?" Mr. Green is standing in the doorway. He has gotten himself up from the table without any help and shuffled his way into the kitchen. "What's going on in here?"

"Nothing's going on, Dad." Chaney pushes the start button on the coffee machine. "You okay? What do you need? Something to eat?"

"I don't need nothing to eat. I need Manny."

"Yes, sir?" I have opened up a package of paper towels. I pull off a square and hand it to Mr. Green.

"What's this for?"

"Your glasses."

He lays it on the counter. "I don't need that."

"Okay." The holder next to the sink is empty, so I move to put up a new roll.

"Leave that for her." He motions toward Chaney. "She can

put that up. You and me, let's head out. Check on the cattle. I'm not sure Alex has been putting out enough feed. I don't know if those steers are gaining like they should."

Chaney catches my eye. *Jealous*. She mouths the word behind his back. She is right. Mr. Green does not like ever to be left out. He does not like for Chaney and me to talk unless he is in on the conversation.

"You want to go right now?"

I would rather wait until the coffee is made and have a cup first. It is smelling really good.

"Course I do. That's what I said. Put your jacket on and let's get going."

My cup of coffee will have to wait.

Friday afternoon, Mr. Green starts talking about what time he wants the three of us to leave for the football game. "We're not getting there late again like happened last week." He glares at Chaney. "Not missing the kickoff."

"Dad, I'm passing on the game tonight." Chaney is sitting with her dad in the living room. I am on my way outside with a broom to sweep off the porch. "You and Manny go without me. I'm going to stay in and do some reading tonight."

"No you're not. You know how much that ticket I bought for you cost? Too much." He slaps the newspaper he was reading down on his knee. "If I'd a known you weren't going to be wanting to go, I wouldn't have bought you one."

"Sorry." She does not look like she is. "I told you I wasn't into football. You were the one who insisted on all of us going. If it's that big of a deal, I'll pay you back. But I'm telling you, I am not going to the game."

"Why the heck not?"

"I don't like football. I never have. What's so fun about sitting out in the cold, watching a game I don't like while strangers scream in my ear?"

"Fine. Stay home. Whatever you want. Manny?"

I am on the porch, but the front door is open so I can sweep the threshold. When I hear him, I stick my head back in the door. "Yes, sir?"

"Let's leave at five. We'll go have us a steak, my treat, then head over to the game."

He aims his voice at Chaney, hoping the promise of a steak will change her mind.

It doesn't.

We are not late to the game this week. We arrive early, but not as early as our seatmate.

"Who're you?" Mr. Green says.

I have parked in the handicapped section and helped him up to our section of seats. He is standing at the entrance of our aisle, not ready to ease his way down until he settles a mistake. Here is the problem. Someone large is wedged into the spot where Chaney sat last week. The man's back is turned so that at this moment we cannot see his face.

"Hey! You're in the wrong seat. That's my daughter's chair."

Then the man turns around. He does not get up, which is probably good because as tightly as he is wedged into the seat, I think getting up and down would be difficult.

The man is smiling. The biggest smile you have ever seen. He is wearing an adjustable Eden Plain Wildcats cap and holding out his hand to shake.

"Mr. Green, it's me! Lee! From Brookshire's. How are *you* tonight? Do you think the Wildcats are going to *win*? I think they are going to win *big*! I think we're going to kick the other team's tail! I'm going to yell *loud*. Loud so that Johnny D. can hear me because he's the best quarterback in the *world*."

Mr. Green backs up from the man. "Son, you're in the wrong seat. The wrong section."

He looks up at the row of well-dressed school board members and bank vice presidents. They are all watching. Listening. Probably glad that someone has finally arrived to tell the man that this section is not where people like him sit.

"General admission is down there." He elbows me. "Manny, go show him. Help him find his seat."

Lee looks confused. His jaw goes slack. I can see his pink tongue between his front teeth.

"I'm in the right seat. This is where the man down there told me to go. See? I got my ticket right here."

He is wearing one of those packs attached to a belt around his waist. He unzips the pack, retrieves his wallet, and gets out his ticket.

"This is where the man said I was supposed to go. Section D, seat seven." His hands are shaking.

Mr. Green's vision is so bad that he cannot read what's on the ticket. He grabs the ticket out of Lee's hand and hands it over to me.

"Get over here." He has me move in front of him so that I'm now next to Lee. "Straighten this mess out, would you? Game's about to start and I want to sit down."

There are still eight minutes left on the pregame clock.

I look at the ticket and it is as I suspected. Lee has a ticket for tonight's game and the next two. Section D, seat seven.

Mr. Green cannot see or hear what is going on. He is not going to be happy when I tell him this.

"Lee, it's okay."

"Somebody gave this ticket to me. A nice lady at my work. Her name is Chaney. You know her. She's your friend too."

"Yes, I know her."

"This is where I'm supposed to sit." Lee looks like he might cry.

"It is okay." I put my hand on his arm. "You're right. This is your seat. It is okay. You can stay there."

"What the—? What do you mean he can sit there?" Mr. Green has leaned forward so that he can hear. "That's Chaney's seat. I paid for it. What's he got, some fake ticket or what?"

"No, he has a real ticket. Chaney gave it to him."

"She did what? Of all the blame stunts she's pulled." His face is as red as Lee's Wildcat hat. "Wait till we get home. This takes the cake."

Lee is looking scared.

"It's okay." I touch his arm. "Don't worry; everything is all right. Stay where you are. You're sitting right where you are supposed to."

So here we are in the high-dollar seats. A rich white man with a walker, a Mexican farm worker who this week has worn Dockers instead of jeans, and a mentally challenged person who probably weighs three hundred pounds and is beginning to smell. The coaches' wives below us and the society ladies above us did not have this in mind when they sat down in their fifty-dollar seats.

This would be funny if Mr. Green was not so mad. His face has gone from red to pale. His arm is trembling, and I can tell his right leg wants to give way. He needs to sit down.

"Sir, come on. Please. Let's take a seat and watch the game. There is no problem. We have good seats. Our friend Lee here has a good seat too. It is almost time for the game to start."

"Okay. But the least he can do is move over one. Let me and you sit next to each other."

But Lee will not move. His ticket says seat seven. He is staying put.

"Well, for the love of Pete."

The band starts to play. The cheerleaders come out. The flag is being raised out on the field.

Mr. Green has two choices. Go home or sit down. He looks at me, shakes his head, then takes a seat on the far side of Lee. Once settled, he crosses his arms over his chest and stares straight ahead. I take the other seat. At least the part of it that Lee is not in.

"This is going to be a great game. We're gonna *win*. Win *big*! You want some jawbreakers, Mr. Green?" Lee unzips his pack and gets a bag out. "Don't you worry. I got enough for all of us right here."

chapter seventeen

MR. GREEN IS MAD AT both Chaney and me. For two days he has said no more words than necessary to either one of us. Chaney is his victim because she gave her expensive football season pass to a grocery store bag boy. He is angry with me because he is convinced, as he puts it, that I was in on the deal. Nothing either of us says changes his mind.

I cook his favorite meal of pinto beans with ham and a pan of jalapeño cornbread, but it does not help his mood. Mr. Green has decided that this Friday he is going to the game without either one of us.

"Dad, be reasonable," Chaney says when he makes this announcement. "You can't go alone. You're not driving yourself. How're you planning on getting there? How're you going to get up into the stands? Who do you think's going to help you?"

"Lori." Mr. Green leans back in his chair and crosses his arms over his chest. "She's picking me up and going with me. I figure me and Lori will get along just fine."

Chaney and I look at each other.

"Don't worry, I'm paying her. Seven dollars an hour."

"Oh," Chaney says, "she's even cheaper than I thought."

"What are you talking about?"

"Nothing, Dad. Nothing. I hope you and Lori have a really good time."

"We plan to. Lori loves football. Some women do, you know."

"That's great, Dad. Just great."

"Think we'll leave in time to get us a hamburger on the way. We don't want to be late though. Lori's looking forward to seeing the game from a good seat."

"I bet she is, Dad. You two go out and have a blast."

Chaney's face does not match her words, but Mr. Green does not notice. Or maybe he does. You never can tell. He really wants to go to the game. But even more, he wants to get to his daughter.

"So."

It is early Friday evening. Chaney and I are standing on the porch watching as Lori and Mr. Green head out to Lori's car, a Ford Taurus that sits pretty low. I hope Lori has a strong back because when they get to the game, Mr. Green is going to need help getting out.

"This gives you and me a night off," Chaney says. "What do you say we do?"

I had not thought of *us* doing anything. Since Mr. Green hates the sound of the vacuum cleaner, I had planned to vacuum the house while he was gone.

"It's Friday night. Come on." Chaney leans against the porch railing. She pushes her hair behind her ears and gives me a small smile. "Let's go somewhere. Get out of the house. Do something fun."

What is this? What exactly does she mean? I have never been asked out on a date by a woman. Is that what Chaney just did?

"Okay. Where would you like to go?" My palms have gone

cold, and I can feel myself begin to sweat even though it is chilly here on the porch.

"I feel like I need to let off some steam. Let's go dancing."

"Dancing?"

"Sure. You like to dance?"

"I like it all right." I look down. There is mud on my right shoe. I scrape my heal against the top step. Some, but not all of the mud comes off.

"Can you two-step?"

I nod. There is mud on my other shoe too.

"Can you swing dance?"

I nod again.

"Great!"

She claps her hands. The dogs run up. They think she is calling for them. When they see she has nothing for them to eat, their tails sag. They go lay down next to the front door.

"Is there anyplace around here to go?" she says. "I'm not all that crazy about bars, but if that's the only place that has a dance floor, we may not have a choice."

I have gotten all the mud off that I can. I am going to need to run the bottoms of these shoes under the hose.

"Ralph's used to be a good place." I have gone there many times in the past, but not a single time in the past couple of years. "It's not just a bar. It is an old-fashioned dance hall. One of the oldest in Texas is what they say. Wooden floors. A little bit shabby, but lots of people go there on the weekends. How do you not know about Ralph's? You don't remember it from when you were growing up in Eden Plain?"

Chaney thinks for a minute. "You know, I sort of do remember hearing about Ralph's when I was growing up, but it wasn't really a place where teenagers hung out. What street's it on?"

"West Fifth. They have a live band there. It's a pretty clean place. Not too rowdy. They serve beer, but no hard liquor. People of all ages go."

"Perfect!" She moves to go inside. "Want to leave about seven?"

"Sure."

"All right then. I'll go get ready. Been so long since I got fixed up to go out, I may have forgotten how. You coming inside?"

"In a minute. After I feed the dogs."

"Okay."

She slams the door shut behind her. I scoop Kibbles 'n Bits into the dogs' bowls, then decide to go ahead and make the rounds of the bird feeders. Mr. Green loves to watch the birds. There are six feeders. I fill each of them up with seed. Then I go inside, down the hall, and into my room.

I head to the bathroom. I showered and shaved this morning, but I think I will do so again. I go to the closet. I am wearing the same thing I wear most every day—blue jeans, a T-shirt, and Nikes.

I own slacks and dress shirts for church, and a dark gray suit for weddings or funerals. My suit is at my duplex. Not that I would wear it tonight, of course. No, tonight I will wear black jeans and a starched white pearl snap shirt. I have a pair of broken-in black roper boots. Nice boots, comfortable for dancing. They need to be polished, but I believe I will have the time to take care of that before we go.

Inside the shower stall, I turn the water on high. For a while I have good pressure but then not so much. The water that was running hot turns cold, then hot again. The pressure is strong, then it is weak. Finally, I realize Chaney is probably trying to take a shower at the same time.

Chaney. In the shower. In the same house as me.

The water runs cold. I rinse, then step out and dry off.

I once heard an expert on marriage talk at my church. He said that if two reasonably attractive, healthy people of the opposite sex spend enough time alone together, something will eventually happen between them. I am not sure I believe what he said. Chaney and I have spent a great deal of time alone in the three months since she came to the ranch. Nothing has happened between us.

Not yet.

Am I interested in her? As a friend, yes. As something else? I must be honest. The answer to that question may also be yes. Chaney is very good-looking. She is funny and outspoken, but inside she is kind. The longer she stays here at the ranch, the more I have come to enjoy spending time with her. But our situation is unusual, and I do not know the rules. She is my employer's daughter, which in a way makes her my employer too.

Mr. Green goes to bed early. Usually at ten. When Chaney first came, once I had helped him get into his bed, my habit was to tell her good night and then go to my room to read or to paint or to sleep. But for the past few weeks she and I have been staying up late, talking in front of the fire sometimes until one o'clock in the morning. Last Monday, we looked up at the clock and saw that it was after three.

During these talks I have learned a great deal about Chaney.

Some things about her surprise me. She has never really come close to being married, and she has had only two true boyfriends in her adult life. Neither of the two were men she wanted to marry.

She does not seem unhappy about not being married. Chaney enjoyed her work, and she misses her friends back in Florida, yet she says she is not sure she wants to go back.

"I feel like my life is at a crossroads, Manny," she said to me the other day. We were working together in the yard. I was cutting the hedges, and she was beside me, raking up the trimmings. Mr. Green was sitting on the porch watching and yelling to us ever so often about how we were not doing it right.

"Like I'm not sure who I want to be when I grow up. When I was a child, all I wanted to do was escape Eden Plain. I went out of state to college. Even spent one semester of my junior year in Italy. Once I graduated and started working, I didn't come back any more than I had to. Now I'm shocked that I actually like being back here. Even with Dad driving me crazy about every other minute." She waved and called to him, "Okay, Dad, we'll do the side yard next."

She bent and scooped up the hedge trimmings. I held the bag for her, and she dropped them in.

"I'm not sure what all this means. And I don't know why I'm feeling this way. You ever go through a time like that?" She stood up, stretched her back, and reached up with her gloved hand to wipe sweat from her forehead. "You know, where you wonder about where your life is going or what it is you're supposed to do?"

I told her the truth. I have not ever wondered about those things. I have never had the luxury. It is not that I have no questions about life. I have more questions than there are stars in the black fall sky. Much of life is a mystery to me, and I spend hours thinking about why the world happens as it does. But as for where I am going or what I am to do? I have known the answer to these questions since that day when I was twelve.

It is simple for a person like me. I have lived in poverty. I have witnessed fear in my mother's eyes and hunger in the faces of my brother and my sisters. I have had no place to live, and I have walked in shoes with cardboard for soles. While Chaney was growing up in this nice house with her mother and her father and nothing more to worry about than which pretty dress to wear, I was working, taking care of my family.

She knows security and safety.

I know what it is to be alone and afraid.

My purpose in life, my reason for getting up each day, is simple. I rise from my bed in the morning to work. When I lay my head down at night, the last prayer that I pray is one of thanks to God for the good job that I have.

Food.

Clothing.

A safe place to live for me and for my family.

When a person obtains these things after living without them, he knows what life is about.

I am outside, on the back steps, polishing my boots when Chaney comes to find me. The cordless phone is in her hand. She is wearing a brightly patterned skirt that goes to her knees. I can smell her cologne. I want to tell her that she looks pretty, but when I look at her face I see something is wrong.

"It's Dad."

Mr. Green does not have a cell phone. He refuses to use one because he saw on TV that they might cause brain cancer. This does not stop him from asking, every time one of us leaves the house, if we've remembered our phone.

"He borrowed Lee's cell phone."

Mr. Green, Lee, and Lori sitting in the stands. All in a row. I can picture what a sight that must be.

"We have to go get him."

"What happened?"

"It's Lori. Seems she brought along some liquid refreshment in her thermos. And it wasn't hot chocolate. Dad's new football buddy is feeling a little too good."

Chaney's blouse is deep green. She has curled her hair and she is wearing lipstick, I think.

"Lori is drunk?"

"Yep. Probably only a little bit tipsy, according to what Dad said."

She looks down at my feet. There is a small hole in the toe of my left sock.

"One thing about Dad—he's never liked women who drink too much. Says it's not ladylike."

On this point, Mr. Green and I agree.

"We've got to get to the stadium. I bet he's so mad at Lori right about now, he's ready to spit."

I stand up and pull on my boot. Chaney has the truck keys in her hand.

"You want to drive or do you want me to?" I say.

She tosses the ring to me. "I'm too mad to drive. Sorry about our night."

Not as sorry as I am.

Chaney buttons her jacket. "I was really looking forward to it. You look nice."

"Thank you. So do you." I would like to say more, but I do not.

Chaney puts her purse over her shoulder. "I was ready to see if

I could keep up with your moves on the dance floor."

"I'm not that good."

"You're lying."

I cannot stop my smile. She is right. According to what people say, I am an excellent dancer when it comes to swing.

"Guess we'll have to take a rain check on our night out, then," I say. "Maybe we'll figure something out so we can try this again."

"I'd love that."

Chaney heads for the truck. I follow behind.

When she walks, the pretty skirt moves around her legs. Her heels click on the sidewalk. I breathe in her scent.

When we get to the stadium, Chaney and I see that the situation is worse than we thought. The first person we spot when we get near the gate is Lori. She is surrounded by three policemen, and she is kicking and yelling and screaming curse words. A crowd has gathered. For them this is better entertainment than the game.

"Get your hands off me!" She tries to jerk away from one of the officers. "I'll sue you! I will. Give me back my purse. Where's my purse? I know my rights."

Chaney is mad. Madder than I ever thought she could be. She marches over to where Lori is and gets close to her face.

"Where's my father? Tell me! Where is he?"

"Ma'am, stay back." One of the officers holds up his hand. "You too, sir," he says to me.

"I want to know where my father is," Chaney says to Lori. "Did you leave him up in the stands? He can't get down by himself, you know. If anything has happened to him, you little . . ."

Lori starts crying. She grabs hold of Chaney's arm and looks like she might fall down, like she might pull Chaney down with her. She puts her hand over her mouth.

I am hoping she doesn't throw up all over Chaney.

"I'm sorry. I'm so sorry. I didn't do nothing. Honey, tell your daddy that they're hauling my butt to jail. He's gonna have to find some other way to get home. I don't have any money. Can you come down later and bail me out? I'll pay you back. I promise I will."

I touch Chaney's arm. "I'm going up to see if he's still in his seat."

One of the policemen cuts in. "Ma'am, if you're looking for Mr. Owen Green, I believe him and that boy that works at Brookshire's are over at the concession stand."

Yes, that is where we find him — past the Booster Club table selling Eden Plain Wildcat mugs and seat cushions, past the restrooms, past the junior varsity cheerleaders and their cupcakes with red icing.

"Dad, are you all right?" Chaney squats in the dirt beside her dad.

"Well yes, of course I am. I'm fine. Lori's the one that's gone and got herself looped. You call them people up. Tell them I don't want her out to the house anymore."

"Don't worry, Dad. She won't be back."

"He couldn't get down the steps by himself." Lee is talking with his mouth full of popcorn. "I had to help him. Two times, he almost fell."

"That was very nice of you, Lee."

"You like my new hat?"

He shoves a handful of popcorn in his mouth, then reaches up and scratches his nose, which leaves a big shiny grease spot on the side of his face.

Mr. Green and Lee are sitting in a pair of folding camp chairs off to the side of the concession stand. Leaning back as if they are at home in front of the TV. I don't know whose chairs these might be. Probably people who have left them to go to the restroom. Some fans around here like to watch from the sidelines instead of sitting up in the stands. I'm hoping whoever these chairs belong to will not think that Lee and Mr. Green are trying to steal them.

"Your hat is nice. Really nice," I say.

"I was talking to her." Lee points to Chaney. It's not hard to tell he likes her better than me.

"It's a great hat," Chaney says.

"I'm ready to go home now." Mr. Green leans forward. The chair sits very low, and I move to help him. "This game's not all that good anyway."

My hands are under his arms. My knees are bent the way I have learned to keep from hurting my back. I lift my eyes to the scoreboard. Near the end of the first half. The two teams are tied.

"Where's your walker, Dad?"

"It's right here." Lee pries himself out of his chair and picks up Mr. Green's walker, which he had folded and laid on the ground next to him.

"I don't know if I can walk," Mr. Green says.

Chaney and I get on either side of him.

"Lee," Chaney says, "can you get the walker?"

Lee picks the walker up, unfolds it, and stands behind it. He moves the walker forward, then takes two steps toward it the way someone who really needs one would do.

"Dad, you think you can make it to the gate?"

Chaney looks over at me. Mr. Green is breathing hard. Even

though the temperature is in the fifties, he is sweating. He does not answer her but moves his feet, which are dragging, toward the exit.

When the four of us get near the gate, I tell Chaney that I will go get the truck.

"We'll get you home, Mr. Green," I say. "Won't be long now."

"What about me?" Lee is still using Mr. Green's walker.

Chaney looks over at him. "You need a ride?"

"Yes, ma'am. I need a ride back to my house. Four three two Apple Blossom Street. Do you know where that is?"

Lee managed to get to the game, but he has no ride home? Where exactly are we going to put him in the truck?

"Okay. It'll be tight, but I think we can all squeeze in." Chaney smiles at Lee. "It was very nice of you to help my dad get down from the stands. I don't know what we would have done without you."

"It was nice of you to give me a football ticket."

Lee looks as if he would like to kiss Chaney for giving him this gift.

chapter eighteen

WE ARE BACK AT HOME after dropping Lee off at his house. I am working on getting the fire going. Since we had planned to be gone for the evening, I had let it die down.

"First thing in the morning, you call those people." Mr. Green is sitting in his recliner, holding the remote, calling over his shoulder to Chaney, who is in the kitchen. "Tell them not to send Lori back. That woman's crazy. I knew I was in for trouble by the time we got to the end of the driveway. You know what she asked me?"

"What?"

Chaney has cut him a piece of a Mrs. Smith's apple pie, warmed it up in the microwave, and brought it to him on a plate. She is showing great control not to remind Mr. Green that she tried to tell him that going to the game with Lori was not such a great idea. I am surprised at her restraint. Thankful for it. This is the kind of situation that usually prompts angry words between them.

"If I'd carry her to Vegas."

"No way." Chaney sits down on the edge of the couch. She leans forward and rests her elbows on her knees. "When did she want to go?"

"Right there and then. She had this big idea me and her could drive to Dallas, catch a plane, and fly out there tonight."

"You've got to be kidding."

"I'm not. I swear. That's what she wanted to do. Like I told you, woman's crazy." He forks a bite of pie into his mouth. "Gold digger is what she is. I knew it all along." He aims the remote at the TV. "What's on tonight, Manny?"

"The news in twenty minutes." I turn my back to the fire and stand in front of the hearth to warm myself.

Mr. Green flips from channel to channel. When he can't find anything he wants to watch, he leaves it on The Weather Channel. He finishes his pie and sets the plate on the table beside his chair.

"So what'd y'all do while I was gone? Anybody call?"

"Nobody called." Chaney has curled up on the end of the couch. She picks up a book she's been reading. "We didn't do much of anything." She catches my eye over the page.

"You sure are dressed up," Mr. Green says. Without the TV to keep his attention, he turns his focus to Chaney and to me. "I just now noticed. Both of you. Chaney, when's the last time you had on a dress? And Manny, what's all this? Nice shirt. Nice pants. Those boots of yours have got some kind of a spit shine on them." He sniffs the air. "And one of you has got on some kind of perfume. I can tell because my sinuses are getting irritated."

"It's lotion, Dad. That's all. I've got dry skin since the weather turned cold. If it's bothering you, I'll go wash it off."

Chaney gets up and goes to the bathroom. While she is gone from the room, Mr. Green does not say a word to me. After a few seconds of silence, I give the fire another stir.

When she returns, Chaney pats Mr. Green on the shoulder before she sits back down on the couch. "You 'fraid you missed something while you were off on your big night out with Lori? Not to worry. You didn't miss a thing. Me and Manny were right here while you were gone. He fed the dogs and put out birdseed.

I emptied the dishwasher and started a load of towels. Same old same old."

Mr. Green's eyes land on me, then move to Chaney. I hold his gaze, but Chaney lowers her eyes for a fraction of a second. Mr. Green opens his mouth, then closes it back. Finally he grabs the remote and turns on the news.

Chaney glances at me. Her look says she believes we are in the clear.

I know we are not.

You may wonder why, since Chaney has arrived and is available to keep watch over Mr. Green, I have not returned to my outside work on the ranch. The reason is pretty simple, really.

"Manny," Mr. Green tells me in confidence, "I need you to keep yourself busy around the house. I know. Chaney's here to look after me. If you were back out on the ranch, me and her'd do just fine. But here's the thing. No telling when she's going to up and take her sassy self back to Florida. When she goes, I'm going to be needing you in the house and for Alex to continue on taking care of the place. I can't take the chance of losing him. If I tell him I don't need him for a while, if I send you out there to help him, he might get his nose out of joint and up and quit on me."

Alex would not do that, but I do not correct Mr. Green.

"Word's got out Alex is a good hand. At least every other week I get a call from some rancher wanting to know if I can spare him a day to help out. Can't take the chance of somebody hiring him out from under me. That happens and we'll be up a creek without a paddle. You savvy?"

I savvy.

He has not asked me what I want, what I plan to do. He only assumes.

Two months have passed since Chaney and I tried to go dancing. Two months and we have not left this house together, just the two of us, a single time. She and I are being watched. Every move, every look, every overheard word that passes between us is being studied. Mr. Green has begun staying up later at night, getting up earlier every morning, and fighting, though not successfully, the nodding off he does in his chair during the day.

"Dad, it's nearly eleven," Chaney says. "Aren't you tired?"

"Nah, I'm wide awake." He tries to hide his yawns. "I want to finish this show. Pretty interesting."

A Discovery Channel documentary about domestic bees and their effects on the pollination of corn.

"But you go on to bed if you want to, sugar. No need for you to miss your rest. Manny'll stay up with me."

Almost every morning, he finds some errand in town for me to run.

"Manny, need you to drive into Eden Plain and pick me up some _____."

You fill in the blank.

"Take your time. Me and Chaney are fine."

I've been sent out for nails, rubber bands, WD-40, legal-sized envelopes, dog treats, weed killer, and hair dye. Yes, hair dye. Grecian Formula for Men.

Lori got fired, but we have Cindy, a new home health aide. She's very good. Dependable and always on time. Her coming would free Chaney to go into town with me on my made-up errand, but when she suggests this to Mr. Green, to take care of a few errands of her own, he tells her no. He does not feel safe alone with the new girl. Chaney can go to town when I get back if she needs to.

This from a man who is a penny pincher and hates to waste gas.

"Remember what happened with Lori. You can't never tell about these people," he whispers loud enough for Cindy to hear even though she is so sweet she pretends she cannot.

The three of us eat lunch together, but most afternoons Mr. Green has me doing something in the yard that does not need to be done. When Chaney volunteers to help me outside, he quickly finds some reason he needs her to stay by his side.

Mr. Green's efforts to keep Chaney and me from spending time alone together would be amusing if not for one thing.

A thing that will probably surprise you. Perhaps even shock you.

As it has surprised and yes, I suppose, shocked both of us.

Chaney and I have fallen in love.

I know. You have questions, probably doubts.

Chaney and I are an unlikely pair. Both of us close to forty. Neither of us ever married. Me a Mexican laborer who only went to school through the sixth grade. She a college-educated white woman who stands several inches taller than I.

Sounds crazy.

But our love and commitment to each other is real.

I am the one who says it first. It is after midnight, three months after our missed dancing date. Mr. Green has been in bed since ten thirty, but neither of us is sleepy yet. So we are in the kitchen making hot chocolate. I retrieve the marshmallows from the pantry and turn toward Chaney. She isn't doing anything special. Just standing in front of the stove, stirring the milk with a wooden spoon, wearing no shoes, only the thick white socks she likes because they keep her feet warm.

All of the sudden, standing there watching her stir, I know I want to be with Chaney for always. I want her to be my wife. All those fears I'd had about getting married, about getting hurt, don't matter anymore. And so I just say it. For the first time. Standing there with a bag of marshmallows, one in my hand, ready to pop in my mouth.

"I love you, you know."

She looks up from the milk and turns her head a little bit to the side, but not in a way that shows even a little bit of surprise. It is as though we both knew it was coming. It just had to be the right time.

"You want to get married?" she says.

I nod.

"Me too."

"How soon?" I move to her.

Chaney sets the spoon down and turns the heat off under the milk. She moves to stand in front of me. Our first time in each other's arms.

"How about Friday?"

chapter nineteen

LIKE A PAIR OF TEENAGERS, we are sneaking off to tie the knot. This morning. It is supposed to be bad luck for the bride and groom to see each other on their wedding day, but Chaney and I do not have any choice. Because we do not want to wait, we are not telling Mr. Green until it is already done. Chaney is afraid if we do tell him, he'll get upset and try to talk us out of it. She's probably right.

"Fried or scrambled, Dad?"

Chaney is standing at the stove, a place that for as long as I live will remind me of the first night we spoke of our love. I can't keep my eyes off her. I can't keep my mind on anything but our plan. In about an hour, she will be my wife.

"Fried. Two. And don't let the yolks cook hard." He lowers his paper and sees me standing there at the coffee doing nothing but staring at Chaney. "What's wrong with you?"

"Nothing. Just waiting on the coffee to finish."

"Looks to me like it's already done. Bring me a cup."

I go to pour him one, but the mug slips out of my hand, and I spill half of it on the counter and down the cabinet front onto the floor. Some gets on my hand.

"You okay?" Chaney leaves Mr. Green's eggs to come over and make sure I am all right.

My hand is red, but of course I am fine. The coffee wasn't all that hot.

Mr. Green gives me one of his looks. "Maybe we should call 911."

"Dad. Stop being sarcastic." Chaney wipes up the coffee with a paper towel.

He raises his hands as though he doesn't know what she's talking about. "I'm just saying. Maybe the EMS people have coffee with them."

I set a full mug in front of him. With two spoons of sugar already stirred in.

"Thank you. Now where's my eggs?"

Those yolks are going to be hard.

It goes just the way we planned. Mr. Green eats his breakfast. Cindy arrives. As soon as she has him in the bathroom for his shower, we dash out the door and jump into my truck. Good thing we don't pass a highway patrolman on the way because I drive like a maniac straight to Grace Baptist, where Mitchell Case, who is still the pastor, is waiting for us in the little library room of the church.

Inside, Mitchell greets us. He has spoken to both of us on the phone a few times during the past four days, but this is the first time he has met Chaney in person. He hugs us both.

"So," he says to Chaney, "you're really ready to commit holy matrimony with my friend Manny?"

She smiles. "I am."

I stand next to her, my arm around her waist. My hand is sweaty. Can she feel how cold it is through her sweater? There was no time to change. Our wedding day and we're both wearing jeans.

"He's a good man. I wish the two of you well. When Manny called the first time to set this up, I knew then you had to be something special. Over the years, I've watched several lovely ladies try to snag this guy. None of them ever got close."

"I'm a lucky girl." Chaney looks into my eyes, then gives me a playful little jab in the ribs.

The moment does not seem real. I know I want to do this. More than anything. But I feel a little bit numb. Me. Chaney. About to get married. It happened so fast. Do I have doubts? Not one. Fears? I confess that I do. Not about making our marriage work but about telling Mr. Green. I should not be thinking of anything but the vows we are about to take, but no matter how hard I try, I cannot stop my mind from jumping ahead. I don't want to hurt him. I don't want him to hurt Chaney. She believes he will be surprised but that when he gets used to the idea he will be fine.

She is more optimistic than I am.

"Okay then, let's get this thing done." Mitchell opens his Bible. He has some notes. "You have the license?"

I hand him the document.

"Rings?"

I take them out of my pocket and place them in his hand. Simple white gold bands, which is what Chaney said she wanted, bought yesterday while on my morning round of made-up errands for Mr. Green. They are the right sizes. Mine because I tried it on, hers because I took one of her rings with me when I went to the store.

I have been to a few weddings in my life. Big, happy weddings. With flowers and music and punch and cake, brides in white dresses and grooms in black tuxedos. I have never been to any wedding like ours.

Simple vows.

A prayer.

All of us wiping away tears when it's done.

"I wish you well, my friends." Mitchell hugs us again as we prepare to leave. "Keep in touch. May God bless you and give you many years of happiness together."

Mr. Green is sitting on the porch when we get back to the ranch. He watches as Chaney and I slide out of the truck. We have done a no-no. Leaving together. Not telling him. He's sitting in a rocking chair, but his body is not moving. His eyes are on us as, side by side, we come up the sidewalk and climb the steps onto the porch. He looks as suspicious as a young child who has just discovered parts of a Santa Claus suit in his parents' closet.

"Something's going on here. I want to know what it is. Where y'all been?"

His hair is still damp from his shower. What is Cindy thinking? It's too cool for anybody to be outside with wet hair.

"Where's Cindy, Dad?"

My heart is beating hard in my chest.

Before he answers, she comes out the front door.

"Okey-dokey. I made the bed and cleaned your bathroom. Guess I'm ready to go." She holds out the paper she has to get signed every time she comes. "See you Monday. Have a good weekend."

"Let's go inside, Dad. It's freezing out here."

"I'm not cold."

He's wearing a short-sleeved shirt and no jacket. His nose is red and goose bumps cover his arms.

"Well, I am." Chaney has her arms wrapped around herself. "I'm not staying out here. Let's go inside. Manny and I have something we need to talk to you about."

Mr. Green just shakes his head, but he does move to get up. I come alongside to help him rise as I have done hundreds of times. But when I touch his arm, he jerks it away.

"Don't need any help. I'm fine."

Mr. Green struggles to stand. Over and over he gets nearly up to where he can straighten his knees, then his strength gives way and his body sinks back down.

Standing back and watching, doing nothing to help, seeing him struggling so hard to be independent, to maintain his dignity and strength, causes me great pain. It is never easy for a man to get old.

Somewhere my own father may be just like this.

Someday this will be me.

Finally, he lets Chaney support his arm. He manages to stand, but he is not steady. His body sways.

"Where's your walker?" Chaney glances around.

"Left it inside. Don't need it."

He can barely lift his feet.

"Okay. Whatever. Let's get you in the house."

Together, they shuffle along.

And I follow behind. I told her I would tell him, but Chaney said she wanted to be the one. We didn't discuss when. After lunch? After his nap? At dinner? Tonight?

She does not wait. As soon as Mr. Green gets settled into his recliner, Chaney moves to stand directly in front of him. No pause. No hesitation. She just opens her mouth and says it.

"Manny and I got married. Just now. We went into town — to a church — and saw a preacher."

"You did what?" His mouth drops open.

"It's done."

I move to Chaney's side. I take her hand. This is the first sign of physical affection between the two of us that he's ever seen.

"We're married, sir."

He tries to say something, but instead he starts having a coughing fit. And it hits me. Mr. Green may have a stroke or a heart attack. Should we have told him before we did it? Should I have asked for her hand? I have no doubts about marrying Chaney, but maybe we were wrong doing it like this.

"Sir, are you all right? Do you need some water?"

Chaney pats him on the back. I go to the kitchen to get him a glass.

Just as I get back with the water, he stops coughing and finds his lost voice. It would have been better if he had not. His eyes bore into Chaney.

"What do you mean, married?" He motions toward me. "Chaney, look at him. He's a wetback. A Mexican. Nothing but a farm worker. What were you thinking?"

His words are like a surprise kick to my groin. There was no way to brace for them. On the outside, I keep myself steady. On the inside, I am doubled over in pain. I need to vomit. Tears sting my eyes.

"Dad, stop it!"

He doesn't hear her. "Get me the phone book. You're obviously out of your mind. I'm calling a lawyer. We can get this annulled."

"I love your daughter." I raise my jaw. I am a man, not a child. Not a dog. I will not speak with disrespect, but he may not disrespect me. "I'll take care of her. I'll treat her well. I give you my word."

"Your word? You're a sneaky one. Yes, you are." Spit flies from his mouth when he speaks. "Pretending to be so reliable, so dependable, tricking me into letting you live under my roof. I treated you like you were my son."

Yes. You made me feel like I was your son. You are the one who used the word, and I believed you. My mistake. You did not see me as a son. It is clear to me now. No matter how kindly you treated me, no matter how pleasantly you spoke to me, to you I was less than a human, not worth as much as one of your animals.

"I gave you the run of my place. I trusted you."

Because I was worthy of it.

"And you do this to me?"

I did nothing to you except take care of you the way I would take care of my own father were he in your place.

"What is it? Money you want? You think you can marry my daughter and be set for life? Ain't gonna work like that, buddy. No way. I wasn't born yesterday. I ain't falling for that trick."

Old man, I cared for you.

I even loved you.

There was no trick.

Mr. Green has not spoken to me in two weeks. Not one word. Anything he needs me to know, he tells Chaney and she tells me. When I speak to him, he turns away. If he is standing up and I say something to him, he leaves the room. He still needs me to get him up in the mornings, and he needs me to help him to bed at night, but we go through our routines in silence.

I zip his pants. I shave his face. I tie his shoes. It is amazing what two people can communicate without making any sounds.

Mr. Green communicates loud and clear.

I am not good enough for his daughter.

He needs me.

He wishes I was gone.

Since my room is on the opposite end of the house from where Mr. Green sleeps, Chaney and I have made that our bedroom. We have a one-way portable monitor we set. At night when we are asleep or during the day when he naps and we come back to spend time together in our room, Mr. Green can call if he needs any help. I am usually up with him to go to the bathroom twice each night—once about midnight, and then again around three.

There has been much to do lately. Many distractions. Decisions to be made. Chaney and I are committed to staying here on the ranch, to caring for her dad. We will be here as long as he needs us, which as I see it will be until his death. She is not going back to Florida except to close off her apartment and pack up her things to have them shipped here.

We have let Alex go, but he has had no trouble finding work with other ranchers in the area. I am back out on the ranch, feeding and tending to the cattle, on the back of a horse or on the seat of the tractor most every day. I work on the fences, the barns, and the outbuildings. On a ranch this size, something always needs my attention. I do my best to keep the place in good repair.

I am back at the work my heart longs to do. I feel a sense of accomplishment at the end of the day. My body is tired, but it is a good kind of tired. Under the blue of the sky and the warmth of the sun, my mind is working to clear itself of difficult things. I am out of the house many hours a day, away from Mr. Green's anger.

Seeing less of Chaney now that we are married is the only bad thing. I miss her. Even though it was difficult for me, I am thankful for the time we had together in this house. She and I would have ended up together. I am sure of that. But without those months we spent cooped up inside, it would have likely taken much longer for us to discover our love.

I cannot tell you how much I love my wife, how beautiful life is with her. Even as difficult as everything is with her dad, I would not change a thing about our lives. I am thankful to God for every situation in my life that has brought me to this place.

It is early morning, still dark outside. Chaney is asleep in our bed. She snores, but softly. Snoring irritates some people, but hers does not bother me. In the quiet of the night, when she is asleep but I am not, it gives me comfort to know she is so relaxed. To sleep as soundly as she does, a person would have to feel safe.

I have gotten up early this morning with the intention to paint. It is something I miss, something I've not spent enough time at these past few weeks. The corner where my easel is set up is lit by a small, dim lamp.

First I pick up a palate knife, then a tube of oil paint. I squeeze out a bit of blue to mix into a dollop of white. The blue is such pure color that it doesn't take much. Only a little bit to get the soft shade I need.

I choose a brush. My canvas has already been prepared. I did that yesterday afternoon. I have already made a few preliminary marks. Just a rough sketch, like a map of what I plan to put where.

I dab the brush into the paint. Then I turn toward my canvas. When I do, an unexpected flicker outside the fogged window catches my eye. It is barely beginning to get light. I move closer to the window to get a better look.

"Chaney. Wake up."

She sits up in bed, startled. "What? What's wrong? What are you doing up so early?"

I am already across the room, in front of the closet, pulling on my boots. I toss her the sweatpants and shirt she dropped on the floor when she came to bed last night.

"It's your dad. In the truck. I just saw him go by."

chapter twenty

"WHAT IS HE THINKING? WHERE'S he going?"

Chaney is barefoot. She and I storm out the back door, tumble down the steps, and run toward my truck.

Mr. Green is headed across the pasture. Thank the Lord, at least not toward the road. Better to hit a cow or a fence than a person. I can hear his engine revving, but the truck is moving slowly. It sounds like he has not been able to shift it out of first gear.

The dogs are barking like crazy. Weaving in and out, wagging their tails, acting like this is some kind of a game. Where were they when he let himself out of the house? Why didn't one of them at least bark?

Chaney waves her arms and calls after her dad to stop. He's got the driver's side window down. I can tell because his elbow is resting half outside the door. But he is already so far away there's no way he can hear her.

We should have hidden his keys. I knew it but I didn't do it. He hasn't talked about driving in months, but still, I should have known.

"He's headed toward the pond." Chaney climbs into my truck and slams her door. "I can't believe this. How did he get up without me hearing him?"

I start the truck and we tear out after him. The ground is so rough and uneven, so full of holes, that we bounce up and down on the seat. Twice Chaney hits her head on the roof.

What was I thinking? I should have checked on him when I first got up. I don't know how he managed to get out of bed by himself.

She's right. The pond's straight ahead. It looks as if that's where he's headed. I would have taken him fishing if he had asked. But then again, it's hard to ask someone to do something for you if you aren't speaking to him.

We're gaining ground, but Mr. Green's still a good ways ahead of us. You can only go so fast when you're driving across a pasture.

Chaney is sitting forward. She has both her hands on the dashboard. "Manny, he's not slowing down. If he doesn't stop, he'll go into the water."

Now we're close. Right on him. I'm honking the horn. All we can see is the back of his head. His arm's not out the window anymore. He must have both his hands on the wheel.

"You think he's had a stroke?" she says. "Maybe he's unconscious."

He's sitting upright. Wouldn't he be slumped over if he wasn't awake?

"I bet it's his feet," I say. "He has so much trouble lifting them. It's always worse right when he first gets up. He probably can't get his foot off the gas to push on the brake."

I pull up beside him. Chaney rolls down her window and sticks her head out. "Dad! Stop! Stop! Dad!"

It doesn't do any good.

I pull up as close to the bank as is safe. It's muddy and I don't want to get us stuck. I slam the truck into park and kill the engine, but Mr. Green doesn't slow down. He steers the truck over a little rise. Chaney and I both jump out and run through tall, dead winter weeds toward the water.

Just as we get it in sight, the truck goes over the rise of the bank and rolls straight down into the pond.

Chaney calls and calls her dad.

I pull off my shoes and run down the embankment to the edge of the water. It's not that deep right here at the edge, but only a little farther out, according to what Mr. Green has told me, it is close to twelve feet.

The truck is sinking fast. Already the cab is submerged. The back end is still visible, but it will soon go under too.

Behind me I hear Chaney screaming. In front of me I hear bubbles rise to the surface of the water.

I draw a big breath. I run a few paces and dive into the muddy winter water. I feel the shock of cold wetness all around me. I am not a good swimmer, but I can hold my breath longer than most men.

The water is so muddy I can't open my eyes. Everything I do has to be by feel.

I go right for the cab of the truck. The window is down on the driver's side. I reach in and feel for the door handle. When my hand finds it, it takes a couple of tries but I am able to make it open. There is resistance from the water, but I brace my feet on the frame of the truck and pull.

The door opens. I grab Mr. Green by the shoulders. I pull and I pull, but he doesn't move.

I am out of air.

I paddle my way to the surface, take two big gulps of air, then go back down again. I am frantic. Swimming as fast as I can. I do not know how long a man can stay underwater, but he has already been down there for too long.

Once again, I find Mr. Green's shoulders. I brace my knees against the frame and pull on his body with every bit of my strength.

At first nothing, then his body does move. First only a small distance, but then it feels as if he is suddenly released from whatever was holding him inside the truck. Once I pull him free, the two of us rise as quickly as a pair of plastic fishing floats.

My face breaks the surface, and I gasp for breath. I'm holding onto Mr. Green by his shoulder, my hand hooked under his arm. He is not moving.

My chest hurts. I am hungry for air, but with my other arm, I paddle toward the shore.

We can get there. We can. *Please, God.* It's not that far.

Only a few more strokes. I feel mud under my feet. We are at the edge. I drag Mr. Green up onto the bank. I try to stand but I can't. I fall down beside him, almost on top of him, still trying to breathe.

"Mr. Green."

I shake him. His head is bleeding from a cut over his left eye, but he is breathing.

"Wake up. Are you all right?"

Nothing.

"Mr. Green. Please, wake up. Look at me. Tell me you're all right."

After what feels like an hour but is probably only a couple of seconds, he opens his eyes. He struggles to sit up and say something, but he's coughing and he can't get any words out. He reaches for me, claws at my chest like a frightened child. Then he vomits down the front of his shirt.

"You're okay," I tell him.

The smell makes me gag, but I manage to keep from throwing

up too. I put my hand on his shoulder. It's all I can do.

"Everything's all right. We're going to be all right."

Oh God, thank You. He's okay. The truck is gone, but he's okay.

I sit up. I lean forward. I haven't yet caught my breath. I rest my head on my knees. But only for a moment because I hear him say something.

"Chaney."

I lift my head. When I dove into the water, she was standing right here. Has she gone for help?

Mr. Green raises his hand to point back toward the water.

Then I see her, in the shallow water near the bank, almost obscured by tall grass, not twelve feet away. She is facedown. Not moving.

"No!"

I scramble on all fours to get to her. The muddy water's only knee deep where she is. As soon as I get my hands under her, I struggle to stand up. I pull her out of the water and lay her on her back on the bank.

She is so heavy. Heavier than I can describe. There is mud on her lips and her hair is all over her face. I push it away. Her skin is pale and her eyes are half open.

Mr. Green drags himself to where I am bent over his child. "Do something! You have to do something!"

I tilt Chaney's head back. I look, listen, and feel. She has no breath. I put my mouth over hers.

Breathe. Breathe. *God, let her breathe.*

Her chest rises when I puff air into her lungs. I stop to feel for a pulse. I think I feel it. Do I? I can't tell.

What should I do?

Please, God. Please.

I breathe into her again. Once more. Then again.

My nose is running. I wipe it on the wet sleeve of my shirt.

Her lips are cold. They don't meet mine. It is as if her face is too soft, sunken in.

Twice more, I check for a pulse. Finally I feel it. Yes, it's there. I'm sure of it.

"Chaney." I take her face in my hands. "Breathe. Please, sweetheart. Just breathe."

What more can I do?

Oh God.

Please.

I can't take this.

I bend forward to put my lips on hers yet again, but when I do, she takes a short shallow breath on her own. Barely a breath, but she draws in some air. Almost a little gasp, but still. It is a breath.

"Come on. Please."

She takes another one. Then she coughs. A small cough.

And she takes another breath.

Mr. Green is on his hands and knees on the other side of her. I look up at him.

"She breathed! Did you see that? She breathed!"

I am crying now. I can't stop it. But I must, because I have to figure out how to get us all out of this terrible, cold, muddy mess.

Mr. Green is in room 203. Chaney in 204. I go back and forth between them, making sure they're all right. Even with all his health problems, the doctors expect to release Mr. Green before they do Chaney. His chest X-ray looked okay. Hers showed pneumonia. All that water. That she smokes made it worse.

One good thing. She told me she's taken her last puff. I believe her.

The doctor said Mr. Green needed to be admitted to the hospital more for observation than anything. Given his age and his poor overall health, they didn't want to take any chances. They gave him a tetanus shot and stitched up the cut on his head. He should be fine. Probably go home in the morning.

Chaney may need to stay for several days. They're giving her antibiotics in her IV, oxygen through a tube in her nose, and every six hours, breathing treatments that look like fog. She has a large bruise on the side of her head from where she slipped and fell trying to get to the bank. The doctor says she probably hit her head on a rock and got knocked out, which explains why a woman who can swim better than I can nearly drowned in less than four feet of water.

She's asleep. Only a minute ago she was laughing and talking to me. Her being so tired worries me, but they say pneumonia takes a lot out of you.

I get up from my chair, kiss her on the forehead, and make sure her nurse call light is where she can reach it in case she wakes up.

Then I go to sit with Mr. Green for a while. When I get to his room, he's up in the chair, sitting by the window, his hands in his lap. His knees are about a mile apart. All he's got on is one of those hospital gowns that ties in the back. Those gowns may be okay for women who are accustomed to wearing a dress. But for men who don't know how to keep the things down, they ought to come up with something better.

"How are you feeling?"

He hasn't heard me come in. My voice makes him jump.

"Fine. Just fine. Chaney okay?"

"She's asleep." I get the blanket off the foot of the bed. "Do you want this over your lap?"

"Thanks. She still breathing okay?"

"She is. Her oxygen level was 97 percent the last time they checked it."

"That's good. Right?"

"Real good. The nurse said it was fine."

I stand there, awkward, the way I used to when I first came to work at the ranch. Mr. Green does not meet my eyes. Instead he looks out the window. He clears his throat. Twice. There is nothing out there to see but the side of a building.

"Been thinking," — he is now looking at his hands in his lap, picking at a bandage on the end of his thumb — "after that fool stunt I pulled yesterday, about putting myself into one of those homes."

I do not need to be standing over him while he tells me something like this. But there is no other chair, no place to sit. So, in spite of my bad knee, I squat in front of him. He may persist in looking down, but when he does, he will be looking into my eyes.

"Sir, you have a home." My voice is low but firm. "There is no need for you to think about living anywhere else."

"You and Chaney shouldn't have to be putting up with the likes of me." He wipes at a tear that has run down onto his chin. "Nearly got her killed. You too. Out on that bank. Lord Jesus, hadn't been for you . . ." His voice fades.

I shift my weight from one foot to the other. "Chaney is fine. It ended well. That's all that matters. In a few days, we will all be home."

"No, that's not all that matters. I done wrong by you. I said things I shouldn't have ever let come out of my mouth."

I swallow hard at hearing these words.

A nurse comes in to give him his pills. He waits until she is gone.

"Things change. People don't stay the same. You came to me as a hired hand. That's all I thought you'd ever be. But then I got to kind of liking having you around. It was terrible losing Karen, but you made it easier in a whole lot of ways. I started hoping you wouldn't ever leave."

My knee is killing me. I can't keep from grimacing.

Mr. Green sees. "Son, get up from there. Take a seat. They won't say anything at you for sitting on the bed."

We both realize the word he has just said. It hangs in the air like a strong smell.

I ease myself onto the bed.

Silence hangs between us for a long moment. Finally Mr. Green speaks.

"I've been a fool." He shakes his head back and forth. "Carrying on about you and Chaney. About you being my son-in-law. Instead of being mad at you, I should have been glad. You're a man of good character. A brave man. A man to make a father proud."

He reaches over and pats my knee.

"If my wife had ever given birth to a boy, he wouldn't have been a better son than you. I'm not your dad, but I wish I was. Your father is one lucky man. I don't deserve your forgiveness. But I'm hoping someday you can see fit to give it to me."

That conversation between Mr. Green and me took place just over a year ago. Chaney and I still live at the ranch. Mr. Green too, though he's now in a wheelchair all the time. We three have worked things out. We have made a good life.

There are still rough times. He gets cranky. Blames too much on Chaney. Likes things done his way. And he still gets jealous of the attention she and I pay to each other instead of to him.

But Mr. Green is a good man. And he does not have much time left. I spend my days doing what I can to see that his life ends with as much happiness and dignity as possible.

Yes, I give to him. But what he has given to me is more than I can explain.

I still paint. I always will. It is forever in my blood. But one thing has changed. Instead of portraits, I paint flowers, birds, landscapes. Sometimes the dogs. For so many years, I was obsessed with painting a picture of my father, of capturing on canvas the look of his eyes.

I'm not anymore. Because to see the eyes of a father, I have only to look across the breakfast table at the man looking back at me.

"Manny," he says to me before every meal, "the blessing?"

I nod. This is my cue. For the word used to stick in my throat but has come to feel exactly right.

We bow our heads, all three of us, and I begin to pray.

"Father . . . we thank You for this day."

bonus content includes:

Reader's Guide

1. Manny broke the law by coming to Texas when he was fifteen. Was his choice justified? Does the need to support one's family supersede the laws of the land? What would you do in the same situation?

2. How should a Christian respond to an illegal immigrant? Does it make a difference if the person is also a believer?

3. How did his father's abandonment change the course of Manny's life? Can a child ever fully recover from a loss of such magnitude? How did the loss of his father affect Manny's ability to trust?

4. How did Mr. Green's attitude toward Manny change? Did he realize his treatment of Manny was disrespectful and patronizing? Were Mr. Green's feelings of superiority related to Manny's race, his education, or his profession? Would he have treated a white farm worker the same as he treated Manny?

5. Are there people like Manny in your church? If not, would Manny be welcomed there?

6. How did Manny view Lee? Did he treat Lee with value and respect? Is it possible to see people unlike ourselves without perceiving them as better or worse than us? Are there specific groups of people to whom you feel superior?

7. Mr. Green appeared to grow genuinely fond of Manny. What explains his angry reaction to the news of Manny and Chaney's marriage?

8. How would you feel if your son or daughter became involved with a person of a different race or socioeconomic group?

9. What challenges will Manny and Chaney face as a biracial couple? How will the differences in their economic and educational backgrounds affect their marriage?

10. How did Manny's views of God change over the course of the book? What prompted those changes? Does estrangement from a biological father always affect a person's relationship with God? Can the damage caused by an absent father be healed if reconciliation is not possible?

A Conversation with Annette Smith

Q. What prompted you to write *A Crooked Path*?

A. Three real-life, seemingly random situations inspired me to create this story.

First, over a period of twelve years, I served on twenty short-term medical mission trips deep into the interior of Mexico. On one of those trips, my companions and I stayed in the apple-scented, dirt-floored compound of a woman who had lived the story of her husband leaving her oldest son at the bus station. Her tale is what inspired the beginning scenes of this novel.

Second, my friend Manuel Ortega, who has a green card, has lived and worked in Texas for more than four decades. I have visited him and his family in Mexico. He has slept under my roof. Our association over the years has given me a peek into the life of a Mexican laborer. I find his assimilation into North American culture fascinating, and his views about our differences both challenging and informative.

Finally, about five years ago, I was working the evening shift, taking care of a frail, elderly rancher who was hospitalized with congestive heart failure. A young Mexican man came for a ten-minute visit. The unexpected affection and tenderness I witnessed between my patient, his wife, and the visitor moved me. Later, I learned that the young man had worked for the rancher for several years and had recently become his personal caregiver.

Q. Did you write *A Crooked Path* as a statement in favor of illegal immigration?

A. No. But it may prompt readers to look at the issue and become more informed. Perhaps it will cause readers to see people with new eyes, to see those of other races and backgrounds with increased compassion and understanding. Immigration is a complicated issue, one my heart wrestles with. My views are not nearly as clear and consistent as I wish. Like Manny, I see both sides.

Q. *A Crooked Path* explores racism and classism. Why write about such topics?

A. I grew up in a loving, multi-generational, Southern Christian family made up of generous, nonviolent people. Yet I remember hearing older family members, most of whom have passed on, use the "n" word in casual conversation. They thought nothing of it.

But I did.

I have always abhorred both racism and classism. Yet I struggle with these very attitudes in myself. I believe our sole purpose on earth is to love God and each other. I find loving God to be pretty easy most of the time. It's the loving others that challenges me. Here is my truth: When I view someone as being different from me, I put distance between us. I find myself dismissing that person, looking at him as someone not worthy of my time or attention, or worst of all, simply not seeing him at all.

Getting inside Manny's heart and soul prompted me to take long, difficult looks at myself. Doing so exposed my own attitudes of superiority and prejudice—attitudes that, with God's help, will change.

Q. Both books in the EDEN PLAIN series are written in the male voice. Any particular reason?

A. I'm actually surprised at this myself. I didn't set out to write books from the male point of view. That's just how both stories came to me. However, I do enjoy eavesdropping on men's conversations, and I find the male viewpoint terribly interesting. I've enjoyed the process of getting into a man's head. My biggest challenge was reaching my word count. I kept coming up short! It's true what they say about men speaking fewer words than women.

Q. Is Eden Plain based on a real town?

A. No. I've lived in small to medium-size Texas towns all my life. Eden Plain is a composite of those places. Mr. Green's ranch is similar to the settings of my childhood. My dad is a cattle rancher—a real cowboy. I gleaned many of the story's ranching details from him.

Q. What do you hope people will gain from reading *A Crooked Path*?

A. I hope readers will find it to be a compelling, captivating story. I hope as they turn the pages, they will enjoy an emotional experience. That's what I seek when I pick up a novel and what I attempt to deliver when I write one. While the book deals with specific moral issues, my intent was to write a story, not a sermon. If readers are challenged or changed by Manny's story, God gets the glory. I am honored to bear written witness, but He's the One who changes hearts.

etc.

About the Author

ANNETTE SMITH is a lifelong Texan, a hospice nurse, and an accomplished storyteller whose book of short stories *The Whispers of Angels* has sold more than 100,000 copies. She is also the author of *A Bigger Life* (the first EDEN PLAIN novel) and the COMING HOME TO RUBY PRAIRIE novels. Annette lives in Quitman, Texas (population 3,000), with her husband, Randy, and an affectionate, shaggy mutt named Wally.

MORE FROM ANNETTE SMITH AND THE EDEN PLAIN SERIES!

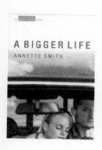

A Bigger Life
Annette Smith
ISBN-13: 978-1-57683-995-9
ISBN-10: 1-57683-995-8

Joel Carpenter's life was never supposed to turn out this way. But after making a careless choice four years ago, his marriage was permanently shattered. Living in a small town deep in the heart of Texas, he now finds himself estranged from his ex-wife, Kari, and sharing custody of their son.

Just when Joel thinks the worst is behind him, he realizes he is facing his greatest challenge yet. And in the midst of deep tragedy, Joel is learning that forgiveness is way more important than freedom. Hopefully it's not too late.